A DISTANT ISLAND

'Often I felt the deep contrast between the sordid
facts of the court-room, the endless fines for
drunkenness, the lash and the cells for more
serious crimes – all that brutality and human
degradation surrounding me, and then the
innocent life of plants. The delicate, fragile blue of
the Austral bluebell – and the sharp pink of
Correa, hanging its head in true fuchsia style, and
the scented bells of *Lomatia* . . .'

A DISTANT ISLAND

Nancy Cato

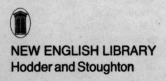

NEW ENGLISH LIBRARY
Hodder and Stoughton

Copyright © 1988 by Nancy Cato

*First published in Great Britain in 1988
by New English Library Paperbacks*

British Library C.I.P.
Cato, Nancy, *1917–*
  A distant island.
  I. Title
  823[F]

Printed and bound in Great Britain
for Hodder and Stoughton
Paperbacks, a division of Hodder and
Stoughton Ltd., Mill Road,
Dunton Green, Sevenoaks, Kent
TN13 2YA (Editorial Office:
47 Bedford Square,
London, WC1B 3DP) by
Cox and Wyman Ltd.,
Cardiff Road, Reading.

ISBN 0-450-41925-3

Acknowledgements

In compiling historical material for this book I have received help from the Mitchell Library, Sydney (Gunn papers), the National Library, Canberra (Franklin correspondence) and the Public Library, Launceston. Much information came from descendants of Ronald Campbell Gunn: Mrs S. L. Napier of Longford, Tasmania, and the late Mr Kenneth Cameron of Blackburn, Victoria, some of it unfortunately too late for inclusion.

My thanks are also due to the Chief Librarian and Archivist at Kew Gardens, Ms Sylvia M. D. Fitzgerald, and the plant expert from the Australian Botanical Liaison Office, Ms Judy West. And particularly to my former editor, Ms Carola Edmond, whose meticulous work of editing was almost complete when tragically cut short by her death in London.

Also to the Queen Victoria Museum, Launceston, for publishing the fascinating book by T. E. Burns and J. E. Skemp, *Some Van Diemen's Land Correspondents*, which first interested me in Gunn more than twenty years ago.

Nancy Cato

JOURNEY OF R.W. LAWRENCE ‒ ‒ ‒ ‒ ‒

JOURNEY OF R.C. GUNN ·················

SCALE

10 5 0   10   20 MILES

TASMANIA

AREA
OF
DETAILED MAP

TO CAPE OTWAY

BARREN ISLAND

CAPE GRIM

CIRCULAR HEAD

WOOLNORTH

ROCKY CAPE

SISTERS HILLS

DENSE
FOREST

HAMPSHIRE
HILLS

ST. VALENTINE
PEAK

CHILTON

BURGHLEY

MAYDAY PLAIN

MACQUARIE HARBOUR

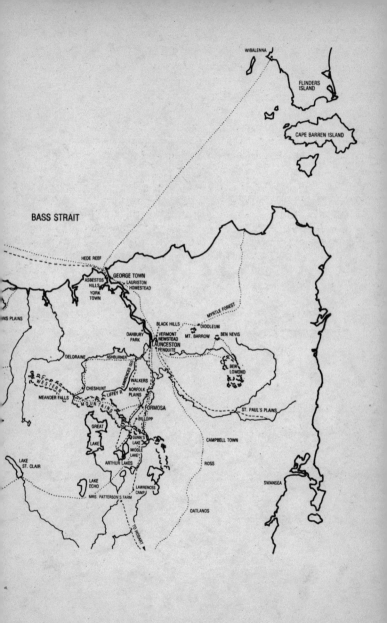

'The geographical distribution of plants, that is almost the keystone of the Laws of Creation'

Joseph Hooker

'A great green book, whose broad pages are illuminated with flowers, lies open at the feet of Londoners' (Kew Gardens)

Richard Jefferies

1

RONALD GUNN looked again at the letter in his hand. He had broken the seal and opened it out with the feeling that he knew already what it contained: another plea from his elder brother William to join him in Van Diemen's Land, where William held a position in the southernmost penal colony in the Antipodes.

William worried about the effect of the West Indian climate, here in Antigua, on his young brother's health, for Ronald had been rather delicate as a boy. In Hobart Town, William wrote, his niece and nephew would grow up in what he believed to be one of the best climates in the world, though somewhat changeable:

> It is truly delightful; you must imagine a continuance for weeks and months together of those halcyon days which are so rare in England and even more so in Scotland, to have any idea of the beauty of this climate.

Yes, thought Ronald, but at least it is never cold here, we don't have the expense of heating the house, and servants are cheap and reliable. And the house went with his Army office job, though he had not yet obtained a commission.

He read his brother's letter through a second time, frowning with concentration. He was beginning to be tempted. Since his father's recent death he had felt little attachment to Antigua, where his father had been Paymaster in the 93rd Highlanders; his own civilian appointment was with the Royal Engineers. But he had spent most of his young life in the tropics or sub-tropics, except when he was at school at home in Scotland. He liked the wealth of tropical fruits, the happy-natured, easy-going people who were established here, having been brought as slaves from Africa many years ago. He looked out from the shady veranda at the feathery green tops of the palms against the perpetually blue skies of the dry season. In a flowering creeper beyond, a gorgeous sun-bird like a coloured bee was probing the scarlet flower for the nectar deep in its throat.

And yet he must think of his family's welfare. There was really no future for him here, he might find himself without employment, without a home, once the present commandant – a friend of his father's – died or was transferred. William had assured him in an earlier letter that he need have no fears on the score of employment if he came to the Colony to join his brother. He could guarantee Ronald's advancement and a position in the vast bureaucracy which ran the convict system.

William was certainly very persuasive. He was as usual singing the praises of Van Diemen's Land and its capital situated on a deep, safe harbour of great beauty, with a high snow-capped mountain towering behind.

Ronald gazed once more into the brilliant garden. As the early sun shone through the crimson petals, the carved jade of the leaves, they seemed to be not so much absorbing light as radiating it, like gems. At once he was reminded of Réunion, that other sub-tropical island where he had spent his childhood: his father had a commission with the Bourbon Regiment which had recently wrested the island from the French. On a day which would always remain as a brilliant background to a sombre memory, he had been leaning in the open window in the regimental quarters, staring out at just such a blossoming, sunlit garden, a glimpse of blue sea beyond. He had been sent to his room for running in the corridor and making a noise, when Mamma was resting. She always seemed to be sick in bed lately. He wondered why everyone looked so serious these

2

days, and why Papa never smiled any more, and was so short-tempered. Then William had come in, looking solemn.

William, who at twelve years old was more than twice his own age, had put a brotherly arm round him. He was always protective towards the younger boy.

'Ronnie, old chap,' he said, and stopped. He seemed to have difficulty in going on. 'Ronnie, you know Mamma has been very sick, and in a lot of pain . . . Well – you have to be brave, now – you won't be seeing her any more, except to say goodbye.'

'*Why?*' He wondered for a moment if he had been so naughty that Mamma was going away, back to Scotland which she often spoke of with longing.

'Because – because God wants her in Heaven, where she won't have any pain.'

'But I want her here!'

'Yes, yes, I know, we all do. But God knows best, and He—'

'I don't care!' And he had burst into tears of rage rather than sorrow.

He had never seen his mother alive again.

The sun-bird flew away, leaving the red flower dancing behind him. Ronald stood up slowly, and carrying the open letter, went to find Eliza, his wife of nearly three years. Once he had made up his own mind to the move, he felt confident he could persuade her. Eliza doted on her children, and would do anything for their welfare.

'Eliza, darling!' He had tracked her down in the spare room they used as a nursery. The nanny stood near the window, folding napkins, looking seven feet tall in her ample skirts and coloured turban. Eliza sat on a low chair with little Ronald James standing in her lap, and pulling at a handful of her red-gold curly hair. Baby Frances slept in her crib.

'Yes, Ronald? Your namesake is pulling my hair out, I declare he has the strongest wrists!'

3

'Give him to Nanny for a moment, my love. I want to talk to you.'

She looked up into his face, reading it with a wife's intuitive knowledge. 'You've had another letter from William with the last packet,' she said, looking apprehensive.

'I have. That's what I want to talk to you about.'

He plucked little Ronald from her lap. He had the same curls as his mother, but with less red in them, and large blue eyes. The West Indian servant doted on the little Celt, offspring of Irish and Scottish ancestors who themselves had inherited their fair colouring from invading Norsemen. He handed the two-year-old boy to her.

'Just mind him for a while, Nanny.'

'Yes, Mr Gunn, sir.'

He led Eliza to the dining-room, where his small library of mainly scientific books was housed in a glass-front case. From this he now took down an Atlas of the World, and opened it to show the new lands of the south, Van Diemen's Land separated from the mainland of New Holland (or Australia, as Flinders had preferred to call it), and not joined to it as in earlier maps. His eye skimmed over the small settlement of Launceston in the north without interest, and settled on Hobart Town, a dot on the estuary of the Derwent which opened into Storm Bay. He indicated it with one long finger.

'This is where William urges us to settle. He tells me an excellent boys' grammar school is established, so little Ronald would not have to go Home for an education. You realise that you will have to part with him here as soon as he is eight or nine; and indeed Frances too, for the effect of tropical climes on young girls is well known—'

'Oh? And what is that?' she asked sharply.

'Premature puberty. Army folk in India have known it for a long time. Even as early as nine or ten, her breasts develop—'

Eliza blushed. 'Really, Ronald, you don't have to go into details! But would it be any better for the children, to grow up in a community where convicts – thieves, forgers,

4

murderers – and wild savages make up the majority of the population? What is William's post? Is it not Superintendent of Convicts for His Majesty's Government? In fact your Van Diemen's Land is but a huge gaol.'

'No doubt there is a normal society segregated from the convict element. The worst offenders, too, are isolated in the penal establishment of Port Arthur, on a peninsula far to the south from which there is no possible escape. And really, Eliza, what is there to keep us here, now that our fathers are both dead? Since Napoleon was banished to St Helena the wars seem to be over: there's no future in the Army. We must think of our children, both present and to come. And William assures me of certain employment, with a home provided for us. Say you agree, my love.'

'Could we not go home to Ireland, or Scotland? You might be able to get a job on that Edinburgh paper again, *The Scotsman*.'

'Ireland! Ireland is finished. Scotland is little better. They are for the old. The newly discovered lands are for the young. Why, William is already a landed proprietor—'

'Only because he knew Lieutenant-Colonel Sorell when he was Governor. I don't suppose Governor Arthur is about to hand you an extensive grant just because you attend the same church.'

'Well, William was lucky . . . But I'm sure I can get recommendations to Arthur from the Commander-in-Chief in the West Indies, if only for Father's sake. And my brother has offered to stand guarantor for a loan to cover a cabin-class fare for all of us – little Ronald will only have to pay a quarter fare, and the baby travels free. He suggests £50 for freight and to outfit us for the voyage, to be paid back out of my salary when we are established.'

'Salary! What salary? You don't even have a position to go to.'

'I told you, William said there are endless opportunities for young men of good family and some education, just because there are not too many over there, except in the Governor's entourage. My brother originally intended to go to New South Wales, you remember, but Governor Sorell persuaded him that the opportunities for advancement were greater in the younger Colony.'

'I don't know. It's so far!' She pushed a curling golden strand away from her brow with a distracted gesture.

'Come now, you are a soldier's daughter, used to living in distant islands.' He wound his arms round her slim waist and kissed her rosy lips. 'Smile and say yes. Come on, smile.' He kissed her again, and this time her lips relaxed.

'I suppose so, if you are sure. Can we take Nanny?'

'I don't think so, we couldn't afford her passage, even if she wanted to go, which I doubt. And we'll have to return to Britain before we sail for the Antipodes, while I raise a loan from the V.D.L. Company or the Australian Company . . . It will cost us at least £200, with the freight on our goods and chattels.'

He became absorbed in the atlas once more, tracing the route by the Cape of Good Hope, which they would follow.

Eliza sat down at the table opposite him, twisting her fingers together. It was true, she was an Army daughter and her own mother had gone wherever her father was sent, uncomplainingly. A wife went with her husband, even to the ends of the earth. But she felt a strange reluctance, almost a premonition, about Van Diemen's Land. Its name did not inspire confidence, somehow. Instead of the Little People of Ireland, its trackless bush was inhabited by demons – black demons, naked savages with spears and waddies – not the dear laughing West Indian natives with whom she had grown up.

'Can I make a visit home to Ireland first? It seems so long since I have seen it, or my brothers.'

'I expect we could manage that. But we should leave for Hobart Town not later than September to make sure of arriving in the summer months.'

'Yes! I don't know how I shall bear the cold winter after being used to the West Indies for so long.'

'So. We leave Britain before the winter begins. Huzzah for Van Diemen's Land, and Terra Australis Incognita!'

6

2

RECONCILED TO the move, even beginning to be excited about the voyage and the new land, Eliza sat down companionably with her husband to make out a list of what they would take with them in the sailing ship.

Eliza wanted to take their four-poster bed, but Ronald thought it would cost too much for freight and they could surely have one made in Hobart Town. But things like chests-of-drawers and wardrobes could be packed with clothing and baby linen.

Eliza stood out for her dining-table of fumed oak, and Ronald declared he must have his book-case and two boxes of books. Chinaware would be packed in a barrel, carpets could be rolled up and packed between the legs of the table – for it was cubic feet of space, rather than weight, which governed the cost of freight. The bath-tub, likewise, could be packed with tin bonnet-boxes, spare bedding and clothing, and cutlery.

For the journey to the Antipodes they would need to take their own cabin-lamp, candles and soap; while Eliza prepared to pack in her trunk for use on the months-long voyage seven bodices, eight petticoats, two pairs of stays and twelve pairs of knitted stockings.

Whatever awaited them in the new land, which was still peopled by savages, they would have the rudiments of civilisation with them.

Passenger vessels from England to Hobart Town were rare; most of the ships calling at Van Diemen's Land were filled with convicts being transported under the care of the military, with a medical officer, and a chaplain the only civilians.

It was not until September 1829 that the Gunns left England's shores in the barque *Greenock*. Now the *Greenock* was flying towards the west coast of Africa before a nor' westerly wind; not quite a gale but it tilted her decks so that the lee rail sometimes dipped through the waves and left an extra trail of white foam among the white-caps. Ronald had found his sea-legs early, and was enjoying a brisk walk on the windward or port side. Going to the rail, he gazed towards the horizon, imagining the vast dark continent out of sight in the haze to the eastward. Because they travelled with the wind, though it bellied the square topsails it did not create much draught on deck.

In the dim cabin with its one porthole, Eliza was singing quietly to Ronnie as she held him on the top bunk to look out at the sea:

> 'And all the little waves had their night-caps on,
> Night-caps, white-caps, night-caps on –
> All the little wa-aves had their night-caps on
> So ear-ly in the morning.'

'More!' demanded Ronnie as he always did.

Wearily, Eliza began again. 'And all the little waves . . .' while he gazed at the dark blue, white-capped sea and clapped his hands in delight.

She did not dare take the children on deck on her own, though they sometimes took Ronnie walking between them, firmly holding each of his hands, while Frances slept in her cot. The first two days, though the sea was calm and the decks almost level, had been a nightmare. Ronnie, at every opportunity, made a bolt for the rails, crowing 'Big barf! Big barf!' And he was small enough to slip between them into the deep blue of the 'bathwater' below.

At least the children had not been seasick, which was a

8

blessing. With the steady wind on the stern quarter the ship did not roll, but it took some getting used to the slope of the decks, so that one corner of the cabin was uphill and the opposite one was down. Ronnie thought it great fun.

It was not the movement of the sailing ship that worried her, she told herself, even when pitching in a head sea; no, it was the bilge-watery, stuffy between-decks smell when the porthole had to be closed, as now. For on the starboard side they were tilted low towards the water, and the foaming break of the bow-wave as the hull hissed through the ocean. Eliza was already losing weight, for she could scarcely force herself to eat. She promised herself a few days of good meals ashore when they reached Cape Town.

Ronald, of course, was enjoying every moment of it. He loved to travel, had been back and forth with his military father to several posts, after being born in the Indies while the regiment was stationed there. Shipboard life held no terrors for him. He took more than his turn at minding little Ronnie, when Eliza wanted to sleep. How they would have managed in steerage, if William had not guaranteed the loan of their cabin fare, Eliza dreaded to think. As it was, the voyage would cost them £300, even though Frances travelled free.

Eliza, having eaten nothing at dinner but some thin soup and dry toast (she craved fresh fruit, but there would be no more till they reached the Cape), had gone to bed early as usual when Ronald came down to the cabin just as she was drowsing off, with the lantern still lit.

'Come, darling, you must come up on deck,' he whispered. 'The children are asleep, they won't miss you for a few minutes. There's something you *must* see!'

Eliza, grumbling, crawled out of the bottom bunk and put on a warm dressing-gown and a shawl.

'What is it that's so important? Can you see Table Mountain already? Anyway it's too dark.'

'No, there's no land in sight. Wait till you see.'

'I'm not going on deck just to see a passing ship! I can see that quite as well from the porthole.'

9

'No, dearest, it is not another ship. Now come on, before you wake the children.'

The wind had abated, and the decks were not so steeply slanted, as he helped her up the companionway and lifted her over the coaming. The masts soared up into the sky, their square sails bellied taut, as the wind sang and keened through the miles of rigging.

'Now look!' He led her aft, away from the saloon lights. He pointed up at the brilliant stars. They seemed to move to and fro among the spars, to the gentle motion of the ship. Behind them the helmsman stood at the wheel, by the ghostly glow of the binnacle lamp.

'See? Just beside the mainmast, a little to the right, and halfway down to the horizon: the Southern Cross!'

'Well, yes, Ronald; I have seen it before.'

'I haven't seen that constellation since I left Réunion, as a boy; and there it used to disappear below the horizon for half of its circuit. From now on we shall see it higher and higher in the sky, until at Hobart Town it will circle without ever setting, round the southern Pole.'

The two pointers, in line above, were twinkling so vividly that they seemed like two white birds rapidly moving their wings. The stars swam slowly to and fro behind the masts. The Pole Star and the Bear had disappeared to the northward, and the southern constellations rose in their place; Argo the ship with its bright star Canopus, and the curve of Corolla Australts.

'The stars are very fine,' Eliza admitted, 'but I am getting cold, and would like to go back to my bunk.'

Ronald kissed her, and helped her back down the companionway, dimly lit by a swining lantern. Then he went back on deck, to gaze at, to be drowned in, the splendours of the night sky.

In Cape Town they had two weeks ashore, and Eliza recovered her spirits. The air was clear and dry, the sky an unbroken blue. They admired the Dutch Colonial houses, the wide streets, the long, sandy beaches, and travelled in two-wheeled carts drawn by fearsomely-decked Zulus in native head-dress. While Eliza took the children to the park, Ronald went with an expedition of a few men from the ship to climb to the top of Table Mountain, from which he could look down on three Oceans – the Atlantic, the Pacific, and the Southern Ocean.

Before they sailed, he acquired some seedlings of acclimatised English apples packed in boxes in damp earth. William had told him that apples, and most stone fruit, thrived in the Southern Hemisphere in the bracing climate of Van Diemen's Land.

After rounding the Cape, they sailed due west in the Roaring Forties towards south-western Australia, where so many Dutch navigators had come to grief before it was properly mapped. The last leg of their journey was saddened by a burial at sea, of a young man who had gone ashore at Cape Town and contracted a fever. All the passengers were well acquainted by now, after three months at sea, and Eliza wept as they committed his body to the deep, tilted from the burying-board from under the bright Union Jack which covered him. It seemed terrible that there was not even a coffin, just a bundle wrapped in sailcloth, vulnerable to the great fierce fish which prowled the deep-blue waters of the southern Indian Ocean.

'What if it had been you!' she wailed, her arms round her husband as she stood with him in a sheltered corner of the deck that night after dinner. What if she'd had to face the unknown land alone, with two tiny children to provide for? But he was alive, even the apple trees were thriving, there was nothing to mar their safe arrival off the Great South Land and that tiny dot in the ocean, away at the bottom of the world, the distant unknown island of Van Diemen's Land.

The *Greenock* had anchored in a beautiful land-locked harbour with deep water close inshore, so that quite big ships could lie at the wharf with no need for lightering. The substantial stone buildings of Hobart Town were spread over some low hills, behind which rose dark, wooded crests and the great bulk of Mount Wellington. Across the wide and islanded waters of the harbour rose the lower peak of Mount Nelson, with the semaphore's wooden arms outlined on its summit.

As soon as a ship was sighted by the watchers on Mount Nelson telegraph station they semaphored to Battery Point the news of 'Ship in sight'. The Battery staff then ran up a flag, a red cross on a white background. Another identification flag would mean, if plain red, 'Ship from England, with male convicts'.

Any ship from England produced a stir of excitement in the town. When a convict transport was signalled, warehousemen in leather aprons, loungers looking for a job rolling barrels of salt pork or lighting-oil across the quay, a few red-coated soldiers from the Military Barracks, merchants hoping for the latest news from the outside world; all would be at the quayside to see the three hundred or so miserable convicts shuffle from the hold in chains. The military detachment which guarded them would then deliver them to the Convict Barracks, or Penitentiary, where Lieutenant William Gunn was the Superintendent. He was reputed to be a just and kindly man, to whom prisoners could make a complaint of any grievance they might feel they had.

It was Lieutenant Gunn's job to call over the names of the new arrivals and inspect them one by one, when they would be questioned about their religious background and ability to read and write; and to ensure that their previous histories, crimes, physical appearance and height were recorded. All were passed under the measuring-stick, given their convict numbers and their prison uniforms, and marched off to the cells.

Prisoners of the First Class – which meant the worst – who had been sentenced to work on the roads, wore the coarse yellow dress with the word Felon stamped upon it. Each morning at six they were sent out in the chain gang,

12

after a breakfast of gruel, to work for twelve hours with an hour off for a midday meal. The men were not chained together, but travelled and worked in a gang of about thirty, each man dragging a heavy chain between his ankles, or holding it up with a twist of rope around his left hand. Quarrying stone was one of their chief occupations, for public buildings and bridges and for road-metal for paving roads.

As the huge wooden gates of the Penitentiary swung open, the road parties would emerge, long lines of men in single file, shouldering their shovels or stone-breaking hammers with one hand, and with the other holding up the heavy iron chains, so that they moved only with a heavy, waddling gait. An overseer armed with a cane accompanied each party, and wielded it on the backs of those who by slowness held up the line, or who dared speak to one of his fellows.

So the splendid roads and bridges were constructed through the Midlands.

Today there was no convict ship. Indeed, there was not a convict in sight. Most of the Hobart Town prisoners had already been marched out to work in the quarries at breaking and carting stone, or on outlying roads. The passengers on the *Greenock* saw that Hobart Town had some well-made, though hilly, roads climbing from the wharf. The town had an indefinibly English air about it which cheered many a migrant's heart on first arrival. Beaches of pure yellow sand fringed each curving bay and inlet, and pretty cottage residences nestled among the trees which clothed the foothills. Only the sombre colour of the foliage, more drab than English green, struck an alien note; and over all arched a cloudless sky of the purest, softest blue imaginable.

After so many years – he'd not seen William since 1822, when he set off to make his fortune in Australia – Ronald felt a little shy as he presented his wife and children.

'Well! So this is my sister-in-law?' said William Gunn, beaming. 'You didn't tell me she was so pretty. May I be allowed a kiss?' He had come aboard as soon as the ship docked.

Eliza smiled shyly at the big man who looked much older than Ronald; his broad face made broader with sandy side-whiskers, his high, bald forehead. Most men these days, even military men, were cleanshaven or had neat side-whiskers. Lieutenant Gunn had the same clear blue eyes as his brother, though smaller, and a cheerful, hearty manner, where Ronald's was diffident. But then William had been a soldier from the age of fourteen; and he looked down on the world from a height of 6ft 4ins.

'Willy, old fellow!' Ronald hugged his brother and stood back to look at him. His face blanched. For his brother's sleeve was pinned to his coat, empty. 'But – but I had no idea you'd been wounded, even!'

'Yes, I lost an arm to a ball from a bushranger's carbine,' said William cheerfully. 'After being a soldier for years without getting a scratch, it's a bit ironic. It was years ago, I'm quite used to it now,' he added, seeing Ronald's look of horrified pity. 'Truly, I don't give it a thought.'

'But why didn't you tell us? Father had no idea—'

'Well, I didn't want to worry you, when there was nothing you could do about it. What the eye doesn't see . . .'

'Poor Unca Willyum,' piped up little Ronnie, standing on tip-toe to pat the empty sleeve.

William laughed and swung him off the deck with his one good arm. 'From having to do all the work, my left arm has become twice as strong,' he said.

'All the same, it's a shock,' said his brother. He told William he had brought letters of introduction, including two from the Commander-in-Chief of the West Indies, Sir Charles Smith; and one from the Secretary of State for the Colonies, recommending him to Governor Arthur for 'some minor post'.

'Some minor post, ha! We'll see about that,' said William, who as Superintendent of the Convict Barracks in Hobart Town, had control over both the men's Penitentiary and the Women's Factory at the Cascades, where there was also an Assistant Superintendent whose wife was Matron.

The newly arrived family, settled into temporary quarters by William, soon realised that Hobart Town, in proportion to its population, contained more thieves and pickpockets than London. Bushrangers roamed the countryside, and marauding parties of blacks robbed outlying homesteads of guns and food. It was so bad in Hobart Town that shopkeepers slept on their counters to watch over their property. Sacks of flour and whole hogsheads of salt meat disappeared from Government stores. But bushranging, according to William, was not as bad as it had been four years ago, when Brady's gang terrorised the northern districts. They would hole up in the rocky hills behind Launceston, in a position which commanded both the road up the west bank to George Town and the traffic on the River Tamar.

Gradually Ronald extracted the story of how William had lost his arm.

Not long after his arrival in Van Diemen's Land, when Brady was the leader of the most desperate gang of outlaws, William had been in charge of a party of ten soldiers hunting for them. The gang had quitted the far north and were raiding properties in the Midlands. News arrived that after burning some outbuildings at Mr Lawrence's property of Formosa, they had crossed the country towards Oatlands.

'We arrived at Sorell late in the evening – wet, cold, and tired. The men were billeted at the local gaol, while the doctor offered me dinner and a bed at his house. My men were just cleaning their firelocks when Brady and his gang arrived, and taking them by surprise they locked them in a cell of the gaol.'

'What incredible cheek!'

'Yes – but Mr Laing the gaoler saw them, crept out of his adjoining house, and ran to the doctor's to give the alarm. I

15

took up my double-barrelled gun and set off towards the gaol. But on the way I was ambushed by Brady and one of his men, known to be a crack shot.

' "Shall I pot him?" asked the fellow.

' "No. He's shown some pluck, coming on his own. Just wing him."

'The man fired instantly, the bullet shattering my arm above the elbow. It knocked me down; the pain was excruciating. I thought I was done for,' said William mildly.

'So they had to amputate?'

'Yes, there wasn't much left of my upper arm. But it healed all right. Now they call me Wingy Gunn.'

William was regarded as a hero in Launceston, and had been given a government pension for catching half a dozen of Brady's gang. Grateful citizens collected a purse of more than £300 for him in recognition of his bravery. As well as his pension, he had been given the government post at Hobart Town, and a grant of land near Richmond.

'So you see it was almost worth losing an arm,' he said cheerfully, patting the empty sleeve that was tucked into the front of his jacket.

'And what happened to Brady?'

'Oh, he was hanged years ago.'

3

A LARGE, imposing building on one of the low hills beside the Wellington Rivulet, of attractive golden sandstone, was marred by the black bars covering the windows. In the courtyard moved women in dark-grey dresses with checked aprons – the prison uniform of those sent to the Cascades, the Female Factory, on their arrival by convict ship.

The women convicts were put to washing clothes and cleaning for two years after their arrival, unless they became assigned servants. Some were assigned almost immediately as servants to families in the town or on outlying farms; many came back again after a year or so. At least half of the women were serving a secondary sentence, sent to the Factory with 'loss of character' for becoming pregnant.

Prisoners who had become pregnant out of wedlock and been sent there to have their lying-in were set to picking oakum for twelve months while they nursed their babies. If the man concerned was willing to marry them, they could get a Ticket of Exemption to allow them to be released into the care of their husbands. Even men who were not responsible for their condition came to the Factory to choose a bride, for there were hardly any free and unmarried women in the Colony.

The only servants Eliza could get were convicts: a ticket-of-leave man as cook, and a hard-faced young woman assigned as nursemaid who had been recruited from among the inmates of the Factory. In her loneliness in her new abode, with Ronald out all day attending private interviews for positions and presenting his credentials,

17

Eliza tried to make friends with the nursemaid. They discussed companionably Frances's dirty napkins and Ronald James' wet beds. Eliza, though perpared to dislike her new home, had to admit that the days were wonderfully clear and sunny, and sheets and napkins dried almost as soon as they were hung on the line. And William told them that in the winter, when it could get quite cold though there were plenty of sunny days, there was firewood lying about just for the picking up.

The girl, Hannah, with her lank mouse-brown hair and sullen expression, was not attractive. The children did not take to her, but she did her work briskly and uncomplainingly. Then Eliza, trying to get past that forbidding mien, made the mistake of asking why she had been transported.

Hannah's face became wooden, expressionless. She went on folding napkins without a word.

'Come now, was it anything so very bad? Perhaps you stole a lady's handkerchief from her pocket? Or were you hungry, and stole food?' Eliza told herself that *she* would steal if it was the only way of feeding her babies.

More silence.

Eliza persisted. 'How long were you sent out for, Hannah?'

'For life.' Hannah lifted her chin and stared out of the window. A troop of redcoats was marching past in the charge of an officer.

'For *life*? Oh dear! Then it *was* for something bad?'

'I was sent out for murder. Lucky not to be 'ung, I s'pose.' She went on folding napkins, but now the words came out with a rush, like water from a breached dam. 'I stole a horse. Fust, that is. I rode 'im up to Lunnon to see me feller. 'E could read and write an' all, but 'e never once writ a letter, not for a whole year. I was in service in the country. I took one of the carriage-'orses and dressed in the livery-man's trousers, and I rode all night till I gets to Lunnon. An' you know what? 'E 'ad a fancy-woman there, and 'e tells me 'e's going to dob me in to the police for 'orse-stealing, so I'd get transported for sure and maybe

18

'ung. So I killed 'im. Stabbed 'im with the kitchen knife orf the table. Then I give meself up. I didn't care no more.'

She looked up defiantly into Eliza's horrified face. 'So now you knows.'

Frances began to cry from her cot, but as Hannah made a move to pick her up, Eliza pushed her away.

'I'll get her,' she said. For the moment she could not bear that woman to touch her innocent baby.

'Ronald!' she turned to him as soon as he came to bed; he had been out to dinner with William and some of his men-friends, and was a little elevated, though not drunk. 'Oh, Ronald! I've been waiting for you to come home, it makes me nervous being in the house with a murderer.'

'What do you mean, my love?'

'Hannah! The nursemaid. She told me today that she was sent out for murdering her lover. I knew she was a convict, but— Good heavens, our cook may have been transported for poisoning someone! It's horrible, it's—'

'It's inevitable, since there are no free men or women of the servant class emigrating. You have the choice of doing all your own work, or employing convicted felons.'

'I wish we had never left Antigua! If only I had dear old Nanny here.'

'Don't say that, love. Give the new country a chance. Things will get better, you'll see. Come, give us a kiss. Come on.'

'You smell of wine.'

'Well at least I didn't smoke a cigar, which was offered to me.' He untied his stock and sat down to pull off his boots, while she looking mutinously over the top of the sheets. 'And you must admit that the weather is delightfully warm.'

'Yes – too warm! And – and I'm going to have another baby.'

'Well – ! I don't know how we can afford it.'

'Is that all you can say?'

'I mean, I'm pleased of course. And at least now you no

longer have to fear getting pregnant, and I don't have to feel guilty making love to you.'

'I don't like that word, it sounds coarse and, and – medical.'

'Well, *enceinte*, then.' He pulled on his nightshirt and jumped into bed beside her. 'Come, my darling, let us make the best of our new freedom.'

'But what about the nursemaid?' She began to cry. 'I can't bear to have her look after the baby.'

'We'll get someone else. I'll ask William to make inquiries from the superintendent of the Female Factory for a second-sentence prisoner.'

'But those women have all been sent there to have their illegitimate offspring!'

'Well dear, if it's a choice between immorality and murder, I imagine you would prefer the former.'

He told her that William had obtained him a post, with the Lieutenant-Governor's blessing, as Assistant Superintendent under him at the Penitentiary. He would start tomorrow and learn the ropes, but it would mostly involved paperwork, which he was well used to. Among other books he would have to keep the Prisoners' Register, the Ration Register, the record of Magisterial Cases, the Prisoners' Character Register, and a register of clothing issue.

Before she could ask her brother-in-law to find her a more suitable nursemaid, Eliza came to revise her opinion of Hannah.

The Gunns' rented house, a cottage built of local brick, was situated on one of the steep, hilly streets in the foothills of Mount Wellington, which towered 4,000 feet above the harbour. Hobart Town was beautifully placed at the head of that deep inlet of the sea forming the estuary of the River Derwent, and from the front windows they had a view of the dark blue waters below, and the forest of masts and spars at Sullivan's Cove.

The English-looking garden, with wallflowers and prim-roses brought in pots all the way round the Cape, and the apple-trees that Ronald had planted flourishing at the back, made a perfect playground for little Ronnie, who pulled his wooden cart along the brick-paved paths. Eliza sat on the porch and sewed long-skirted baby clothes in the May sunshine of a tranquil autumn. The sky showed a cloudless, ethereal blue behind Mount Nelson.

A picket fence enclosed the garden, and a double gate which was kept closed. But looking up dazzled from the white material in her hands, Eliza slowly realised that for some reason the gate was ajar, and the little boy nowhere to be seen.

She gave a scream for Hannah.

'Come quickly! Master Ronnie—' She struggled to get out of the low chair which she had pulled to the edge of the porch to catch the morning sunlight on her work. She was already heavy with the five-month pregnancy which had begun in Cape Town. The chair tilted and spilled her over the edge of the veranda, two feet above the path, with a fearful jolt.

Hannah came flying out of the front door and threw up her arms in horror.

'Oh Mum, be you all right? I'll just help ye up—'

'*No, No,* leave me, I'm all right. But the gate was not latched, and Ronnie must have pushed it open and he's out on the road. Quick, quick! For heaven's sake, *leave* me.'

Hannah ran to the fence and looked over. She gave a cry of concern. Ronnie was pulling his little cart down the middle of the road, and over the brow of the hill came a loaded dray, nearly out of control, the driver pulling urgently at the reins and brake. She was through the gate in a flash, pushed the little boy to the side of the road away from the horse's hooves and the iron-bound wheels, then leapt up and grasped the big horse's reins. The wooden toy cart crunched beneath the wheels. The driver, as soon as the horse was brought to a standstill, hitched his reins to a gate-post and helped carry the yelling child inside.

'Yer not frightened o' horses, I see,' he said admiringly.

'Brought up with 'orses, I was,' said Hannah smugly.

Eliza sat on the gravel path below the porch from which she had fallen, the chair lying on its back beside her. She held her stomach and rocked herself to and fro, moaning.

The drayman looked rather shaken, but he touched his hat and told Eliza that 'this 'ere girl of yours' had probably saved the little boy's life by her prompt action. Ronnie, still indignant over the loss of his toy, was thrust inside the front door, yelling loudly. The cook came and took him off to the kitchen for a piece of brownie, and the drayman and Hannah helped Eliza to her feet. Having got her to bed, Hannah sent the man for Dr Bedford, and to ask the doctor to let Mr Ronald Gunn, at the Convict Barracks, know that 'Missus Gunn is taken crook'.

'It's the baby, yer see,' Hannah confided. 'Reckon she might lose it.'

She did lose the baby. Dr Bedford told her it was a boy, but he had been too small and weak to live.

'Very bad luck, my dear,' he sympathised with her. 'You are basically healthy, there is no reason why you should not have another. But you have lost a lot of blood, and just now you must rest and recover your strength.'

Eliza had made friends with a couple of Army officers' wives – her own father, Lieutenant Ireland, had been an officer in the 93rd Regiment – who had been travelling out to Hobart Town garrison in the same ship. They called on her and brought her the town gossip. They'd both been invited to a soirée at Government House, and met Colonel Arthur's large lady who had already presented him with twelve children.

Eliza shuddered. 'I find two quite enough to cope with, without proper servants,' she murmured. 'But I must say that Hannah, my present nursemaid, is a tower of strength in an emergency. I am going to ask my brother-in-law Lieutenant Gunn to ask the Governor for a pardon for her; you know she saved my little boy's life.'

'No doubt she'll get her ticket-of-leave soon, anyway.'

'I think not. She was transported for the term of her natural life, and has been here only six years.'

William Gunn listened sympathetically to Eliza's appeal on behalf of her nursemaid. He explained that Hannah would have to make a written application, or it could be made for her, to the Lieutenant-Governor, which should be supported by two depositions on her character by persons who had known her for a number of years, and a list of any ameliorating circumstances which might influence the Governor's decision.

Lieutenant Gunn himself could vouch for her good behaviour over the last five years, and another 'character' might be obtained from the Matron at the Female Factory where she had spent her first two years before being assigned; and from the family she had last worked for, if they could be found.

The result was that, after much grinding of the cumbersome wheels of State, Governor Arthur indicated that he would issue a Conditional Pardon to one Hannah Roberts, per ship *Susan*, if such was agreed to by the Colonial Secretary in London. Once the pardon was gazetted, Hannah would be free, though not allowed to leave the Colony of Van Diemen's Land.

Eliza was delighted, Hannah suitably grateful. But she confided in her mistress that she would be applying to leave her service very soon, for the dray-driver (a farmer from the Richmond district who was a widower with two young children) had asked her to marry him. He had been struck by the girl's brave and prompt action, and had been to call on her in the servants' quarters several times.

'Why, Hannah! I am so pleased,' said Eliza warmly. 'But I'll be sorry to lose you, and Master Ronnie will miss you, I know.'

'Oh, you'll get someone else, Mum.'

Now that she was happy, Hannah's hard face had softened wonderfully. Eliza had given her a new hairbrush, a great luxury, and her hair had lost its lankness and even tended to curl a little.

Her conditional pardon was gazetted the following year – though copies of the Gazette did not reach Hobart Town for another five months – and by that time poor Eliza had been uprooted once more and had gone to live in the northern capital of Launceston, a hundred miles away.

4

WILLIAM GUNN, stretching his long frame in front of his brother's fire in Macquarie Street – and it was many years since Ronald had sat by a wood fire –, told him that Governor Arthur had decided to do something drastic about the Aborigines and their increasingly bold forays against the white settlers. They were not only murdering shepherds in isolated huts, but making organised attacks on homesteads as soon as they saw the men were away in the fields.

'Martial Law has been in force for the last two years, outside the settled districts,' said William. 'And then His Ex. issued a solemn Proclamation directing them to stay outside an invisible line – a proclamation which of course they couldn't read, though it was set up on posts for their edification.'

'So what is he proposing to do now?'

'Well, it's going to be open war. The armed "roving parties" under people like Jorgensen have helped to keep them quiet, but very few have been captured. They're very wily, and excellent bushmen, and their aim with the spear is deadly. Mr Edward Curr had been petitioning the Governor to do something; they're not only spearing the Van Diemen's Land Company's sheep in the north-west, but his shepherds as well.'

'It's not just in the north-west,' said Ronald. 'There was a report the other day of two men working in the open on a farm at Oatlands, who were speared to death at midday. And a child clubbed to death with a waddy. Something will have to be done.'

24

'Yes. That's why Governor Arthur has called a conference of government officers and leading settlers, to work out a plan. He wants the whole community, private settlers as well as the military, to act *en masse* against "the savage tribes which infest the country", as he now calls them. His plan looks excellent, on paper.'

The idea was to beat or drive the most hostile tribes from the northern and central areas towards the south, where they could be herded into the southernmost tip of the island, Tasman Peninsula. As this was joined to the main island by an extremely narrow neck of land, it would be easy to bottle them up there and close off the neck with a cordon. Then they could all be deported to one of the islands in Bass Strait.

'Of course, Colonel Arthur is a soldier to his bootstraps,' said William. Arthur had worked out all the details with military precision, drawing up a detailed map or 'Field Plan of Movement of the Military', showing the lines of advance of the various parties marked in red: 'Each group will be divided into smaller parties of nine men under a leader, who will be responsible to the Army officer commanding the group . . .' 'I'll get you leave to join my party, if you like.'

'Do you think His Excellency will allow us both to leave Hobart Town?' asked Ronald.

'Arthur is so keen on his plan to drive them like a mob of sheep; he wants everyone he can get in the field,' said William. 'And I think it might succeed.'

However, some of the members of the Executive who were at the meeting had queried the neatly drawn plan. 'Er, excuse me Colonel Arthur,' said one, 'but this right-hand section marked 'A-A-A' on the eastern side of the Great Swanport River; how is this detachment to do anything effective, when it can only move down to Oyster Bay without joining the next detachments?'

'Oh, this is a purely military operation,' said Arthur rather loftily, 'which you, as a civilian, would not understand.'

'Perhaps not, Colonel. But if you propose to capture the wily Blacks with merely *military* manoeuvres, I fear Your Excellency may find yourself much mistaken.'

To which Arthur replied only with a smile of contempt.

Among the leading settlers who sent volunteers was Mr W. E. Lawrence of Formosa, in the northern Midlands, a wealthy landowner who had properties dotted over a wide area from Launceston to the Arthur Lakes. He sent his twenty-year-old son Robert to represent him, with nine men including three from the property Vermont, which Robert managed for his father.

On October 5th young Robert Lawrence set out light-heartedly with his men to rendezvous with Captain Donaldson's troop in the high country. All over the island, landowners and their servants, gardeners, and shepherds were starting on what promised to be a delightful picnic excursion, with a chance of taking a shot at the 'Black Crows'.

For the assigned servants taking part in the exercise, masters were expected to provide a good pair of spare shoes and a blanket, and seven days' provisions of flour, salt meat, tea and sugar. Prisoners holding tickets-of-leave would be supplied from the government depots at twenty different locations in the countryside. Only the most trusted men were to be allowed to carry firearms.

The time of year was early Spring. The pastures in the midland valleys were still green from winter rains, and dotted with new lambs. As Robert and his band left Formosa, the sun was just rising, gilding the dew-wet leaves of the gum-trees and shining on the golden puffballs of acacia, the wattle of the bush. Over all arched a perfect sky of delicate blue, a blue which filmed even the nearer hills with a mysterious veil, while the mountains, purple with distance, were still capped with snow.

Robert was looking forward, not to taking pot shots at the natives, but to collecting some rare plants for his new correspondent, Professor William Hooker, Professor of Botany at Glasgow University. He had already pressed

26

some of the common though beautiful *Epacris* for him, and had begun a herbarium of dried native plants.

A fortnight later, with their shoes wearing out, clothes torn on sharp rocks and branches, rations running short, and a cold wind with sleet driving in their faces, his men were wishing themselves back home, even at work.

Robert Lawrence had spent a miserable twenty-first birthday in the bush, cold, wet and hungry. He could not even write up his notes on the new species of casuarina and hakea he had found, because he had to write reports for Captain Donaldson every night, to be forwarded to Colonel Arthur in the field.

High on the cold central plateau, the party was benighted on the way to a rendezvous at Lake Echo. With the prospect of being out all night in the pouring rain, without blankets or anything to eat, the men were all bad-tempered and argumentative. Each one swore that the lake lay in a different direction, and each announced that he would make his own way there.

'You would be mad to split up,' said Lawrence. 'In this driving rain you can't see a yard in front of you. And if you get lost, a lone traveller will almost certainly be speared. Even if the Blacks don't get you, you could easily die of cold and exposure, or fall over a cliff. I cannot allow any man to leave.'

'Y' can't stop us, neither,' sneered a wizen-faced shepherd who had been complaining loudest about the cold and wet. 'We carn't even light a fire in this, and I'm not stoppin' out all night.'

'Me neither!' 'Too right!' There were growls of agreement from half a dozen others. Lawrence snatched up the gun of the only other armed man, and pointed his own gun at the disaffected group. 'I'll shoot the first man among you who makes a move to leave,' he said violently.

Grumbling, the men gave in, huddling with their backs against an outcrop of rock. The next day the sun came out

27

and dried their clothes, and with some aromatic shrubs and dry underbark from a melaleuca, they were able to light a fire and cook the duck and kangaroo Mr Lawrence had shot.

Captain Donaldson came over that night to complain about the size of their fire, which he said would give away their position to the enemy.

Yet Colonel Arthur himself, having called Captain Donaldson's men down from the high lakes to help pen the supposed captives in the south, next ordered a double line of huge fires to be kept up all night, and every third man to be on sentry duty. The arrival of the new division from the north meant that four hundred men could scour the country down to the isthmus. Yet no one seemed to have set eyes on a single Aborigine: they had melted away into the undergrowth.

The weather was foul. As Lawrence noted in his field diary, 'The men are becoming more ill-tempered, which makes the situation of a leader anything but pleasant.'

To make matters worse, they got into a thick and almost impenetrable scrub, where they made only about four miles a day. After passing through another patch of scrub, mostly prickly Moses, a dwarf acacia, and yellow bottle-brush, they came on five native huts made of bark near the trees from which it had been stripped. One of the men picked up a spear which had been newly made, the sap not yet dry in the wood. After that there was no more talk of going off alone.

Lawrence collected a foxtail orchid, and pressed it in the pages of his diary to send to Professor Hooker. His bush-jacket's button-flap pockets were full of seeds and berries.

The rumour now spread that no Aborigines had been seen ahead of the parties for days, but they had been robbing huts again in the north – in short, they had slipped quietly through the lines, and two thousand men had captured so far only one old man and a boy, while two more had been shot.

All the military detachments were now milling about in the narrow neck of land between Pittwater and the east coast. They closed the entrance to Tasman Peninsula – no more than a few hundred yards across – and within the trap they found one old woman.

In spite of a complicated manoeuvre which Arthur called 'cross-scouring' the country, this was the sole result of an operation costing some £30,000; plus the deaths of five soldiers from falling over precipices or getting drowned in rivers. The despatches to and from the field, from Arthur's 'Camp Sorell', exceeded the number forwarded and received by all the Allied armies in the recent European war against Napoleon.

The abortive Black Line was abandoned in the last week of November.

On the final day before departing for their homes, Lawrence and some of the other leaders of the various parties were asked by Captain Donaldson to take an *al fresco* meal and a bottle of wine with him in the bush, while their men were each issued with a tot of rum.

Among the leaders were Lieutenant William Gunn, and his brother Ronald on leave from his new position as Assistant Superintendent of the Penitentiary. The two young men, Robert Lawrence and Ronald Gunn, were introduced, and took a liking to each other at once: the dark-eyed, thin Englishman, full of nervous energy, and the tall young Scot, long-headed, easy-going and blue-eyed.

Looking for a notebook to write down his new acquaintance's address, Lawrence happened to pull out a handful of seeds and moss. He explained how he had become interested in botany of late, besides the other natural sciences.

'I have found a kind of prostrate wild cherry, and several ferns that I believe are quite new,' he said.

Ronald told him he'd heard that not less than 150 different native plants had been collected from Mount Wellington and on the banks of the Derwent at Hobart Town.

29

'Have you ever done any collecting or botanising yourself?' asked Lawrence.

'Never. My duties are all at Hobart Town – they keep me pretty busy. And then I'm not a free agent with a wife and two little ones. But if I come across any unusual plants would you like me to send them to you?'

'I should indeed. I'd be most grateful. Until the late campaign my collecting had been all in the north and the midlands. If you ever come up to Launceston, you must do me the honour of calling on me at Vermont. It's on the North Esk, just beyond the town. Spend a day or two if you can.'

'I'd be delighted, my dear Lawrence.'

So it was arranged. Neither of them thought much more about it, for it was a full day's journey from Hobart to Launceston and it was likely to be a long time before they met.

Lieutenant-Governor Arthur had thoroughly enjoyed himself. He sent some self-justifying despatches to London, pointing out that even if the Black Line had not succeeded in its main objective of rounding up the dangerous tribes, at least the sight of so many men in the field had had the effect of intimidating them and deterring them from their aggressions. He reported to the Colonial Secretary in London that the operation 'had not been fully successful', adding that of course 'no undertaking can be more arduous, in any country, than to capture savages; and in this colony . . . the country is perhaps the most rugged on the face of the earth. In spite of the fertility of its valleys, no country that I am acquainted with has so large an extent of wild, rugged mountains and dense tangled forests.'

No sooner had he written than he received new reports of several daring murders committed by 'these miserable savages'. The settlers had lost patience. They wanted all the natives shot, or banished forever.

In all this there was one ray of hope. A Mr George

Augustus Robinson, who had been Superintendent of a native settlement at Bruny Island in the south, had volunteered to go unarmed among the troublesome west coast tribes; and had even induced some of the most hostile to accompany him freely to Hobart Town, whence they were sent to a camp upon Swan Island in Bass Strait. It was thought that Mr Robinson should be encouraged in his mission, and should also visit other Strait islands to induce the sealers there to give up the native women they had abducted – one of the main causes of hostility towards the whites.

Ronald Gunn saw Mr Robinson outside his house in Murray Street, after his triumphal march into Hobart Town with the fierce chief Towterer and the 'Arthur River mob': men, women and children, the small children carried by their mothers, the men carrying nothing but their spears and waddies. The women's hair was curly, cut close to the head with sharp shells; the men's was decked with an extraordinary mixture of grease and dried red ochre, which produced the effect of a cap made of overlapping red leaves.

Ronald watched them give a display of spear-throwing which was certainly impressive. A melon was split neatly in half from a distance of sixty yards. After studying them carefully and speaking to some who had a knowledge of English – though it was a form of pidgin which almost needed an interpreter – he was impressed with their intelligence and decided they were not as low in the human scale as some had placed them, somewhere between an ape and a human being.

The mothers were evidently much attached to their children, and there was great affection between the old chief and his wife. Yes, they were human beings with human feelings, however different in appearance from European man. Yet he knew that whole tribes had been exterminated, shot down with no more compunction than if they had been animals.

He expressed these ideas to his brother, who like him

deplored the actions of settlers who went out hunting 'Black Crows'.

'The Aborigines certainly showed us up in the matter of the Black War,' said William. 'Everyone agrees that their eyesight is phenomenal and their bushcraft far superior to ours. Colonel Arthur has been made to look foolish. He is now pinning his hopes to a peaceful solution, with this man Robinson going into the bush after them.

'Have you met him? He's a funny, pompous little man, but driven by an almost religous fervour; not too well educated but with a good opinion of himself. Yet he's done what no one else has managed: gained the trust of the blackfellows, and induced them to come peacefully to the settled areas. They call him "The Conciliator".'

5

ONLY TEN months after the family's arrival in Hobart
Town, Ronald Gunn was promoted to the position of
Assistant Superintendent of Convicts in northern Tasmania, covering both the Female Factory and the men's
Penitentiary. The following year he was to become Superintendent, and soon, at only twenty-four years of age, he
was in control of all convicts in the Northern Division, the
distribution and assignment of convict servants, and the
conduct of chain gangs. A year later he was appointed
Magistrate as well.

Once they graduated from the chain gang, or First Class,
convicts could be assigned as servants either in town, as
house servants, or in the country as stockmen, shepherds,
and farm labourers. Good cooks were in demand in the
towns, and educated prisoners were put in a class by themselves, after working their two years on the roads, and given
positions as clerks and scribes and allowed out on parole.

By temperament Ronald Gunn was not suited to be a
supervisor of prisons, and too often he felt sympathy for the
prisoners, particularly for soldiers transported for 'insubordination' and for educated men sent out for political
crimes, or for ingenious forgeries; or even, 'abduction of an
heiress'. One man, Hartsoke, who had been transported
for twenty-one years for the 'attempted murder' of a
rascally uncle, had such an open, honest countenance, and
such a gentlemanly demeanour, that Ronald was half-
inclined to believe his story that he had been wrongly
convicted.

As a registered Passholder Hartsoke was allowed to take employment, or if unemployed was lodged at the Police Barracks in Hobart Town with other partly emancipated prisoners. While lodging at the 'Tench he had been sent with twenty-five others to Launceston, in care of a constable who had himself been a prisoner.

Ronald Gunn became interested in the 'gentleman prisoner', and offered him some unpaid office work, with time off in the afternoons. With a signed pass Hartsoke could walk freely about the growing town of Launceston, the capital of the north, situated on the broad Tamar estuary forty miles from the sea. He had served in the Madras Cavalry in India, so they both had an Army background. Knowing that there was a former officer of that regiment with a property in the Midlands, Ronald wrote to him and suggested Hartsoke as a tutor for his three boys. The officer had for some time been looking for someone suitable, but there was no one available in the free community.

So Hartsoke, full of gratitude to Superintendent Gunn, set off to walk to the south, with a 'swag' of blanket, tea, sugar, a pint-pot for boiling water, tinder-box, frying-pan, a threepenny loaf and a pound of fresh mutton. He wrote on arrival that he had enjoyed 'a pleasant pedestrian trip with *al fresco* meals' and was his ever grateful, J. P. Hartsoke.

Eliza found the northern town dull, and less congenial than Hobart in spite of the purple ramparts of the Western Tiers, and the great flat-topped bulk of Ben Lomond behind the town.

Besides, she had left behind her only women acquaintances, and had to train a new batch of convict servants. Ronald's duties kept him away from home every day in the week except Sundays. Young Ronnie was going through a difficult, self-assertive stage and Frances was cutting milk teeth. Eliza began to wish they were back in the colourful islands of the West Indies; sometimes, even, that *she* was back there, young, carefree and unmarried, the Captain's

34

pretty daughter who flirted with all the young officers. Her life now was bounded by the nursery and the bedroom.

As Superintendent, Ronald had much paper work, checking records of new arrivals and keeping track of Passholders, ticket-of-leave prisoners and 'trustees', as well as dealing with endless correspondence over the assignment of servants. Masters wrote complaining of servants, or sent them in with a note for punishment; servants wrote, if they were sufficiently literate, to complain of ill-usage and ask to be assigned elsewhere.

If it had not been so time-consuming, so that he had to work long hours even though magistrates' courts closed at four in the afternoon, he would not have minded the paperwork. He took a physical pleasure in the act of writing, in seeing the neat, sloping letters appearing from under his hand and marching across the page in ordered lines.

When his recent acquaintance Robert Lawrence wrote to complain of a drunken servant at Vermont, and to apply for a new assigned servant to take the place of a man who had just received his ticket-of-leave and left for Hobart, Gunn remembered how much he had liked the young man on sight. He answered the letter officially but added a postscript:

Do you recall our meeting in the bush outside Hobart Town last year? I know you shared my feelings about that farcical 'Black Line', tho' it gave me a welcome opportunity to get out into the country. I look forward to calling on you, if I can get away from my multifarious duties. How goes the plant and seed collecting?

He had not so far had time to look for any new specimens for Lawrence – who had entered rather bitterly in his diary, 'Received an assortment of native seeds from Circular Head collected by Dr Hutchinson, one of the few whom I have known to keep their promises.' Hinks Hutchinson was the only medical man at the small settlement of Circular Head nearly a hundred and fifty miles to the north-west.

When Ronald arrived on his first visit to Vermont on a

Sunday afternoon, he found Robert Lawrence engaged in a careful anatomical examination of what he called 'the male organs of generation' of an opossum, with pencil sketches of the parts.

'I thought botany was your great interest, not physiology,' said Ronald, apologising for not having done any collecting yet.

'I'm interested in all branches of science. Geology, chemistry' – he pointed to a double row of high shelves containing coloured crystals and powders in glass jars – 'zoology, horticulture, and above all botany. I've been on this island for five years and I'm still finding fascinating new specimens of birds, animals and plants: in Van Diemen's Land we have a whole new land, full of fresh and undescribed species, an almost unlimited field for scientific activities.'

'I'm afraid I know little of science. I've been with the military most of my life since I left school, and then a journalist for a brief time in Edinburgh; but I prefer scientific books for reading matter.'

'Well, I left school in England at sixteen to come out here, and have taught myself from books. Would you like me to lend you some books on botany? I have a good microscope, too.'

'Why yes, I'd be interested. But I wouldn't dare borrow such valuable works. Perhaps I could come over one weekend and spend some time studying?'

'Of course, my dear chap! Professor Hooker has sent me the essentials, Brown's *Prodromus*, and a copy of his *Botanical Miscellany* – both totally unobtainable here of course.'

'And all totally unintelligible to me, I expect. But I'm willing to learn. I like reading, and find the lack of a good public library or a decent bookshop nearer than twelve thousand miles away one of the trials of exile.'

'We will visit my father's town house in Launceston when you get the time, and you can browse in my father's library. He has some original papers of the great Jeremy Bentham.'

36

'I believe he actually *bought* a ship to transport his goods out from the Old Country? He would not be limited in what he could bring. I had to content myself with £50 worth of freight, I'm afraid.'

'You can read Latin, I suppose?'

'Tolerably well. It's better than my Greek.'

Robert washed his hands in the small sink in his laboratory, and hung up the dust-coat he had been wearing for dissecting.

'Come along and I'll get that lazy cook to make us some tea.'

'Is he the man you've been having trouble with?'

'No, that's Morgan, the gardener. He's been drunk the last three weekends and not fit to work on Monday. Also I could do with another assigned man.'

'Are you going to send him in for sentence?'

'No, I'm hoping the threat of punishment will be enough. But if not—"

'You know, I don't like this business of having to sentence men to secondary punishment. They're already being punished by their exile from home and family – though I had an application the other day from a woman who has followed her husband out here, and has asked to have him assigned to her as a servant!'

'Is that possible?'

'Certainly, if she came free and can afford his clothing and rations. She seems respectable enough.'

'I don't like the lash myself, but if your man is sent to the chain-gang you lose his labour. I would ask you just to give Morgan a reprimand and fine him a few bob, so that he can't afford tobacco for a week or two, if I do send him in.'

'I don't like it either, but if you have a convict constable in charge of a consignment of two women for the Factory, who takes twice as long as he should to get here from Hobart, and the women complain of indecent assault – well, what else can you do but give him thirty, *pour encourager les autres*? Or a few weeks in the chain-gang. But most prisoners prefer a flogging, and get it over with.'

Ronald had grown up seeing soldiers flogged for misdemeanours in the Army, but when possible and for minor transgressions like drunkeness, he preferred to impose a fine.

'It seems a shame, in a way,' said Lawrence, 'that a new country with such pristine natural beauty should be occupied by the outcasts of society. Though some emancipists have already made good citizens.'

'I don't know . . . Van Diemen's Land has been given a good start in a material sense: such substantial buildings, stone bridges, handsome churches, and roads from south to north all built by cheap convict labour. All produced by the System.'

'Yes,' said Robert Lawrence. 'And my father has profited by it too. But it will have to cease eventually, and the population be made up of free immigrants and Currency lads, born here.'

'That won't be for a long time yet, if ever.' Ronald, whose very livelihood – and that of his brother – was dependent on the continuance of 'the System', could not contemplate its end with equanimity.

Unlike most young men of their acquaintance, young Lawrence and Gunn found as they got to know each other that neither was interested in a social round of hunting, dancing and drinking. As a single man of ample means, Lawrence had more opportunity to indulge in these activities, but he regarded them as a waste of time. As it was, the days were never long enough, filled as they were with his many interests including gardening and chemical experiments, zoology and botany. He kept a daily diary of his excursions and discoveries:

'Sowed early peas . . . Forest trees of several kinds, native to this island . . . Dissected a specimen of the Cormorant family . . . Succeeded in several experiments on the Gases . . . Made an excursion in search of young plants suitable for transportation . . . Was fortunate in finding some plants of several rare species.'

38

After being away on one occasion for a few days in Launceston, Lawrence had found his garden, the fruit of three years' work, completely destroyed by cattle which had broken down the garden fence – two hundred head had spent the time treading into the ground whatever they did not eat. The new peas, which were in a different enclosure, had been attacked by grubs.

As he said to Gunn, 'Truly I am an unfortunate devil as I have most truly said. How often are our fondest hopes denied us!'

To his surprise Ronald found his wife in the sulks when he returned home, late on Sunday night. He was full of enthusiasm for microscopes and dissection, and fired with the spirit of scientific inquiry. Eliza declared that she did not want to hear the disgusting details of the anatomy of a platypus.

'But it's a fascinating creature, so strange that naturalists in England thought the first specimen sent Home to be a hoax; a furred animal with a duck's bill, which is oviparous and lives in water. Which is why they have given it the Latin name of *Ornithorynchus Paradoxus*. It is a monotreme—''

'I don't care if it's a mammoth! I am *sick* of being here all the weekend with no one but children and servants to talk to. And – and I fear I am expecting – again.'

'There – you see, that's why you're feeling moody. I'm sorry to have left you all alone, dearest, and that you felt left out. But I couldn't take you with me. Mr Lawrence is unmarried and it's very much a batchelor establishment . . . That is where I am more fortunate, in spite of his wealth. *You* are my treasure.'

He folded her in his arms and though she stood unyielding within his embrace, once they were in bed she melted and met him with a passion which surprised him. He wondered uneasily if such activities might not harm the coming child; but he took her gently, from the back, while Eliza lay on her side and moaned with pleasure.

She still wanted him, and he presumed that wise old Mother Nature knew best. Dozing off with a hand cupped round one of her firm young breasts, he thought drowsily that he would not exchange for all Robert Lawrence's wealth and freedom, the present felicity that was his.

On another visit to Vermont, Ronald was invited to dinner and stay over Saturday night. On Sunday they visited Mr Lawrence senior's home, Formosa, and Ronald was introduced to the library and to the weeping willow which grew in the coutryard and was now in full leaf. It had been grown from a cutting taken from Napoleon's grave at St Helena when the *Lord Liverpool* cutter called there on the family's voyage to Van Diemen's Land. Several apple trees, too, were flourishing, brought as cuttings from acclimatised trees in Cape Town like the ones he had established in Hobart Town. These healthy transportees showed that living Tasmanian species might also be sent in a reverse direction to the British Isles.

6

THE NEXT time Ronald was away from home it was on a less pleasant occasion. He was called to jury duty at a coroner's inquest into the murder of two white men, for which three Aborigines had been arrested and had just been brought down to Launceston from the goal at George Town.

Two women were with them, one of their own tribe who said she had witnessed the murders, and another 'tame' native who spoke some English and acted as interpreter. The Superintendent of the Launceston lock-up had seen to it that they had a fire in their quarters – almost as much a necessity as food to the naked black men – and that they were fed, but reported that when he went to see them they were sulky and sullen as a cage of black cockatoos.

In court, the first witness described how Captain Thomas, a settler near Port Sorell on the north coast, rode down to the landing with his overseer, Parker, to supervise the unloading of some stores. A few members of the Big River tribe were standing about and begging as usual for 'breadlie, tea, and tchugar', for they had acquired a taste for the white man's food. One settler had retaliated after the theft of flour from his hut, by concealing a possum trap with iron jaws in a bag of flour, and an Aborigine lost an arm as a result.

Captain Thomas, who had always been on good terms with the Aborigines, directed that they should be given some goods, and while conversing in pigdin English with the men, learned that the rest of the tribe were camped not

41

far away. As the latest advice from the government in Hobart Town was that 'conciliation' was important, he decided to go with them and visit the camp. His overseer then protested: 'Surely you're not going to trust yourself with those blackguards who'll kill you directly they're out of our hearing!' But Thomas replied: 'Oh, they are not so bad as they are painted. I'm not afraid to go with them.'

Parker, uneasy and mistrustful, shouldered his double-barrelled gun and went along with the small group of guides, who were smiling and indicating the way.

When the two men had not returned, the carters with the load of stores, having waited till sundown, set off for the homestead, whence four servants were despatched in the morning to look for the missing men.

Meanwhile, some women of the tribe had turned up at Northdown, followed by three of the men; and the servants, becoming suspicious, secured them in a strong-room, then sent them by boat to George Town gaol.

An officer of the Van Diemen's Land Company then gave evidence of how he had interviewed one of the women in the gaol, with the help of another woman interpreter, and found that Captain Thomas and his overseer had been murdered by the tribe. The woman offered to guide him to where their bodies lay, about two miles into the dense bush behind the port.

The witness, a tough adventurer who had been a leader of one of Colonel Arthur's 'roving parties', shuddered and covered his eyes with his hand, recalling the grisly sight.

'The first I saw,' he said, 'was a mob of crows flying up. Something dead, I thought. Then I came on the overseer. He was *nailed* to the ground by spears. A dozen shafts were driven right through his body, and his head had been smashed in with waddies; not just with one blow, but his skull smashed into little pieces.

'The body of Captain Thomas lay about sixty yards further along the native track. He had ten spears through him . . . According to the story of this woman, through the

42

tame native, they had planned the whole thing. The overseer's gun had been suddenly snatched from his hand by one of the prisoners, and he was set on by half a dozen men. Captain Thomas had tried to run for it, but the fastest runner among the men overtook him, catching him by the skirt of his frock coat. He was knocked over and speared where he lay. And yet he'd always been kind to the Blackfellows, encouraged them to come round his place. He'd done nothing to hurt them.'

After two more witnesses had been called to testify that the only intercourse between Captain Thomas and the Big River tribe had been friendly, the VDL Company's witness, McKay, was recalled to interpret the black woman's evidence as transmitted through her friend. But to his consternation she had completely altered her story; the three men present had nothing to do with the murders, she insisted. They were 'sitting down' back at the camp. McKay turned in exasperation to the jurors.

'It's quite evident to me,' he said, 'that a plan has been laid to get the prisoners off by getting her to contradict her former evidence.'

The jury retired to consider its verdict. 'I'm inclined to believe McKay,' said Ronald Gunn, and the others agreed with him. If the three men had nothing to do with the murders, why had they followed the women and tried to get them to come away, as had been told in evidence? They were obviously afraid the women would 'talk'.

After some discussion the twelve returned a verdict: the men had a case to answer for premeditated murder, and should be committed for trial accordingly.

Ronald had studied with interest the three Aboriginal men in the courtroom. They were all rather small in stature, but muscular; all had fierce dark eyes, the whites rather bloodshot, beneath overhanging brows. One man looked a real villain, with his plastered red wig and wide, cruel mouth. The other two were younger, one of them quite prepossessing if fear had not made him bite his lips and roll his eyes continuously. But Ronald felt sure that they should hang for the horrible crime they and their tribe had committed: it could not go unpunished.

The case had caused extraordinary interest and consternation all over Van Diemen's Land, but particularly in the northern capital. Feelings among the white settlers ran high when the eccentric judge, the Attorney-General of the time, refused to prosecute. He felt that there was a lack of evidence that the right three men had been caught. He discharged them into the care of George Robinson, 'The Conciliator' and banished them with his other willing captives to an island in Bass Strait.

'It's unbelievable!' said Ronald Gunn to his wife. 'If they didn't actually strike the blows, those three men – and the woman said at first they *had* committed the actual murders – were technically guilty with the rest of their bloodthirsty tribe.'

The local press bitterly criticised the judge for letting the murders go unpunished. Mr Edward Curr, the absolute ruler of the Van Diemen's Land Company and its 500,000 acres of land and 400 men, was particularly upset, because he had lost several shepherds over the years to the 'Big River mob'. In the latest atrocity the victim, who was known to have abducted an Aboriginal woman, had been battered and horribly mutilated; his genitals cut off and stuck mockingly in his mouth.

The Company had acquired 250,000 acres between Woolnorth and the Middlesex Plains, on top of their original grant of 250,000 acres on the coast. The Company imported artisans and shepherds from England, under indentures, besides employing two hundred convicts as assigned servants. Curr had built a magnificent mansion, Highfield, on the bluff beyond Circular Head.

Robert Lawrence, who managed Vermont for his father, knew that there was no love lost between Curr and Lawrence Senior, who had fallen foul of Colonel Arthur. Edward Curr was a member of the ten-man Executive Council, which Lawrence Senior had not even been asked to join.

Lawrence, like other settlers, had trouble getting enough competent servants and stockmen, and had had several brushes over farm labourers, for good men were scarce. So when a strong, sensible-looking man came to Vermont one day looking for a job, he was employed at once to look after one of the huts and the stock pastured there. The man said that he had been employed by the Van Diemen's Land Company's station on the Middlesex Plains, but it was too cold and wet for him.

'Bejesus, it's a cold place!' he exclaimed. 'It's not even fit for sheep, let alone hooman beings, I don't reckon. I've seen a hundred lambs dead in the mornin', after a night of frost. At dawn the grass is covered in ice, at noon it's drenched with the thaw, and in the evenin', there's a cold dew that turns to ice again by mornin'. No wonder the feed rots on the ground.'

Robert Lawrence knew that there were rumours of heavy stock losses on the Van Diemen's Land holdings, and that Mr Curr himself had said that the Port Phillip District across the Strait in New Holland had a climate much better for sheep. What Robert did not know was that his new man was one of the free labourers imported from England by the Company, which paid their passage out and engaged them for three years on fixed wages. Men sometimes escaped from the service, where the pay was low, and offered themselves to private settlers who were prepared to pay better.

Robert Lawrence, riding out with his gun one morning towards the stock-hut occupied by the new man, called in to ask if he had seen anything of a Tasmanian Wolf or 'Hyena' which had been sighted along the River Esk. He not only wanted to stop the animal killing his sheep, he wanted a stuffed specimen to send back to England. The *Thylacine* was an interesting carnivorous marsupial, sometimes called 'tiger' by the settlers, but it was more dog- or wolf-like in appearance, though its back was striped like a tiger's.

'I ain't seen hide nor hair of 'im, Sir,' said Gale, squatting on his haunches to lift a billycan from his open fireplace,

45

after scattering a handful of tea in the water. 'I've seen 'em many a time in the Hampshire Hills, though. Them things would kill even a full-grown ewe if she was down.'

They were companionably sipping the near-boiling, milkless tea when there came a shout from outside. 'Hey there! You, William Gale!'

The man blenched at the sound of the voice. He set down the mug of tea with a shaking hand.

'Tis Mr Curr himself!'

'Of Highfield?'

'The same.'

Robert Lawrence stepped out of the door to greet 'the Potentate of the North'. Gale followed reluctantly.

Curr's appearance and bearing were in keeping with his reputation as a despot. He sat on a big chestnut stallion, now restively pawing the ground. His hands were gloved, and he carried a short plaited whip. He dismounted, handed the reins to the man accompanying him, and came up to the other two, hands on hips. He was a very large man with a broad head and big side-whiskers which made it seem even larger, and there was a haughty droop to his eyelids.

'Robert Lawrence, sir; this is my father's property,' said Robert, feeling absurdly young and inexperienced before the great man.

Curr did not hold out his hand. He nodded briefly, and asked, 'You are employing this man Gale as a stockman?'

'Yes, he's an excellent man, I find.'

'No doubt you do. He was trained on Company property, at Company expense. Goldie, bring this man's indentures over here', he called imperiously. The second man dismounted, led the horses over and handed across some papers.

'Now, Gale! (Come here man, don't skulk in the doorway. I know you're there.) You'll admit that you are indentured to our Company for another two years? That you absconded without permission?'

'Well. Y'see the cold was affectin' me health. I've got a crook chest, see.'

46

'And you thought you could get better wages elsewhere, no doubt.'

'Too right I could. And Mr Lawrence is a decent master, treats a man like a hooman being—"

'That's enough! If you will glance at these papers, Lawrence, you will see that you are illegally employing this man. Goldie! Tie his hands behind his back. You're coming back with us, my man.'

Gale stepped back, sheltering himself behind Robert. 'I'm not going nowhere!' he said.

Robert had set his loaded rifle against the front doorpost when he went inside the hut. Now he picked it up and turned on his visitors.

'This man is not a convict,' he said quietly. 'He's a free man, and you can't take him back by force.' He aimed the gun at Goldie's chest. 'Don't take another step, or you'll be sorry.'

He crumpled the indentures into a ball and threw them on the ground. Edward Curr's face was red, his big grey eyes bulging with anger, no longer heavy-lidded but open to their fullest extent.

'And I'll thank you to get off my land, both of you.'

'That man cost us sixteen pound for his fare out, besides his keep—' began Curr in his nicely-rounded baritone.

'You'll have my bank order for sixteen pounds shortly. It's well worth it to keep a good man. And now, good-day to you.'

Curr turned on his heel, mounted his horse and rode away without another word, followed by Goldie, scowling.

Robert told Ronald Gunn, who did not know Curr personally, that he might have been more cooperative if Mr Curr had not been so arrogant; but his manner made him feel obstinate. As for Goldie, the man had a reputation for shooting Aborigines, including women, in cold blood, and with the tacit blessing of Mr Curr. Robert was not sorry he had ordered them off his land, though it meant he had made a personal enemy of one of the most influential men in the Colony.

47

7

Dear Sir,

Give me leave to introduce to you my friend Mr Gunn; a gentleman who has lately acquired a passionate taste for the science of Botany, and who has become an enthusiastic collector . . .

So wrote Robert Lawrence to Professor William Hooker, his botanical correspondent in Glasgow, who had encouraged him with kind letters and praise of his own collections.

On his second visit to Lawrence, Gunn had become engrossed in Robert Brown's *Prodromus*, a first book of Australian wildflowers with many Tasmanian species. Before long he was collecting with even more enthusiasm than his friend, whose interests were scattered through all the sciences of which botany was only one.

To Ronald Gunn, a new world opened out. Behind and beyond the world of his work, the brutality of the chain-gangs and the lash, the prisons, and the solitary cells, was this other delicate, intriguing, infinitely varied life form which was his to explore, and to discuss with his dear friend Robert Lawrence in his lamplit study when they returned from a collecting excursion.

William Hooker had urged Lawrence to 'climb mountains; there the most interesting varieties are invariably found.' So Ronald set out with two of his men, Noonan and Dredge, on a weekend expedition to the top of the Western Tiers, and the source of the Meander and Mersey rivers.

It was a perilous ascent, only a few tufts of grass for a handhold, and a footing of loose earth and stones. Noonan was in the lead, and Dredge followed behind.

'If at any time our footing had given way, certain death would have been the consequence,' he wrote afterwards. 'I was not going to show it in front of the men, but I was petrified. I held on and climbed with a dogged resolution not to give up first, but was at no time easy in my mind.'

Among some high tree ferns and sassafras, they came on a deserted Aboriginal camp. It was the turn of the men to be uneasy. But Gunn knew that the natives often travelled in very small parties of half a dozen people. Their camp was a primitive one, consisting of a prostrate tree with sheets of soft bark stripped from other trees laid over it to form an open shelter. There were the remains of a fire in front, and a few animal bones strewn about.

They cooked a meal of a few green parrots he had shot, damper baked in the ashes and billy tea. Crawling through dense scrub, mostly waratah and prickly *Pultanaea*, it was intensely cold and damp. They lit another fire to dry out, roasting one side while the other was frozen.

Next day, his continual digressions to right and left in quest of plants amused the men, as he told Robert Lawrence later, when 'I found a pimelea to my delight unbounded. You know how it is – only a Botanist can imagine fully the pleasure of finding a new plant!'

The waratah was in flower and in places formed masses of beautiful crimson flowers. It was so thick and level surfaces were so few that in spite of the sacrilege they had to light their evening fire on top of a splendid waratah in full bloom.

The next day, coming out into open country, they counted 150 kangaroos in one mob. In the distance, the long, narrow plains were green as if under crops, the groves of myrtle and eucalyptus by contrast a sombre tawny green; and visible fifty miles away a band of blue sea showed the direction of Bass Strait.

Descending from the high country they entered a forest

of myrtles, some of the trees forty feet in circumference and tall in proportion. They came on another deserted camp of Aborigines with shelters built of bark, and trees with notches made with stone axes for climbing after possums. But the natives remained invisible, not even the smoke of a fire indicating their silent presence. Many had already been collected by George Robinson and shipped off to Flinders Island.

By now Gunn's knapsack was bulging with specimens, including mosses collected in wet, shady ravines, with some flowering forms, and lichens found growing on rocks.

When he returned he heard of some new raids among the V.D.L Company's flocks in the far north-west; there were still hostile natives about, though they showed up only occasionally. Robinson had arrived in Launceston, on his way to try to collect them, and he called on Ronald Gunn. He knew that Gunn was one who did not underestimate the work he had done in making life safer for everyone who lived and moved outside the towns.

'I've just come back from an expedition to the Tiers,' said Ronald, welcoming him. 'It was strange to come on a deserted camp, and know that travelling had become so much safer than it was two years ago.'

'I'm on my way to the west coast at present,' said George Robinson. 'An interesting country; when I was last there it was bitterly cold, and the country covered in snow. I am no botanist, I'm afraid; I have not made a study of the arboraceous flora of this interesting island.'

Arboraceous! Good gracious! thought Gunn. 'But have you come across the cider tree?' he asked.

'Yes, I have tasted the mellifluous sap of this tree; it rather resembles a blue gum, but the leaf is different. The sap, when fermented by the aborigines, tastes like rather sweet cider. They are inordinately fond of this drink; it can make them a trifle merry.'

'Do you remember where you saw the trees? I wish to collect some seed for Sir William Hooker.'

'I think it was on the far side of Lake Echo, that is the

50

northern shore. They were growing on the edge of an extensive plain.'

'I shall make an expedition there before long. You have seen more of this interesting island that most white men.'

'And you, sir, have had your adventures in the bush.'

'Yes; on this last I broke my journey, with my men, at the hut of Dalrymple Briggs. You know, the half-caste daughter of one of the sealers' women. The one who received a grant of land from the Governor for beating off a party of marauding Aborigines single-handed.'

'Yes, I brought her mother from Penguin Island in 1830,' said Robinson. 'The mother is now on Flinders Island. The Settlement has been moved, for the last time, I hope, to Peajacket Point.'

'Mrs Briggs is a credit to her mother's race. But there was no room in her hut, though she gave us a good evening meal. As it was a bitterly cold night, Noonan and I slept in some straw in the shed. Unfortunately the fowls were roosting in the rafters, and favoured us all night with their donations.' He laughed. 'And I don't mean eggs! Those hens hardly slept at all.'

'Er – hem!' Robinson permitted himself to smile briefly. 'My worst night was in a camp on the Arthur River, when the Aborigines' fleas transferred all their attentions to me – my skin being softer, perhaps.

'By the way, several settlers have expressed to me a strong desire that some mark of approbation should be awarded to me, as a token of gratitude for the many advantages that have resulted from my work among the hostile Blacks . . . I feel the extreme delicacy of bringing it up myself . . .'

Ronald promised to write to his brother in Hobart Town.

From his expedition Ronald was able to pack up a case of specimens to send to Professor Hooker in August 1832. He wrote:

Mr Lawrence excited in me a few months ago a taste for Botany and Collecting, and has since induced me to

51

trouble you with the result of my six months' labours. The collection is in many respects very imperfect and poor; although my rambles were very circumscribed I was successful in obtaining a few things that Mr Lawrence had never seen . . .'

He suggested that if Hooker did not want his services, so modestly offered, the professor could perhaps recommend him to some botanist friend, who might send a few books in return; as he was as yet ignorant of botany and had no means of acquiring information, as no books on the subject could be obtained in V.D.L.

He added sadly; 'Mr L.'s collection of books was at my service in his own house . . . but he has now removed *28 miles* from Launceston, previous to being married, and where he will in future reside.'

He felt that with such an accomplished collector as Lawrence, Hooker would not want him for another correspondent. But although Gunn did not know it, Hooker had not found any of his Van Diemen's Land correspondents quite satisfactory; some had sent only packets of seeds, or dried plants without the flowers or fruit which made each one distinctive. Some did not bother to reply to his letters.

Now at last, with the first letter from Ronald Campbell Gunn, Hooker had found the ideal plant collector and a scrupulous and interesting correspondent who was to keep in touch with him by letter for many years; who would prove himself to be courageous, venturesome, unafraid of discomfort, meticulous in noting the sometimes slight variations which separated one sub-species from another, and careful in recording the habitat. He was also careful and ingenious in packaging, whether pressing dried plants between sheets of paper or sending live mosses in damp soil.

It was not just that Robert had moved away and their delightful rambles were no more – there was rarely time to get as far as Formosa, where Robert had gone to manage his father's estate – but he had inevitably distanced himself from their friendship in his new absorption in the company of Miss Elizabeth Wedge. Ronald thoroughly approved of his choice and felt he could recommend marriage to his younger friend, but while happy for him he felt a pang for the loss of their old intimacy. Robert Lawrence had become like another brother to him, one who shared all his interests. Though he and William were on the best of terms, they really had nothing in common. William was a soldier of many years' standing, an easy-going and popular official, and had not the slightest interest in natural history. In fact he felt that collecting flowers was rather an effeminate occupation, though he liked growing them – English ones, that is.

William became aware of Ronald's new hobby on a visit he made on official business to Launceston in September. He brought the news that he too was soon to be married, to a young lady called Frances Arndell whose father had been a medical officer at Norfolk Island Penal Colony.

'That's wonderful news!' said Ronald, clapping his brother on the shoulder. 'It's about time you stopped being a bachelor; eh, 'Liza? We'll make an old married man of him yet.'

He opened a bottle of claret to celebrate the engagement. The wedding was to be quite soon, in early December.

'You two will have to come down to Hobart for the event,' said William heartily.

'We shall have an addition to the family by then,' said Ronald. 'It will be a bit difficult travelling with three children, but we'll manage.'

'If only we could get a good girl for a nurse, like Hannah,' sighed Eliza.

'I think I've found a girl who might suit you. I can have her transferred up here, as she is due for parole this month.'

'What was she sent out for?'

'Shoplifting. You know it's among the commonest crimes among women prisoners. It seems they are overcome

53

by temptation, to have something nice which they could never afford. Susanna Davies stole a pair of black silk stockings. But she's had no secondary convictions since she arrived. I believe she is basically a good girl.'

'Well, thank you, William,' said Eliza. 'I really am going to need a good nursemaid after the new arrival is born.'

After dinner, as they sat before the fire in the drawing-room which Eliza found 'odiously small', Ronald asked his brother if he had a microscope, or even a good magnifying glass, as such a thing seemed unobtainable in the Colony; he needed it for studying sections of flowers and seeds.

Eliza, who had taken wine with her dinner and was now sipping a glass of maderia, burst out with a sort of pent-up irritation which surprised William and disconcerted Ronald:

'But he would buy one if he could, oh yes, even if I have to use an old mildewed hand-mirror on my dressing-table because we couldn't afford a new one! He spends money on great sheets of blank paper and uses it for pressing flowers, no, not even flowers, dreary old weeds and bits of slimy moss and rubbish that he brings back from the Hills, going off for days on end and leaving me to cope with the children and a convict maid—"

She stopped to drain her glass of maderia, and looked expectantly at her husband who rather reluctantly filled her glass again. Eliza in this mood was hard to stop, and after a couple of drinks she was inclined to air her grievances to anyone present, her voice becoming rather strident and shrill compared with its normal soft tones. He had heard her, too, screaming at the children in a way that was most unlike her; but as she was so near her time, he made allowances for her condition.

William Gunn, though he felt sympathy for her, was embarrassed at being included in the family quarrel. He excused himself soon after dinner and left, to stay in the quarters for visiting officials just across the way from the Superintendent's quarters. Ronald agreed that though they could find him a spare bed, he would get a better night's rest out of hearing of young Frances, who was having sleeping troubles and nightmares. He told himself that Eliza's edginess was due largely to lack of sleep, and once the child settled down she would be more like her old self.

Still, he felt irritated at being deprived of his brother's company, which he always enjoyed, so early in the evening. His usual good nature was also wearing thin after weeks of disturbed rest, for he took his turn in walking the floor with the screaming child at two and three in the morning.

'You have a right to criticise me, in the privacy of our room, if you have cause for complaint,' he said stiffly as he got undressed, 'but I would ask you not to embarrass our guests with domestic squabbles. William left early because of your behaviour.'

'What nonsense! He wants to go and yarn with some of his military friends at the barracks, and drink port with them, and tell men's stories. Anyway, I would have gone to bed and left you two to talk about your boring police work. But he left almost as soon as the meal was over.'

'Yes, because you drove him away. And another thing. I think you should restrict yourself to one glass of wine at dinner while in your condition. Indulgence cannot be good for the coming child.'

'Oh, fiddlesticks. Now I cannot even have a drink to help me bear the discomfort of another baby.' And she began to sob.

Ronald could not bear to see her cry. He lifted her into bed and soothed her gently till she fell asleep, sniffing and hiccoughing like a child.

8

CHRISTMAS IN Hobart was blazing hot, with bushfires burning on the mountain and the sun a deep bronze in the smoke-stained sky. The exiled Europeans who lived there, both emancipated and 'came free', as ordinary migrants were termed in official records, nevertheless ate their roast goose or turkey, hot plum puddings with brandy sauce, and all the other traditional Christmas fare of a cold climate. There was no holly with red berries, no mistletoe (though on the mainland of New Holland a similar plant was parasitic on gum-trees).

Ronald, who loved his children, had been delighted when Eliza was brought to bed of a healthy boy. They named him Robert, not without some bitter quarrels over the name – for Eliza insisted that he was perpetuating the name of his friend, while Ronald argued that he was naming the boy after his Uncle Robert in Scotland. He was usually easy-going and could be moved by argument or tears, but this time he refused to budge, and the baby was christened Robert. Eliza immediately shortened his name to Robbie.

With considerable effort, and some misgivings on the part of Eliza, the Ronald Gunn family packed up the two-month-old baby and his new nursemaid, the older children and themselves and clothes for a week, and set off by coach from Launceston.

'I feel very nervous,' said Eliza fretfully. 'Only last week I read in the *Examiner* of the bushrangers holding up the Launceston coach near Deloraine, and robbing the passengers of jewellery and watches.'

56

'But no one was hurt,' said Ronald cheerfully, 'and no doubt they'll soon be caught and hanged. Did you hear about the lady passenger who was inclined to faint with the shock, but her husband asked her would she mind waiting for a more appropriate time, as he had been bound hand and foot by the robbers and could not assist her? So she bravely retained consciousness until they had made off, and after untying her husband fainted into his arms. I hope you would show the same restraint, my love.'

Eliza did not smile. She took all his remarks literally.

'I hope I shall not have to show any such thing. It is bad enough, Heaven knows, travelling with three children in the heat.'

The wedding ceremony, held in the Presbyterian Church of which William Gunn was an Elder, was to be performed by the Reverend John Lillie, who was born in Scotland and had recently come out to the Colony to take charge of St Andrew's. He was acclaimed as a preacher of great eloquence and power; and was also known to Robert Lawrence as a man deeply interested in science and natural history. Ronald looked forward to meeting him.

After a day's rest following the long journey to Hobart, Ronald and Eliza left the new maid (who had turned out well so far) to give the children their lunch and their afternoon sleep, while their parents went to the late-morning ceremony.

In the church, William Gunn towered over his diminutive bride, in cream lace with a veil of needle-run net covering her thick dark curls. William had said that Frances Arndell's grandmother was Italian; her grandfather, Surgeon Thomas Arndell, who had come out with the First Fleet, was a nephew of the sixth Baron Arundell, but had changed the spelling of his name. As Dr Arndell was dead, Francis was given away by her brother.

Standing beside William as his best man, Ronald was reminded of his own wedding six years before. As the vows were exchanged he turned to smile at Eliza in the front pew, looking pretty in her new straw bonnet lined with

57

palest pink stuff in fine pleats, sarcenet she called it, which enhanced her fine complexion. She smiled back at him dreamily, sadly, as if she too were remembering, and wondering what had happened to that eager young girl who had vowed to love, honour and obey till they were separated by death.

'Those whom God hath joined together, let no man put asunder,' intoned the preacher, and Ronald breathed an inaudible 'Amen!' The reception was held at the Arndell family home on Knocklofty, a high terrace just below Mount Wellington, which enjoyed an uninterrupted view of the deep, dark-blue harbour within its ring of hills. The house was long and low, with French windows opening on to the veranda, each framed with green wooden shutters which could be closed against marauding Aborigines at the time when the house was built. Now that the natives were mostly rounded up and deported to Flinders Island in Bass Strait, the shutters with their slots to take a rifle were kept against possible attack by bushrangers. The house backed upon wild uncleared bush, and there had been some uneasiness about the bushfires until the wind changed.

Before they sat down to the wedding breakfast, Ronald had a chance to talk to Mr Lillie about his new hobby of collecting wildflowers, and to discuss the *Thylacine*, of which Robert Lawrence had shot a fine specimen. It was supposed to be less destructive to sheep than the dingo of the mainland, killing only for food where the dingo would rampage through a flock, tearing out the animals' throats for the mere love of killing.

'I fear, sir,' Ronald said to Mr Lillie as they partook of a glass of sherry-wine, 'that many of our unique animals may become extinct. It strikes me that a few pounds employed in collecting emus, the different species of kangaroo, wombat, and so on would be well spent. And their food, being grass alone, there would be no expense beyond enclosing a piece of ground. There is that immense Government Garden and the Domain attached to Government House—"

'Quite, my dear Gunn, but our Governor is not interested in natural history, I'm afraid, any more than he is in botany and our indigenous plants. He is using the land to grow cabbages and carrots for the table, and for his horses.'

Ronald Gunn snorted in disgust. 'Cabbages and carrots! Do you know that our emu is already extremely rare, and in a few years will be quite gone? No means have been taken to domesticate or breed them. Kangaroos have been killed in tens of thousands for the sake of their skins, and people may live here for months without seeing one!'

'It's true I've never set eyes on a kangaroo, but then I've scarcely been out of Hobart Town . . . Ah, I think we're being called to take our places at the wedding feast.'

Ronald went to collect Eliza. She was talking to the bride's sister who had been matron-of-honour at the wedding.

Eliza had a half-empty glass of champagne in her hand, and a bright flush in her cheeks. He noticed uneasily that she was talking rapidly and rather loudly: ' – and of course there's absolutely no social life in Launceston, as far as I can see, and we never entertain, except of course when dear William comes on a visit. It's not as though I had any relatives here myself, not even a sister, they are all in Dublin and my parents are dead—'

'But you have your children, after all.'

'Ye-es . . . I hope they're all right, we've had to leave them in the care of a convict nursemaid, and—'

'Dear, we are being asked to take our places.' Ronald bowed to the sister-in-law and removed Eliza's glass, which was tilting dangerously in her hand.

'Ouf, it's so *hot*!' said Eliza, fanning herself with a lace-edged handkerchief, as they found their places at the long table. In fact there was a pleasant breeze up on Knocklofty, it was far cooler than down at sea-level. They sat at the top of the table with the bridal party, Frances looking happy with her veil thrown back, William beaming and pouring champagne with his one arm. Eliza took her glass back and drained it; William leant forward to fill it again.

'Don't forget,' Ronald whispered in her ear, 'that you

59

have to feed little Robbie in three hours' time.'

Eliza lifted one shoulder towards her ear, as if to shut out mention of maternal duties when she was out for once enjoying herself, and did not reply. She quickly drank half her glass of champagne.

Then there were toasts to 'The King, God bless him' – King Billy after whom the western pine had been named – and to the bride and groom, and each time Eliza drained her wine.

Ronald made his modest speech. Eliza, with a sweeping gesture towards him as he sat down, knocked over her own glass. The cold wine flowed across the table and into her lap. She gave a shriek, and then a helpless giggle. Her bonnet was awry, her pink gown stained. Ronald, dreadfully embarrassed, told her in a whisper that she had had enough to drink and had better pull herself together.

'Have I? Then so have you.' And with a deliberate movement she knocked his full glass over as well, while he was still distractedly mopping at the puddle the first had made. The gentleman on her left and the lady on his right stared stiffly ahead, pretending not to notice this extraordinary behaviour. Eliza giggled some more, while Ronald stood up and dabbed at his frock-coat and trousers with a damp table-napkin.

'Please excuse me – a slight accident,' he murmured, mortified as he noticed William's new sister-in-law staring from across the table; William, leaning across to share a joke with his brother-in-law, appeared not to have noticed. Ronald took Eliza's arm in a steely grip, jerked her to her feet and guided her out of the long dining-room, past what he felt was a row of disapproving backs, and asked a servant the way to the bathroom. There he rubbed his clothes with a dry towel, and made Eliza splash cold water on her face, while he sponged her dress.

He wondered how she had managed to get so drunk so quickly, for drunk she certainly was. Perhaps fatigue after the long coach journey, and then the fizzy wine on an empty stomach, had been too much for her. He guided her to the

60

bedroom which had been set apart for the ladies to remove their bonnets and titivate if they wished to. Fortunately she was now becoming sleepy. He lifted her onto the big bed where a few ladies had left their reticules, and took off her satin boots. She put her arms round his neck and tried to draw him down with her. He firmly tucked them back at her side.

After a while she began to breathe heavily, and he stole back to the wedding feast. He was very conscious of the wine-stain on the front of his pale trousers, and deeply ashamed of the scene in front of his brother's new in-laws. He muttered to William before he sat down that Eliza had a headache, and was lying down till she felt better. But the happy pair had little time for anything but each other, and William scarcely seemed to have noticed their absence.

One of the servants had mopped up the spilled champagne. Ronald resumed his place, a space between him and the nearest guest on his left who stared pointedly ahead of him, or conversed with his next-door neighbour, showing Ronald the back of his head. The sister-in-law opposite raised her eyebrows in inquiry, and Ronald muttered, 'She is lying down for a while.'

He had lost interest in the excellent food and the brilliant gathering, with military officers in their crimson and gold and the wives of high-ranking officials decked in satin and lace. He sat and worried. Had Eliza for some reason become more susceptible to drink, or was she just drinking more? She had never shown signs of taking too much before they moved to Launceston. He told himself that she had probably swallowed her wine too quickly to overcome her nervousness in this Hobarton society where she was not at home. Yes, that must be it.

He hoped that she would sleep it off, and that he could get her back to the Macquarie Hotel without any more embarrassing scenes. He believed that William had noticed nothing, but no doubt some new relative would soon put him in the picture.

He gave a dark glance at the sister-in-law opposite, who was daintly taking a single sip from her nearly full glass.

9

ROBERT LAWRENCE told himself he was the happiest of men. Not only was his young bride beautiful and loving, but she shared his scientific interests and was learning to skin birds for him to send home to England. She copied his letters in her fair round hand, or wrote them for him at his dictation, and was as excited as he when he found a new plant in flower. He had gathered that Eliza Gunn did not approve of Ronald's botanising, and that he carried on his scientific pursuits in the face of both silent antagonism and occasional vociferous opposition.

Packing up some bird skins for Professor Hooker, whose son William was a budding ornithologist, Robert added some notes written by Elizabeth: *The Bronze Wing Pigeon*, 'An excellent bird for the table and when alive very beautiful'; *Black Cockatoo* with yellow-barred tail feathers, 'The principal food of this bird is the seeds of the Banksia and a large variety of grubs inhabiting that tree, much sought after and eaten by the Aborigines of this Island.'

He made a visit to town to try to trace a consignment of willow and poplar cuttings which Professor Hooker had sent from England, which had gone on to Sydney in the ship by mistake, and come back after three months. He found them stored at the warehouse – every one of them dead! The wharf officials responsible for the mistake shrugged it off; it made him furious.

He called on Ronald and complained bitterly.

'It's so distressing to lose much-needed plants so unnecessarily,' he said, and Ronald agreed. 'But such is the ignorance of the officials who take delivery here – they actually asked why I was worried about "such trash"! – that it's impossible to get living specimens handled with proper care.'

Robert said he was already mapping out a course of scientific education for his first son when he should be born.

'Except that it might be a daughter,' said Ronald.

'Well, she can still have a scientific education.'

He had recently been on an expedition up the mountains in the neighbourhood of Formosa, and told an envious Ronald how he had collected *Lomatia*, the sweet-scented guitar plant, a new hakea and several species of the yellow bush-pea.

'I've sent a sample collection to Professor Hooker,' he said. "It's nearly two months since I collected them, but though it was still officially summer we struck some appalling weather, with rain and squalls and freezing cold. We had to camp halfway up the Flat-Topped Mountain till the weather cleared, then when we got to the summit we had snow. It was so cold that there was actually unmelted snow on each end of a log that was burning in the middle. I've written an account for Hooker's *Journal*.'

'I've still had no reply from Professor Hooker, you know,' said Ronald despondently.

'Well, you know how slow the mails are. And there's always the chance of a ship going to the bottom between here and England. I have Elizabeth make copies of my letters and descriptive notes, and send a duplicate on a different ship always. And she has a neat hand, like yours – mine is such an impatient scrawl, my brain races ahead of the words.'

Hooker later published extracts from the diary of this journey of Lawrence's in his *Botanical Miscellany*:

The high country here presents a rugged and romantic appearance, being constituted of small wet plains over which are scattered projecting columns of Basalt, and hemi-spherical masses of a species of Moss, resembling beautiful green cushions, and occasional masses of rock calling to mind ruined Castles . . .

A severe storm came on and the men returned unsuccessful from hunting. It was exceedingly cold, so much so that the men's kangaroo skin caps were quite stiffened. Snowing all night, a fall of several inches . . . however the sun when rising promised us a fine day. Saw numbers of fine Forester kangaroo, and observed the excrement of the Hyena. Collected *Richea*, and a trailing *Exocarpus* (Wild Cherry). Ascended the Peak, 500 feet above the plateau. The wind blew very strong and in less than an hour the thermometer fell 10° . . . Abundance of lichens here. As we approached the top it became very precipitous, and with the high wind I became too nervous to be able to ascend further though I made several attempts. My friend Mr Curzon, however, went right to the top. His small figure was an advantage, and he mounted with apparently the ease of a kangaroo.

A very cold night indeed, with a considerable fall of snow. On our descent next day of the Flat-topped Mountain, we passed fine specimens of the Mountain Lilac.

They had arrived at level ground at the foot of the mountain just as it was darkening, and reached Formosa at about 11 o'clock at night, after a walk of about thirty miles over rugged country.

Elizabeth, not knowing when to expect him, was already in bed asleep. One of the servants let him in, and he had a hot bath before climbing quietly in beside her, but he still felt chilled after a week on the high plateau. When she woke with a murmured endearment and turned to him, he buried himself gratefully in her softness and warmth.

Some time later, spreading her long dark hair on the pillow in silky strands, he exclaimed, 'I must be mad! To think that I could have been here in our bed, and instead I've been wandering about the mountains in ice and snow and wind and rain—'

'Yes, darling, but you positively *enjoy* discomfort when it's in the cause of science. And I wouldn't love you so much if your only interests were in sheep and wool. Did you find any interesting new plants for Dr Hooker?'

'Yes, indeed. I'll show you in the morning. Did you see our campfire the first night out? We made it very large so that you could see how far we'd ascended.'

'Yes. I was watching, and sent a prayer after you for your safe return. I couldn't bear it if anything happened to you, my dearest one.'

He held her tightly. 'Nor I, if anything happened to you. Indeed, I don't think I should survive you long . . . Dearest girl! Let us hope we'll grow old together, and have lots of children, and grandchildren, and I'll still love you when you're a great-grandmother.'

They fell asleep still conjoined, their breathing softly synchronised, so that as he drifted into unconsciousness he felt that they were mysteriously one flesh, one being, of which one half could not exist without the other.

Ronald Gunn came over for a weekend to see the new specimens before the case was sealed for Hooker, and Lawrence told him the happy news – he was to become a father in the spring. Ronald wrung his hand and congratulated him.

'Eliza and I have had our third, it's not quite as exciting as the first. I suppose you would like a boy?'

'I don't care. I'd like a little girl if she turned out as sweet as her mother.'

'You're very happy together, aren't you?'

'Very happy.'

Ronald Gunn heaved a sigh. He and Eliza had been happy once. Now he dreaded his return home, knowing that he would face sulks and recriminations. It was almost as if Eliza were jealous of his friend. Surely she couldn't be jealous of another man?

And yet he himself had felt a twinge of unworthy envy.

Robert Lawrence was such a fortunate fellow: son of a wealthy and indulgent father, his own master, able to take a week off to go exploring whenever he pleased, and apparently without his wife objecting; in the first flush of a loving marriage to an intelligent girl who shared his interests.

Of course his own Eliza, after seven years, was not quite the lovely girl he had married; but she was the mother of his children, and the living link to the shy young man he had been, fresh out from Scotland, in 1825. He still loved her, if only for their shared past.

On his return on Monday morning from his brief visit to Lawrence's home, he found as he had feared that she lay prostrate on the sofa. She had not recovered as fast as usual from the birth and still suffered from swollen ankles.

'It's not fair!' she pouted, fretfully pushing back the heavy red-gold curls which fell rather untidily over her forehead. 'You can go off visiting and enjoying yourself, while I have to stay home and mind the children when I'm not feeling well. The new girl is useless, as usual. Like all these convicts . . . sulky, sullen—'

'Dear, I have only been away for two days. Robert Lawrence goes on week-long expeditions of some dangers, and *his* wife does not object.'

'But she does not have three little ones to look after.'

'But Robert tells me she is expecting. And a first child is always the subject of some anxiety.'

Eliza was silent. There came the waking cry of the baby from the nursery. Then: 'Ronald, I don't want any more babies!' she almost wailed.

'Stay there and rest. I'll see to him,' he said. The nursemaid he had glimpsed through the window, hanging out clothes and napkins on the line, with Ronnie and Frances running about her feet.

He picked up the warm, wet bundle of little Robert and tossed him in the air. The baby boy gurgled with delight.

'I have to go to work, old chap,' his father said, as he expertly removed the wet things and pinned on a dry

66

napkin. 'I'll take you to Mamma now, but don't make too much noise, she has a headache.'

He wondered why Eliza always made him feel guilty. It was a man's place to be the breadwinner, and a woman's to bear and bring up the children which were almost an inevitable part of marriage . . . And it was not as if she didn't enjoy the making of them as much as he did. She had tried packing herself with a tampon of vinegar and soft paper, without success; as soon as she stopped nursing one child she started another. But for the miscarriage following her accident at Hobart Town, they'd already have a family of four. At least she was healthy and had no complications at the time of birth, he thought. It was to be hoped that the delicately beautiful young Mrs Lawrence would be equally fortunate with her first child. A healthy son would make Robert's cup of happiness overflow.

10

THERE NEVER seemed to be enough money coming in to balance the outgoings in household bills. For some reason the bills had increased markedly, while Ronald's salary had not. When he had time he went out with a cart and an assigned servant and picked up free firewood in the bush around Launceston.

This man, Thompson, had been transported for seven years for poaching. He was a native of Buckinghamshire, had lived in the country most of his life, and had a countryman's eye for birds and plants. Ronald had asked his brother to look out for a man skilled in bird-skinning, or even better a transported taxidermist, for though he shot some interesting specimens during these excursions into the bush, he made a botch of preparing the skins.

Thompson proved an excellent plant-collector. Ronald took the man with him at first just to carry bags of specimens for him, but Thompson was soon collecting as avidly as his master, and looked for no reward beyond a few words of praise when he found a new specimen. Ronald also gave him tobacco for his pipe. Camped out sometimes at night, with a bright camp-fire burning and the billy boiling for their black tea, Thompson puffing on his pipe and Ronald writing up his field-notes by the light of the fire or the moon, they reached a sort of companionship which transcended for the time being the positions of master and servant, of prison superintendent and convict.

Ronald Gunn had still not received any reply from Professor Hooker to his letter offering himself as a second correspondent. His letter had taken several months to reach Glasgow, and though Hooker, always meticulous in answering his correspondents around the world, had written at once, the mails were so slow that *his* letter was to take eight months to arrive by sea.

Meanwhile, Ronald wrote again rather despondently, once more asking for any botanical books and offering to pay for the more expensive ones; what he desired particularly was the *Prodromus* of Dr Robert Brown, a first book on Australian native plants with illustrations by Dr Ferdinand Bauer. He wrote of the discouraging circumstances of having no botanical library and no way of knowing what he was collecting.

All the time, Brown's *Prodromus* and Hooker's own book on foreign mosses were on the way and would arrive safe and sound with some back copies of the *Botanical Miscellany*, and some heavy paper for pressing plants. An encouraging and grateful letter arrived in October of 1833; the dried plants had reached him in most excellent condition, 'only last Friday'; and he hastened to say how happy he would be to have another valuable correspondent besides Mr Lawrence, 'his beat being a considerable distance from yours. More than one Botanist will be needed to exhaust the riches of Van Diemen's Land, where there is so much that is new.'

Ronald's joy was shortlived, for in the same month occurred another event which cancelled out his happiness at Hooker's acceptance, and was to haunt him for years to come.

On the first day of spring, September 1st 1833, Ronald left Formosa after a visit of two days, spent botanising with Robert Lawrence and discussing with him the possibility of inventing an instrument for taking, perhaps, pictures of plants in their native habitat – something more portable than the Camera Obscura.

Young Mrs Lawrence was heavy with child, but happy and in excellent health. On September 3rd she was delivered safely of a daughter. A few days later, when

Ronald Gunn received the news of the birth in Launceston, it was accompanied by more alarming news; the man who had brought it had ridden over from Formosa to fetch a doctor, for Mrs Lawrence had developed a high fever and was delirious.

'Bad news travels fast,' and at the beginning of October came the terrible news that Robert Lawrence's young bride was dead. The note which Robert had sent was almost illegible and begged him to come.

I am in such a state that I fear for my sanity, [his friend wrote.] I cannot bear to look at the child who caused this bitter loss by coming into the world. I have dosed myself with laudanum in an effort to get some sleep, but its only effect seems to be to depress me further. At least come and help me through the funeral, to be held on Saturday.

Ronald arranged for his assistant to take over for a few days in the following week. When he told Eliza he must go to the funeral, she said, 'Why can't I come too?'

He stared at her. 'Why, you scarcely knew Miss Wedge – Mrs Lawrence – and you didn't like *him*. Why should you want to come?'

'At least I'd be getting out of the house. A funeral is better than staying at home day after day.'

'Listen, this is not an *entertainment*. It is an appalling tragedy. I fear for the effect on Robert's mind, for he worshipped that girl. I must go and stay with him, help him over the worst of his loss. Perhaps I could bring him back here to stay? – yes, that might be best – new surroundings, where he will not be haunted by memories of their happiness . . .'

He was thinking aloud, and did not see Eliza's mouth turn down, till she asked, 'And would you be so distressed if it was me who had died?'

He stared at her, scarcely able to take in her words, his mind was so full of his friend's suffering.

'Oh, don't be so daft. You know you are healthy as can be, and apart from that one miscarriage you've never had any trouble with your pregnancies. Why, do you think you ought to see the doctor?'

'No, I'm healthy as a horse, or rather a brood mare. Don't worry. And bring Robert back here, I'll get the spare room ready for him.'

'Thank you, dearest. And look after yourself, don't do too much.' He kissed her tenderly, noting with only a corner of his distracted mind that there was a taint of brandy on her breath. It was only as he was riding out towards Formosa that he recalled it. Spirits in the morning? Well, perhaps she had a toothache . . .

He drank brandy with Robert that night, encouraging him in fact to get a bit drunk, so that he might sleep. He had been shocked at his friend's wild appearance – hair unkempt, eyes swollen and bloodshot, clothes looking as if they had not been changed for days.

'I tell you, Ronald, I don't know how I survived that first day. How – how I didn't . . . Excuse me, old friend. It's impossible to express what . . . I don't know, I can't conceive how to go on living without her, we had become so entwined that at the moment – the moment of her dissolution I felt as if an integral part of my own self had been cut away.'

'You have a little girl, old chap – she is a part of her too, you know. You must live for your daughter's sake.'

'I told you, I can't bear to look on her. If it weren't for her my dearest Elizabeth would be alive still. That's the hardest thing to bear; that *I* am responsible for her death, that *I* planted the fatal seed which grew and killed her; and she was only nineteen! Her mother has taken the baby, perhaps it is some comfort to her. It is none to me. Only a living reproach.'

'You mustn't feel like that. The ways of Providence are inscrutable. Perhaps—'

'Providence! An all-wise, all-knowing, all-loving God in the sky? Have you ever thought of the sheer in-built cruelty of Nature, Nature with its red fangs and dripping claws, its helpless insects bound and waiting for the spider's sting to go in, the little birds swallowed alive by snakes?'

'Yet nature is responsible for the orchids, the stars of clematis and the scented lomatia—'

'And the drosera, the pretty Sundew that traps flies and then dissolves in acid their helpless bodies . . . Plants *seem* less aggressive, I grant you; but if you could see the growth of a climbing vine or a trailing creeper speeded up, you would see it snaking out and enveloping other plants in its horrid coils. And all the plants in the rain-forest are fighting, competing for the light and air, struggling upward and smothering each other . . . Did I tell you I attended a hanging in Launceston, while you were still in Hobart?'

'No. The two young bushrangers, was it?'

'Yes. One of them demanded a clean shirt, and went bravely to the scaffold. The other was craven, and wet himself with fright. Yet afterwards, when I helped to dissect the bodies, there was nothing to distinguish between them. The brave man's viscera could not be distinguished from the coward's. His heart was no larger. They had been reduced to the level of dead meat.'

Lawrence's voice rose hysterically, and to distract him Ronald made his suggestion – that after the funeral he should come back to Launceston and stay with them.

'It's not exactly peaceful, with three children in the house; but at least it won't be lonely. You will come?'

'I suppose so. I'll go mad if I stay here alone.'

So it was arranged. As Ronald Gunn wrote to Hooker,

After the funeral I brought him into town with me, and amused him in various ways, and he spoke with great pleasure of the satisfaction you had expressed in your last letter relative to his collections . . . On 8th October I accompanied him some miles out of town on his return, and many future plans were made . . .

Less than a fortnight later, Robert Lawrence was found

72

dead in his bed. It was his twenty-sixth birthday, and the first anniversary of his wedding. Clutched in his hand was a lock of dark hair he had cut from the head of his dead wife.

W. E. Lawrence was an influential man, and he went to see the editor of the *Launceston Advertiser*. There would have to be an inquest, he realised; but he told the editor that his son had long been subject to fits of apoplexy, and he had apparently expired in a fit. Such was the evidence he and his son's manservant would give.

The inquest was held at Formosa, before the coroner and 'a most respectable jury' which returned the verdict, 'Died by the visitation of God.'

It was well known that young Lawrence was an amateur scientist, chemist and biologist and that he had whole shelves full of various poisonous substances of which he well knew the properties. The coincidence of his death occuring on his wedding anniversary, only a fortnight after his young wife's death, was enough to convince many people that the death was not an accident. But the Establishment drew together to protect its members, and the cause of death was duly recorded.

'I was, I might say, almost his only friend on earth, and we were brothers to each other – ' Ronald Gunn wrote heartbrokenly to Hooker, a man he had never met, on the other side of the world.

Our pursuits and feelings were alike, and it will be long ere I shall be able to fill the blank his death has made . . . He led me to commence the study of Botany, in which I have spent many happy hours – he was years ahead of me in experience of Botany and the plants of V.D.L. – I can only however promise to do *all I can*, and trust time will improve me.

When a reply eventually came from Hooker, Ronald read that the beautiful forest iris, Libertia, had been named *Libertia laurencii* after his dead friend.

To distract himself from the misery, he immersed himself

in botany. He sat up late at night comparing, classifying, and writing notes for William Hooker, the Professor of Botany twelve thousand miles away who was now his only conversible friend. No one shared his interests as Robert had. And he went over and over in his mind his friend's last hours; the loneliness and despair, the visit perhaps at midnight to the shelves of chemicals in his laboratory . . . He blamed himself for letting Robert go home alone to Formosa at such a time. Yet he had seemed so much cheered, and they had made plans to meet soon and go botanising together. It was the return to that house full of memories, to that bed where his beloved wife had died, which must have brought him to the decision that he could not go on living without her. The guilt which the living feel because they are still alive . . . He could only expiate it by joining her in the same grave.

Ronald could not talk to Eliza about his loss. He knew that she could not share or even comprehend the depth of his feelings; must even (dreadful thought!) be almost relieved that her 'rival' was no more. So he shut himself in his study with the botanical books Hooker had sent him. He cut himself off from her.

One night when he came to bed, as usual, at about two in the morning, she did not stir. He always tried to creep in without waking her, but this morning he dropped a boot, which crashed loudly on the floor. Looking at her in the light of a shaded candle, he noticed that she was breathing stertorously, with her mouth open. He shook her slightly, but she seemed comatose. Her head rolled loosely on the pillow.

He remembered her pointed question, 'Would you be so upset if it was me who was dead?' In a panic he shook her harder. Her eyes came open, but did not focus on his face.

'Lemme alone,' she muttered, flinging herself on her other side.

'Eliza – darling – are you all right?'

He leant over to kiss her, and recoiled from her breath, which reeked of brandy. Looking beneath the bed, he found a nearly-empty bottle. Not even a glass! She was drinking from the bottle like a hardened toper.

It was no use trying to remonstrate with her in her present state. He put the bottle on the bureau and got into bed, prepared to have it out with her in the morning. How much was she drinking? And was that why the household bills were so high? He fell asleep while still puzzling over it.

11

'ELIZA, WE must have a talk.'

She pretended to be engrossed in buttoning one of little Robert's bootees as he sat on her lap, bending her head so that her curls fell forward and hid her face.

'Eliza, look at me.'

She looked defiantly. He noticed anxiously that her face had a rather bloated look, and there was a puffiness beneath her eyes. She did not look well. Eliza buried her face in the baby's stomach, making him laugh.

'Put the child down, and listen to me.'

She bent from her chair to put Robert on the floor. He crawled energetically to another chair, where he tried to pull himself upright.

'Eliza, I should like to see the housekeeping bills. How much have you been spending on brandy?'

'Why, we always have brandy in the house for cooking, and in case someone is taken faint, as you know. I keep it under lock and key, of course, one can't trust the convict servants not to drink it,' she said virtuously.

'I will look after the key in future.'

'And shame me before my own servants? How dare you suggest—'

'I am suggesting that I found a nearly-empty bottle of brandy beneath our bed last night, while you were almost comatose. Pray how did the bottle get there?'

'I was – I got up to fetch some warmed water for little Robbie, who was fretful, and I added a drop of brandy to make him sleep. That is all. It wasn't a *full* bottle.'

76

'Great Heaven! You'll make the child an alcoholic next.'

'It was only a *drop*. And then I took a drop or two myself to help me sleep, because you come to bed so late, and I can't rest until you do.'

'Perhaps I had better sleep in the spare room for the present.'

'No! Already I hardly see you except at meals, away all day at the Magistrate's court and doing your rounds, and at weekends off collecting your miserable weeds, and writing about them half the night. Pray don't start sleeping away from me as well.'

'Very well. But your keys – and the accounts for the last month, please.'

The cupboard where the brandy and sherry-wines were kept revealed only one full bottle of brandy; but the accounts showed that four bottles had been bought for the month. That was a full bottle every ten days! Or perhaps some of them were hidden about the house, in the wardrobe or the chimneyplace. He felt a curious reluctance to look. If she had reached the stage of secret drinking, he didn't want to know.

'And when the cook asks me for the brandy—'

'You will refer him to me.'

'Oh! You are treating me like a child.' She began to cry.

'Because you are not behaving like a sensible adult.' For once he would not let himself be moved by her tears. He couldn't believe that she had a serious drinking problem, but he had to think of the children and their safety; in a fuddled state she might drop the baby, or set fire to the nursery . . . He wished he could confide in the nursemaid, but Susanna Davies was no solid, respectable English servant, but a woman from the Cascades who had already had one baby there, born out of wedlock. She had to give up her own child to an institution. She seemed fond of the Gunn children though.

For a while he thought his measures had worked. He admitted that he had left Eliza much to her own devices, and began coming to bed at a reasonable hour. Before long

77

Eliza was pregnant again, and blamed him bitterly for her condition. But once the discomforts of the first few months were over, she seemed to settle into a more contented frame of mind.

In his loneliness without Robert Lawrence, Ronald wrote lengthily to thank Hooker for his kind letters and gifts of books, adding that he had purchased nearly forty acres in the suburbs of Launceston on which to commence a private Botanic Garden, to which he could attend along with his official duties. He noted sadly that 'Mr Lawrence's Father had taken possession of all his Books and his Herbarium . . . the Books will be kept by Mr W. E. Lawrence as his own inclination runs a little that way . . .'

He would have appreciated a few of the botanical books and had hoped he might at least be given one or two as a memorial of his friend, for it was Robert's books and enthusiastic feeling for plants which had made him adopt botany in preference to any other science in the first place.

In May 1834 he wrote a respectfully begging letter to Governor Arthur, asking for the loan of three labourers for about two months, rationed by the government. He explained that he now had at least 1,000 species of plants, both native and exotic, ready to transplant from their seedbeds; also a large selection of plants 'of the late Mr R. W. Lawrence of Formosa, whose garden would soon be broken up and the property sold'.

Promptly came an answer from His Excellency's Secretary:

H.E. regrets that under all the circumstances he cannot asquiesce in this application; he would however were it at present practicable have pleasure in establishing a public Botanic garden in Launceston.

Ronald threw the letter to the floor. 'Stupid old fool!' he muttered. 'He has all those acres in Hobart Town, and as many labourers as he wants, and what does he do with them? Grows carrots and cabbages for his horses! A

Botanic Garden "if it were practicable", forsooth! Of course he doesn't consider anything which does not show an immediate financial return to be "practicable".'

He slaved in the garden himself whenever he had some free time, if he was not out collecting. It was utterly frustrating to have to let all those valuable plants, both native and exotic, simply die for want of a man to help transplant them. If Robert Lawrence had been alive he might have asked him to lend a gardener, but he did not feel he knew Mr Lawrence senior well enough to ask such a favour. The older man was stoical in his grief, but he knew it was shared by Gunn and that was a bond between them.

Ronald had bought the forty acres impulsively, not really able to afford the price. One day they would be valuable, as part of the suburbs of Launceston city, but just now his purchase was only a big white elephant, and little grew there but weeds. He determined to do a little digging there every evening in summer, after his long day's work at the courts. It would give him some needed exercise since he had no time to go on extended walking expeditions to the hills. He did not care to leave Eliza for long in her present condition, fearing she might have recourse to the brandy-bottle again if she felt herself neglected.

One bright spot in his melancholy over Lawrence's death was the arrival of Messrs Backhouse and Walker, two Quakers who had been sent to Van Diemen's Land and New Holland to inquire into the conditions for convicts in the penal colonies. As he answered the searching questions of James Backhouse about the penal system he had been sent to investigate, Ronald decided to give his honest opinion even if it made him unpopular with the authorites.

'I have not found the Penitentiary to permanently reform any of the men confined within it,' he asserted. 'In fact, generally it has a tendency to make the men worse, from the majority being so very bad. Men of the better class, employed as clerks, mechanics, and farm labourers and builders, are confined with men of bad character – a

79

hundred men in each of the two wards, all crowded in together.

'They are divided only by whether they are chained or not; there are no rooms of detention or lock-ups, just the two big wards where they sleep and eat.

'The bedding is aired once a week in summer, and on fine days in winter, and the health of the prisoners on the whole is good.

'But there are too many crowded in one room together at night. The practice of having the men sleep on straw mattresses on a large shelf is an unwise arrangement – leading to immorality and the inevitable harassment of those still virtuous. They would be better in hammocks.'

He added that he thought crimes like disobedience and neglect of duty should be punished perhaps by adding a month to the sentence, not by subjecting the man to the degrading and demoralising punishment of flagellation.

One reform he had introduced was to keep two hundred extra shirts in the store, so that each man could be issued with a clean shirt on the Sabbath, the day they were given soap and a towel to wash with. And a school had been started which at least half the prisoners attended voluntarily on Sundays.

The worst hardship came from the poor quality of the shoes issued every six months. The men sent out on road parties and to the quarries breaking stones, found that their footgear soon wore out and gave them little protection while they waited for the next half-yearly issue – even though a shoemaker was kept constantly at work repairing prisoners' shoes.

'My duties include furnishing the Principal Superintendent in Hobart Town with daily returns, and making requisitions for bedding, clothing and stores of which I keep an account in my office.'

James Backhouse, who was the son of a nurseryman in York, took a great interest in plants and was busy collecting specimens for Robert Brown in England. He was kind enough to give Ronald, whose arduous and ardent collecting had been mentioned to him by Hooker, some of his duplicate specimens. 'From him I gleaned much information,' Ronald wrote to Hooker.

Excitedly, he planned an expedition to the Meander River with Backhouse and Walker, who were indefatigable travellers on foot. They had walked by the stock route of the Van Diemen's Land Company all the way from the Hampshire Hills, where they were entertained by the Company's resident surgeon, young Dr Milligan.

'My dear fellow,' said Backhouse on receiving the invitation. 'There's nothing I'd like more!'

Ronald beamed.

'But – I'm afraid we have a religious meeting tomorrow, and then must be on our way. We've already overstayed our time in Van Diemen's Land.'

Ronald hid his bitter disappointment. But one good thing came of the visit – they suggested he correspond with Dr Milligan, who had some interest in botany.

Soon he had enlisted the doctor as a plant collector of great enthusiasm if not great knowledge, in an area from which he had not been able to do any collecting himself. It was a tenuous relationship, yet he felt less alone as he unpacked the parcels forwarded by his new correspondent.

'I just don't understand it,' said Eliza.

'Understand what, my love?'

'How you can have become so obsessed with plants and botany and all that. You never showed any interest in the plants of Mauritius or Antigua.'

'No. I had no idea then of becoming botanical.'

She did not smile. 'No. And I doubt if I'd have married you, had I known how you would change.'

'Oh, come now! We were but children – I certainly was at eighteen, at all events. A man must have a hobby, something to take his mind off his daily work – especially work like mine. Do you realise that I have to sentence from forty to eighty poor wretches *every week* in the Magistrate's

81

court? Some to flogging, some to short rations, some to the chain-gang. Yesterday I had to fine a woman assigned servant for drunkenness—'

'Oh?'

'Yes; it is sad but true that women as often as men are brought up for this offence in Van Diemen's Land. My brother remarked on it in Hobart Town.'

'Indeed.'

'And women having a weaker constitution than men, are more likely to be overcome, to ruin their health . . . That is why I am so relieved, my darling, that you have given up any over-indulgence in alcohol—'

'Then may I have the keys back?' He did not notice the cunning look from under her curls which accompanied this request. 'It is so shaming to have to tell the servants that I am not allowed the keys of my own liquor cabinet.'

'Well—' She looked very appealing in a loose rose-coloured morning gown which hid the swelling of her figure. From being thin she had become rounded all over, not just her belly but her breasts and arms, their creamy Irish skin showing beneath the turned-back sleeves of her gown. Pregnancy suited her, even her red-gold curls seemed to spring with life, pinned up carelessly and caught with a comb on top of her head. Formal ringlets shaped like sausages and lying decorously on the neck and shoulders were the fashion, but not half so becoming as Eliza's unruly curls.

'Well – I suppose so. But promise me, if only for the sake of the child – just one small brandy after dinner, and no more.'

She promised eagerly, while aware of what an impossible vow it would be to keep. Just a tiny nip in the morning, to get her through the day, and perhaps one with her afternoon tea . . . This time she would know when to stop, though; she must never let him catch her in that state again.

12

THEIR FOURTH child, a lovely little girl with Eliza's fair complexion and Ronald's dark hair and blue eyes, was born early in 1834. Eliza fell into a deep depression after the birth, indifferently suckling the infant when it was brought to her by the nursemaid, but taking no further interest in it.

Fanny, little Frances, was now five years old and a motherly little thing. She liked to push the baby's perambulator or sit and nurse her on her tiny lap. She was not the least bit jealous of this new sister, but was fascinated by her; endlessly counting her rosy fingers and toes, and keeping little Isabella amused. It worried her terribly that Mamma lay on the couch all day weeping quietly to herself. But Papa came home every night and swung her up in his arms. 'Well, how's my little nursemaid?' he asked. She was his favourite, as little Robbie was his mother's.

The doctor came, and gave Eliza a bitter-tasting tonic with iron in it. When this had no effect, he made the suggestion, 'Perhaps a glass of port every day, or a tot of spirits might help. The condition is not uncommon after several pregnancies. Perhaps the mother's nervous system is depleted in some way.'

Ronald Gunn did not tell him of his wife's weakness for alcohol; indeed he thought Eliza a reformed character and did not know she had been going out and buying brandy, apart from the usual household stores. She had become cunning and never indulged in a real drinking bout unless he was away for a few days on business visit to Hobart or an expedition to the hills.

She had her last drink in the afternoon and washed out her mouth with peppermint. Brandy had become a daily necessity to her and it was partly the result of her abstinence, in the two weeks when the midwife was in attendance and kept her resting in her room, that had led to her shakiness and depression after the birth.

Now Ronald actually suggested a glass of port or madeira after dinner to help her sleep. She was able to get about the house again and secreted a nearly-full bottle of brandy in the wardrobe under some folded winter garments; but until she was stronger she could not get out for more supplies. Meanwhile her depression lifted and she felt more like her old self, but the brandy bottle had become a prop without which she could not function.

In mid-year two letters arrived from Hooker, together with a box of books which sent Ronald into a seventh heaven.

> Your most valuable present of Books, for which I really know not how to make sufficient recompense, and which placed me most woefully in your debt, came in good condition, and have made my Botanical library almost complete . . . I suppose I need hardly tell you how proud you have made me by naming the Mountain buttercup after me, *Ranunculus gunnianus*.

But he had the depressing task of receiving by the same ship, the *Tamar*, a parcel addressed to Robert Lawrence, which he duly delivered to Lawrence senior. He was reminded once again of his friend's untimely death and the terrible void it had left in his life.

Another parcel addressed to Ronald was no consolation. The *Tamar*, a paddle-steamer of 88 tons, with sails, had been built on the Clyde and sailed out for trading on the Tamar River between George Town and Launceston. Even with steam – and she was the first steam vessel ever to arrive in Launceston – instead of making a fast voyage she took nearly nine months; delaying in Ireland from January till March, and then spending three months at the Cape of Good Hope.

As a result the carefully packaged seeds and living plants were mostly ruined. Only the bulbs and dahlias were still good, while most of the seeds were rotten. He wrote despondently, 'I do not think one seed hardly of Mr Lawrence's or mine will vegetate . . .'

A letter arrived by the same ship from a Mr T. K. Short, with a parcel of seeds from England; but the letter was pompous and ill-spelt and Ronald was not impressed. However he sent an affable reply as the young man seemed to be a protégé of Hooker's. He thought no more about it.

Since his appointment as Police Magistrate on top of all his other duties, he'd found it increasingly difficult to get out of town to do any collecting. If he disappeared for an hour or two he was hunted after in all directions, so that an escape after plants during the week required all his ingenuity. His Sundays he felt he had to devote to his growing family, who were a delight as they grew out of babyhood and became small people he could teach and talk with.

In April he managed a trip to the top of Ben Lomond. This great bluff nearly fifty miles away was visible from Launceston and seemed to call him with its blue beckoning shape. In four days he rode the ninety miles there and back, ascended the mountain and slept two nights on its summit. He would not have minded the rain and cold and discomfort if the collection had been worth it – but there had been an excessively dry summer in Van Diemen's Land and the plants had not flowered at all, their young shoots burnt up and some dead or dying altogether. He collected some seed of *Bellendena montana*, the cream-flowered mountain rocket; and two species of snowberry of which he nobly ate only a few – though they were pleasant to eat – so as to preserve them for seed; some everlastings, helichrysum, and *Epacris*, the coral-pink native heath. It reminded him faintly of Scottish heather, though not such a wine-red and with a larger flower.

In the next months he was able to get another magistrate to take over for him for a week – he'd not had a holiday for more than a year – and made another expedition after the winter rains. This time he went far to the west of any of his earlier rambles and discovered a series of ridges interspersed with green fertile plains.

There was no longer any need to be on the lookout for Aboriginal marauding parties with spears, for George Robinson had followed his remarkable first successes in 'conciliation' by rounding up the last of the tribes and settling them on Flinders Island in Bass Strait. This singular man had gone into the bush completely unarmed, guided by an Aboriginal woman from Bruny Island, Truganini, and her husband Wooreddy. Now the Government was congratulating itself on solving 'the Aboriginal question' satisfactorily, 'without the British name being disgraced by exterminating the original possessors of Van Diemen's Land'.

Among the new plants Ronald collected was a beautiful correa, the native fuchsia, with a flower of crimson and green, a new clematis, and some *Wahlanbergia gracilis*, the delicate austral bluebell, still with a ball of earth about its roots; and *Lomatia tinctora*, the sweet-scented guitar plant. Best of all were two beautiful orchids, both new to him. Elated by these discoveries, besides several new mosses and ferns, he returned to find his home in chaos.

Eliza was lying drunk and half-stupefied on the couch, the baby Isabella screamed from her crib, and two-year-old Robbie was in the kitchen, pouring honey over himself and the floor from an open jar.

He shook Eliza into wakefulness and demanded to know where the other children were. His usually mild and open features were so contorted with rage and fear that even in her fuddled state she was alarmed.

'I do' know . . . They went – went—'

'*Where* did they go? Wake up and answer me! Where is the nursemaid? And the cook?'

'Gave cook – the day off. Others gone for a walk, with Nanny.'

'Oh my God! Thompson!' He called the manservant who was unpacking their camping things on the back veranda. 'Clear up this mess in the kitchen, will you, and give Master Robert a wash. I've got to see to Baby.'

Isabella, scarlet in the face, stretched her little dimpled arms towards him piteously as he entered the nursery. The curtains were half-drawn and the room was dim. She had evidently been put down for her daytime sleep before the others went out for their walk.

Her sobs subsided into shuddering gulps which shook the whole of her little body. How long she had been crying here alone, he hated to think. As the scarlet in her face subsided, he saw that her whole forehead was still mottled with red, while her eyelashes were so wet that they were gummed together in starry spikes. Even her black curls were damp with tears.

He held her over his shoulder and she buried her face in his neck with a pathetic hiccough.

'Here – blow!' He held a handkerchief for her and wiped her swollen nose before he changed her sodden napkin with practised hands. She kicked her legs in the air and gave him a watery smile.

'You poor little mite,' he murmured. 'Papa won't leave you for so long, ever again.'

And he had been away a whole week! He shuddered to think how long his wretched wife had been at the bottle, the children at the mercy of a convict cook and a willing but not very bright servant girl. The manservant was a good all-round help, from gardening to setting fires to keeping the boys amused by whittling wooden whistles and other toys for them. But Ronald had also trained him as a collector, and he was an invaluable help in the field.

In a revulsion against his all-consuming hobby, Ronald pushed all the new plants into an oblong trough with damp soil packed around them, and left them in the shed attached to the back of the house which was his workroom and housed his extensive herbarium of dried plants. He would not classify or annotate them now, though he longed to look up the new species in his botanical books. He was beginning to be pleased with his progress as an amateur botanist.

But his young family must come first. Obviously he must take back the keys and keep the liquor cupboard firmly locked.

Robbie was full of questions about where he had been and what he had seen, but his father asked him sternly, 'Why didn't you go to your sister when she was so upset? You must have heard her crying and crying.'

'She's mad. She jus' yelled. So I wen' – I wen' to get her some brenanhoney.'

'Well, that was a thoughtful boy. But you spilled most of the honey on the floor.'

'Ess. Robbie not know honey's so runny.'

He sat Robbie and Isabella on the carpet with a big pile of building blocks, a game which usually ended with Robbie hitting his sister for demolishing his carefully-built towers. Then he went to tackle Eliza.

The best thing, he decided, was to put her to bed, and try to carry the fiction that the mistress was not well, though it was unlikely the servants had not seen her in this case before. He found the keys of the liquor cabinet in the pocket of her gown, and took them away. The bottle on the floor under the couch was empty.

'Now, Eliza, get up,' he said sternly.

'Don't want to get up. I'm qui' comf'table here.'

'*Get up*! I don't want the older children to see you in this state.'

She sat up slowly. Her hair was falling down, its bright curls contrasting with the pasty pallor of her face.

'I don't know! If you can't think of your children, you might think of yourself! You're ruining your health. Now come to bed.'

He half-dragged, half-carried her to their room. As he

started to undress her and get her into a nightgown, she put her arms round his neck and tried to kiss him.

'No, Eliza! I want none of that. And we want no more children, when you're not fit to look after your own. I shall move into the spare room to sleep.'

13

Things were worse than he had realised. With the next week's post came a staggering bill from the liquor store 'for spirits supplied on credit'. Eliza had been running up bills for brandy instead of ordering it through the household accounts, which he checked regularly.

He had to write and explain that he could not meet the bill immediately, and to ask the manager formally not to supply any liquor to Mrs Gunn in person, or to any of his servants.

When he told her, Eliza was furious. 'You have made a public spectacle of me!' she cried. '*Everyone* will know that I am not allowed credit, I shall be unable to order anything in the shops, I shall be a laughing stock—'

'Whatever you will be, you will have brought upon yourself,' he said quietly. 'Can't you see you will ruin us with your drinking and extravagance? If you attempt such a thing again, I shall have no recourse but to advertise publicly, in the Luanceston press, that Mr Ronald Gunn will not be responsible for his wife's debts.'

'You wouldn't dare!'

'Oh yes I would, if only for the children's sake. Already the household bills take all our income, with scarcely a penny left over. Young Robbie needs some new boots, and Isabella needs walking shoes soon, and there's the cook's wages, and the laundrywoman once a week.'

'And paper and packaging and freight on your parcels of rubbish for Mr Hooker, and franking letters and, and—'

'Eliza, my hobby is not an expensive one, and Mr

90

Hooker has more than returned any outlays I have made in his most generous supply of botanical books.'

'Books! Musty old scientific books, with pictures of nothing but dissected plants and animals! If he would send a few copies of the *Ladies' Home Journal* – I wish you had never taken up botany, and become such a fanatic about it.'

'And I wish you had never taken up drinking.'

'What else was there for me to do?'

'You should take pleasure in running your household, and bringing up your children, as other ladies do.'

'I have no friends in this godforsaken penal settlement on the edge of nowhere.'

'If only you liked gardening, or needlework.'

'If only we had stayed in Hobart, even.'

They continued to talk at cross-purposes, without answering each other. Eliza was sulking because he continued to keep to the spare room. She was not suffering from the locked liquor cabinet, as she still had some bottles secreted about the house. He was uncharacteristically short-tempered, because he was not used to sleeping alone. And though she was still his wife, he felt that she was no longer the person he had married. Sometimes he wondered if he still loved her at all.

He'd still not had time to classify and annotate his new finds, but he sprayed them with moisture each morning and watched anxiously for any sign of wilting. So far they were fine.

He had been extremely busy catching up on correspondence over assigned servants at the office after his time away. He was amused at the strange spelling of so many of the letters, and not only those of the servants.

Elizabeth Neil was one of the more literate:

Sir, i hope you will excuse me for being so bold as to trouble you as i doo but its necessity as makes me apply being that i am totally destitute of things to keep me clean & wholesome, Mr Deane an't sent me none of my things . . .

Her former master had replied indignantly that 'hit is no fault a mine that Eliz. Neil's things as Not Been sent, but Sir i did not No whear to send them . . .'

Ronald added an ironic note to these letters:

Query: Who writes better – Eliz. Neil or her master?

John Leach, a farmer, wrote to him for a book of recipes of 'Bible cures of sheep and cattle': 'Perleas honoured sir i shall be very much a bligt to your honner . . .' The tone of this letter suggested that the farmer was a former, now emancipated, convict; 'your honour' being a usual address to an official when asking for anything.

Yr honour i write to say i mimoriald for a ticket of leaff in November, Robert Pegler per ship Lord Luddock, your humbul sincerest Robert Pegler in the service of Mr. Roak . . .

In the matter of James Brown, assigned servant, his master came into the Magistrate's office to complain. The master was not very prepossessing, in fact he looked a thorough villain, with one eye that rolled wildly while the other was fixed straight ahead.

'James Brown, that Your Honner assigned to me, is useless and what's more e's very sassy whenever I asts 'im to do anything. Says 'e's not fit for service on account of 'is 'ealth.'

'What's supposed to be wrong with him?'

'Well, 'e *says* as 'is back 'as gone on him. I've kept 'im this last fortnight a'doin' nothing, so I come to petition for another servant seeing as 'ow he's useless like I said—'

'Yes, yes. I'll get the Surgeon Superintendent to examine him. He knows that the penalty for malingering is thirty lashes, no doubt, so there probably *is* something wrong with his back. Send him in tomorrow morning. Meanwhile I'll assign another man to you.'

Each new servant cost his employer a pound for a suit of

clothing in place of the prison garb; the only expense after that was for three pairs of boots annually, four shirts, one cap or hat, and rations. No wages had to be paid, but free rations included ten pounds of meat and ten pounds of flour a week, with seven ounces of tea and sugar, and soap.

No wonder Gunn had complained to William Hooker of the endless correspondence that went with his job, and the difficulty of getting away for more than a day.

Having dealt with a week's backlog of correspondence, Ronald had to go on a visit of inspection to the two Houses of Correction. After a return to the office to tidy his desk he arrived home . . . late.

The children were in bed, the servants had withdrawn to their detached cottage in the grounds, and all was peaceful. He dreaded to find Eliza comatose again, but she had dinner waiting for him and was wearing a pretty gown, with ribbons in her red-gold curls. Only two hectic spots of colour in her cheeks, and a rapid way of talking, made him suspect that she might have been drinking.

The plates were left in the kitchen for the servants to wash in the morning, and the two of them sat by the fire in the drawing-room. Alone in the intimate circle of firelight and candlelight, it was almost as if they were in the first years of their marriage, before the children were born.

Suddenly Eliza, who had been staring into the fire, jumped up from her chair and flung herself on the couch beside him. She wound her arms round his neck and kissed him with open mouth. He felt his own inevitable response, but the smell of wine on her breath, from the two glasses she had taken with dinner, reminded him of all that had happened. They *must* not have any more children, at least not until Eliza was cured of her drinking.

Firmly he put her away from him. She stared at him in disbelief.

'Ronald!' she pleaded.' Please come to bed. I miss you.'

'I miss you too, but my mind is made up. We must sleep alone for the present.'

Her eyes darkned with rage. She snatched up a candlestick

from the low table and threw it at him, burning candle and all. The heavy brass object grazed his cheek, the candle went flying to the carpet, where he stamped out the flame.

'You beast! You are doing it to punish me. I hate you!'

She rushed from the room and he heard the bedroom door slam behind her. The noise woke Isabella, and he remembered with a hardening of the heart how her mother had left the child to scream till she was sick. He went to pick her up and brought her by the fire, where he rubbed her pink toes in one hand.

'Sit there while Papa gets you some warm milk.'

'Mickle.'

He nursed her till she dozed off – he rarely had a chance to spoil his children – and as he was tucking the warm and sleepy bundle in her cot, he felt a great tenderness and pity for his little daughter. One day she would grow up and become a woman and have daughters of her own, and a husband with whom she might or might not be happy.

Eliza lay and cried as if she would never stop. Oh, it was dreadful to be a woman, you couldn't take what you wanted, but had to beg for a little love; and then when it was refused, you felt utterly shamed and rejected.

Never again! When he grew tired of this celibate existence, and came creeping back to her bed, she would be the one to refuse him. She felt her heart had turned to stone. At last her sobs ceased, as if some well of misery had finally dried up; she had no more tears.

She felt under the bed for the half-full brandy bottle.

Ronald hesitated towards the back door. He could work on his plants instead of going to bed. But it was late, and cold, and he was tired after his long day. He took his candle and went to the cold and empty single bed in the spare room. Passing Eliza's door he heard her sobbing, but he felt he was meant to hear it, and she would soon stop when it brought no result.

She did not get up for breakfast, and when he went to the bedroom to say he was leaving for the office, she would not speak to him.

He anxiously checked to see that he had the keys of the liquor cabinet safe, and he locked away the Madeira bottle from the dining-room sideboard. As he looked in on the nursery breakfast, Isabella held up her arms from the high chair. He bent to kiss her. The others, busily spooning up porridge, sang, 'Bye Papa!'

'Bye Papa!'

'Bye Papa!'

Well, he had four beautiful, healthy children, he thought as he went out into the sunny morning, whatever might have become of his marriage. So many little ones died in infancy; but the healthy climate and fresh food in this south land seemed to counteract the dangers of childhood mortality.

When he came home again, having got away early with the idea of at last dealing with his new collection of plants, he found Eliza drunk and sprawled on the drawing-room couch. She was still in her dressing-gown, had not even bothered to get dressed, which meant that she must have supplies in the house – was she bribing one of the servants?

He carried her to the bedroom and dropped her unceremoniously on the bed. She glared at him mutinously while he frowned angrily at her.

'Eliza, I've had about enough. You can't keep on like this! Where are you getting your supplies of drink? Tell me!'

He shook her, but she only laughed at him. 'Look at you! Actually losing your temper for onesh . . . Ronald Gunn, always the gentleman. Why doan you beat me? Eh? Why doan you? Wait'll you see your preshus plants, what I did – Ha! Ha! Ha!' She went into peals of drunken laughter.

Ronald's heart went cold with dread. He rushed out to the shed which housed his collection. The trough of earth was upside-down on the floor. The plants, except for a few green shreds, were gone. Half his herbarium of dried and pressed plants, the result of years of work, were torn up and partly burnt. He sank down on the earthen floor, his head in his hands. This was the worst thing she had ever done to him.

In a cold rage, with trembling hands, he gathered up the fragments. Some of the dried plants could be re-mounted. But many of the notes and numbers that went with them had been destroyed. He stalked back inside. The children, fortunately, were having their nursery tea and did not hear him.

'You spiteful woman,' he said in a low voice. His face was white with suppressed rage, his blue eyes glittered in a way she had never seen before, even his soft brown hair seemed to stand on end.

Eliza pulled the covers up to her chin, and stared up at him, beginning to be afraid. Now he really would strike her.

'You're not content with ruining your own health, neglecting the house and the children, trying to ruin me financially – you have to destroy my one simple pleasure. Eliza, unless you can promise to give up the bottle at once, and altogether, I shall have to send you away to your relatives at home in Ireland. Perhaps there you will recover your health and sanity.'

'Send me away!' She had never thought of this. 'Away from my children? Oh, you woulden – you woulden do that to your poor 'Liza!'

'Wouldn't I? We'll see. I'm going to write to your brother and your married sister tonight.'

'Ohh-ow!' She began to cry noisily, but he turned on his heel and walked out. His heart was like stone towards her. From now on, as far as he was concerned, all was over between them.

He turned for solace to his distant friend in Glasgow.

I can hardly record with patience what has happened, [he wrote.] My servant [he could not write 'my wife'] has lost or damaged my whole collection from my last expedition, into entirely new territory; and what is worse I had not made a record of what they were, tho' one was a new orchid . . . During my whole Botanical life of two and a half years I certainly met with no loss that annoyed me so much. Fortunately the seeds I collected are still safe in the pockets of my bush jacket . . .

He was half-prepared for the next blow Eliza had arranged for him. As wife of the Chief Police Magistrate she had had no trouble in borrowing money from a money-lender, at exorbitant interest, to finance her drinking. The first he knew of it was when a bill came due, for £172 including 25 per cent interest for six months.

Once again he lost his temper, though he knew it was bad for the older children to hear them quarrelling, and even the little ones must be aware of the tension in the household. The servants withdrew with scared faces after dinner, as they heard the shouting from the front bedroom.

'My oath, the Master's in a fair paddy, idden 'e?' said the cook. 'Wonder what she's done this time?'

'I dunno. But Mr Gunn don't lose 'is temper easy. Even when 'e fell in the Meander in the middle o' winter, 'e just laughed. But that was pretty mean, burning all 'is plants.'

'Yair. Well, it's not our worry.'

Ronald was striding up and down the bedroom, brandishing the bill.

'How do you suppose I'm going to pay this? I already owe a hundred to the liquor store. I'll just have to let it accumulate more interest. Do you realise you've run up bills that amount to more than my whole year's salary?'

She looked sulky. 'You wouldn't let me have any money.'

'No, because I knew what you'd do with it. Have you looked at yourself in the mirror lately? Pasty-faced, with great bags under your eyes, your hair's a mess—'

'I don't care!' she screamed at him suddenly. 'Do you know why I look like this? I'm going to have another baby, that's why.'

He stopped short, staring at her. He grabbed her by the shoulders. 'You're lying! It's not possible. Or are you telling me—'

'Oh, you're hurting me! Let go.' She gave him a nasty

97

smile. 'See, you needn't have been so careful the other night. If you don't believe me, ask Dr Pugh. He examined me today. It's due about next January. Must have been begun about April.'

He slumped into a padded velvet chair, clutching his head. 'And how are we going to afford it? You have just about ruined me.'

'Well you can't send me away now, not in my condition.'

'Not before you've had the baby anyway,' he said ominously. His anger was gone; he felt old and tired, old before his time. He had no friends, no parents he could turn to for advice.

William! His brother had always been a pillar of strength, a sort of surrogate father to him. William was happily married with two children. He would ask him to help. Not financially, of course. Even if William could afford it, he would not ask. But perhaps he could talk to Eliza, write to her family and explain that for everyone's good, including her own, she had better go back to Ireland until she could be weaned from her unfortunate addiction. Otherwise the whole family was heading for ruin.

14

WILLIAM GUNN came up to Launceston and was shocked at his sister-in-law's condition. Soon after the birth of her baby boy in January she managed to get a bottle of brandy and drank herself insensible. Her milk dried up, which perhaps was as well for the baby.

As Superintendent of Convicts and responsible for all assignment of servants in the northern district, Ronald Gunn was able to choose the best available wet-nurse from the latest shipment from the south; a strong, healthy, cheerful Irish lass whose baby had died in the Female Factory in Hobart – she had become pregnant to one of the ship's officers on the voyage out – and who lavished affection and plenty of milk from her full breasts on little William.

'Eliza's drinking herself to death,' said Ronald to his brother in despair, 'and me into the Bankruptcy Court! She's not fit to look after the child, and her milk has failed for the first time. I've managed to get a wet-nurse, an excellent woman. What do you think, Willy – I feel the only solution is to send her back to Ireland for a time. I've written once—'

'To her brother?'

'Yes, and her married sister. It is too easy here to bribe servants, to get favours for money. I stopped her credit; and then she went and pawned her engagement ring. It's a kind of madness. She'll do anything to get strong drink.'

'I think you're right, old man. It's the only solution. What *is* it about this place that drives so many to tippling?

You know yourself the number of cases of 'drunk and disorderly' that come up before the courts . . . Like that fellow Jorgensen, apparently a highly intelligent feller, speaks several languages and has published several books – he gets a free pardon, and what does he do? Spends his time drinking with an illiterate, drunken Irish washerwoman! We fine 'em five shillings and they go out and get drunk again.'

'Yes . . . In Eliza's case of course there's no public scandal, but you know how servants gossip from house to house. It must be common knowledge that the Chief Superintendent and Magistrate in Launceston has a drunken wife. I was forced to stop her credit at the liquor store, and then she raised a cash advance from a moneylender, at an exorbitant rate of interest. For the children's sake, I can't let her bankrupt me.'

'No; well, look, Ronald, I know how difficult it is; I'll write to her brother for you, put the whole situation before him, and tell him to expect her home not later than the end of this year. She couldn't take the little boy with her?'

'Impossible! When not drinking, she's so sunk in apathy that she would let him fall overboard without noticing it. You can see the state she's in. Doctor says her liver is affected, and her kidneys are in such a state that she was lucky to survive this last pregnancy. For her own sake she must be put out of harm's way. I can't stay home from my work to watch over her. In Ireland, they can get a reputable nurse to live in; tell them I'll contribute what I can to her keep. I—I—'

His sensitive mouth trembled. He felt like weeping, but held back the tears that he knew would embarrass his bluff soldier brother. He bit his lip, and muttered, 'Thanks. Thanks, old chap. I didn't know where to turn.'

'Forget it. Glad to be of help. I'm only sorry I can't offer some finance, but Louisa and I having two of our own and one on the way—'

'Yes, I know. If you'd just write for me.'

*

In early May, the southern autumn of calm sunny days and blue skies, he saw Eliza off from a ship that called at Launceston on its way through Bass Strait from Sydney.

The parting with the children was the worst. Little Fanny kept saying, 'Don't cry, Mamma! Please don't cry!' while the tears kept rolling down her own cheeks. Eliza was still indifferent to the baby, but she clung fiercely to little Robbie, who looked so much like his father, and smothered him with kisses. Ronnie stood stiffly by, rather embarrassed by all this emotion, at eight years old feeling he was too much of a man to cry. Isabella clung round her neck, not really comprehending that Mamma was going far away over the sea, for years and years, but affected by the general feeling.

'You will be good for Papa, won't you?' said Eliza, kissing them all again.

'Yes, Mamma.'

'And Ronnie, you look after the little ones.'

'Yes, Mamma.'

She buried her face in Isabella's dark curls with a cry: 'My poor motherless babes!'

'Come, Eliza.' Ronald had decided that it was best for the children to say goodbye at home. He was ready to take her to the wharf, where her baggage had already been loaded. 'We *must* go. The captain won't hold the ship for you, he has to catch the tide. Come, my dear.'

He had ordered a closed cab, which was waiting at the door. Eliza pulled a veil over her swollen eyes, and leaning heavily on his arm, left the house.

In the small cabin, she shed floods of tears and clung to him, and he kissed her wet face and tried to comfort her. 'You must understand, dear, that it's for your own good. The doctor says you are killing yourself with drinking so much.'

'I want to die. I'd rather die than be sent home in disgrace.'

'It's not that. Your brother understands, he agrees with me that a holiday with your own people, in new surroundings, is just what you need to get back on your feet. Your sister has invited you to stay, too—'

'And what about my babies?'

'They won't forget you in a year, or two . . . Come Eliza, dry your tears.'

She took off her bonnet and stood close to him. 'If only you could come too!'

'Dear, the cost of your passage-money has taken all my remaining funds. The captain's wife is travelling on board, and has promised to be your companion and look after you.'

'You mean, keep me from getting a drink.'

'That too. Because you must give it up entirely if you are to be cured. And you must *want* to be cured.'

'Oh, I do, I do!'

She sank down on the bottom bunk and gazed up at him pathetically, her face pale and gaunt, its youthful beauty almost lost; yet her hair was still bright. She held up her arms like a child.

'Ronald! Kiss me goodbye. I'll try to be brave.'

'Oh Eliza! Whatever has happened to us? We were so happy, once.'

'I don't know . . . It's this place, this Demons' Land! I hate it, I always have.'

He sat beside her and held her in his arms.

'Oh, *Ronald*! Won't you make love to me for the last time? Just this once? It's been so long—'

'But Eliza—'

'Please, please!' She was kissing him passionately, urgently, and he felt himself weakening. After all, he might never see her again. The doctor had told him there was an even chance that Eliza's system was damaged beyond repair. Suddenly it seemed the most natural thing in the world. They were lying in the bunk together, perfectly fitted like a hand in a well-used glove, and for those minutes all was as it had been.

The pain of imminent parting increased the pleasure. Eliza moaned on a rising note, 'Oh, oh, *oh*!' and then they both reached a climax together as they nearly always did. There had been nothing wrong with this part of their marriage.

There were sounds of the anchor-chain being hauled up by the capstan; the ship was ready to sail. Ronald hastily got up and straightened his clothes. She lifted up her tear-streaked face and he kissed her for the last time.

'Now promise me not to cry any more. You will come back to us in better health, and we'll try to make a new start.'

He gently disengaged her clinging hands, and stumbled up the companionway to the deck. Eliza got up slowly, the tears beginning to flow again, and noticed for the first time the bunch of Tasmanian wildflowers he'd had placed in a vase on the chest of drawers. Beastly wildflowers! She picked up the vase and with a scream flung it and its contents against the cabin wall. She wanted no reminders of Van Diemen's Land.

'Where my Mamma?' The question he had been dreading came from young Robbie, who had been trotting round the house looking for his mother. He had not understood the explanations which the older ones accepted. Now little Isabella too set up a cry for 'Mamma!'

Ronald took one on each knee, and with his arms round them tried to convince them of the incomprehensible: that Mamma had gone away, away across the sea to Ireland, and they would not see her for a very long time ('perhaps never,' he said to himself).

'But I *want* Mamma!' cried three-year-old Robbie indignantly.

Ronald was reminded of his own reaction when told by his older brother that Mamma had decided to go off to Heaven and leave him. Like Robbie, he had been increasingly separated from his mother by her declining health, but he still could not bear to part with her. Seeing that Isabella was preparing to join in a long wail with her

103

brother, Ronald hastily distracted them with a peek at his latest collection of insects. He had some small, papery-blue butterflies, moths with orange 'eyes' on their wings, and a grasshopper with its pretty yellow-striped wings extended. Unfortunately there was no cork to be had in Launceston for lining boxes, so the pins would shake out easily from the hard wood.

'Ooh, butterflies!' The little ones stood on a chair to examine delightedly the box of treasures.

'Careful, Robbie!' he warned, but inevitably by a sudden movement the child jerked the box, out came the pins, and legs, wings and atennae flew off.

'Oh dear! I was afraid that would happen.' By an effort he kept his temper. It was his own fault for bringing the box within reach. Young Ronnie was always extremely careful and could be trusted to help mount specimens, but Robbie was too young.

Soon after his wife's departure Ronald had a visit from the extraordinary Dane, Jorgen Jorgensen, an emancipated convict who had once been on an adventurous trip to Iceland with William Hooker, and had incidentally saved his life in a burning ship. Now he was sunk very low, shabbily dressed and not too proud to beg from anyone; while his domestic situation, Gunn knew, resembled his own in one particular: his wife was a hopeless drunkard.

In his fellow-feeling he gave Jorgensen a small hand-out, knowing full well that it would probably go on drink rather than nourishing food. Jorgensen asked pathetically for news of his 'old and dear friend' Hooker, to whom he had written a long letter but received no reply.

Hooker in fact made inquiries about his former friend, whom he had helped out of scrape after scrape and even saved from an English gallows; but the report he received from Lieutenant William Gunn, Superintendent of Convicts in Hobart Town, had convinced him that Jorgensen was a lost cause. The thinly-concealed requests for money in Jorgensen's flamboyant letters made his motives for writing suspect.

Poor Jorgensen! It seemed there was no hope for him; he was a flawed character, in spite of his brilliance. To send him money would do him no real good, Hooker told Ronald Gunn: 'I have scores of letters from him, begging – and all on gilt-edged paper!'

Gunn, busy as a father, as a magistrate, and with endless correspondence in his other position as Superintendent of Convicts, yet found time to write long letters of many pages to Hooker in his neat, sloping hand, the lines as evenly spaced as though written on a machine. He wrote of his loneliness without any botanically-minded person to exchange thoughts with: 'Therefore I appreciate your correspondence, more especially since death has removed poor Lawrence . . . I still sadly feel his loss, to me irreparable.' Yet he felt every day more satisfied with his progress in botany. It was strange; he felt almost as if the dead botanist and friend was guiding him, helping his ideas, urging him to collect more.

The house felt empty without Eliza. However flawed their relationship, he now missed her daily company, and began to dream of her at night, dreams in which she was young and fresh as in the early days of their marriage in Antigua . . . Had he been wrong to bring her to Van Diemen's Land? The Demon's Land! She had remained an exile, while he had come to love his new abode, the trackless bush, the often delicate colours of the wildflowers, the subtle scents of boronia and wattle.

He wrote a letter by the next ship after the one in which she sailed, in time to reach her soon after she arrived. Unless the ship made an unusually slow passage, she would be spending Christmas at Home. Her brother sent a short note to say they were expecting her before the New Year.

For a while the younger children kept asking for Mamma, but they gradually accepted her absence. Young Ronnie never mentioned her. Perhaps he remembered her drinking bouts with distaste, for he was old enough to know what was going on; perhaps he felt she had deserted them.

The baby, William, was a sickly child, fretful and underweight, spoiled by the wet-nurse and the nanny, who competed for his lop-sided and toothless smiles.

William Hooker was startled to read, in a letter acquainting him of the imminent arrival of a Thomas Keir Short in Van Diemen's Land, and full of botanical details of some new plants found near George Town, a few lines which told him more about his young friend Gunn's domestic situation than he had ever expected to know:

Should my wife, who has recently gone to Dublin, apply at any time to you for money you will oblige me much by *not* giving any – she has unfortunately acquired a habit of extra-indulgence in drinking, which after a marriage of ten years has forced me to send her home to her relatives in the hope of effecting a cure – success is doubtful – but her being able to procure money would spoil all, and from her knowledge of our continued correspondence I thought it probable she might apply to you. – A hint to you is enough.

It had cost Ronald Gunn much effort to write these laconic few lines.

Books continued to arrive from Hooker, such generous gifts, and always exactly what he wanted. He began to feel woefully in his debt; he even cautioned Hooker not to send any compensation for his labours beyond his means, 'for I am aware that like myself you have a large family'.

Hooker, aware of his V.D.L. correspondent's melancholy and lack of a congenial companion, had been pleased to send a letter of introduction with the young man, Thomas Keir Short, when he left for the Colonies. He knew Short as an agriculturist and a collector of seeds, and that he was of a respectable family.

When Short arrived in Launceston, Ronald, feeling the loneliness of the house without Eliza, asked him to bring his things from the hotel and stay. He looked forward to having someone to talk to at meals, with similar interests; someone who would perhaps help with the chores of drying, packing, and forwarding plants to Glasgow. Besides which, Short had brought with him a whole trunk of valuable books, which to book-starved Gunn were like a tray of sweets to a child.

At first he was rather taken aback. Anyone less like the late Robert Lawrence would be hard to imagine. The young man was fair, sandy, with a smooth ruddy complexion; he was short and fat, and also, as Ronald soon began to realise, incurably lazy. His pale blue eyes surrounded by pale lashes, and a rather blob-like nose, gave him the look of a well-dressed, very clean pig. Yet he was a cheerful, lively, loquacious guest, and as they sat over their wine at dinner – and he had brought some good wines with him – Ronald felt the pleasure of his company.

After three months, however, he wrote to Professor Hooker:

I am, *entre nous*, much disappointed. He can give me no information in Botany or any other science – and his collection of Books, though expensive, is very badly selected – his seed collection ditto . . . He is however a good hearted young man, but very ignorant.

One thing that endeared the guest to Ronald was that he got on so well with the children.

'Come, children, you can help me this morning!' he would cry, after putting away a large breakfast of two eggs, bacon, toast and coffee. If the eldest boy had to stay in the schoolroom, and the baby was too young, he would take the other three with him to ramble on the shores of the Tamar estuary, collecting shells. The girls liked this occupation, though they laughed at him a little: 'Papa, he cannot *bend*! We have to pick up Mr Short's shells for him.' The boys would go with him on weekends to collect insects, not plants, of which he seemed 'positively more

ignorant than myself', as Gunn wrote disappointedly to
Hooker. Yet Short had apparently asked the Professor to
recommend him as Government Botanist in New South
Wales.

He wrote to Hooker from Launceston:

I am at Preasant with Mr Gunn and a most delightful
companion he is we go out together on every spare hour
we have to collect, and he is very anxious for an answer to
his last vollominious letter to you . . .

After a few more months, Ronald was glad to see young
Short of on a 'collecting' expedition to New Zealand. He
had made a friend as well as a house-guest out of the young
man, in spite of his faults – one of which was vanity, and a
wish to be thought a great collector and naturalist without
doing any real work in natural history. But he was growing
tired of Short's untidy ways and greed at meals. He had not
ascended one hill or mountain in Van Diemen's Land or
slept one night in the open air since his arrival, and had not
seen nine-tenths of the commonest native plants in the
field; yet in conversation with others he would draw the
long bow about his explorations and discoveries.

His manners were rather boorish and uncouth, and he
kept the one manservant constantly attending on him, and
dressing bird skins for him; his bedroom was so untidy that
the maidservant complained she could hardly get in to
make his bed. Altogether it would be pleasant to have the
house to himself again, Ronald thought. He was getting
tired of Mr Short's long stay.

He had originally intended to charge for board and share
the household expenses, including many bottles of wine,
but did not press the point, yet Short had come as a cabin
passenger and seemed to be well-off. When he had to
borrow £25 towards his New Zealand trip, and at the last
moment asked for another £5, Ronald felt a twinge of
unease. But Thomas Short looked at him with his round
piggy eyes wide open, blue and innocent; as he said, 'Just

till a remittance comes from Home, old chap, you know how it is; the mails are so slow!'

Short came back from New Zealand with extravagant tales of how he had been entertained by Maori chiefs in remote areas where white man had barely penetrated before; Gunn received these stories without comment, and without believing them. Short's collections from New Zealand were scanty and of little interest, and he suspected that even these had been bought rather than sought out in the field.

'He is very indolent as a Collector and always begs or buys in preference; and is supremely ignorant, vain and conceited,' he wrote, admitting to himself and Hooker that he was heartily sick of the young man. So when Short announced that he thought of returning to England – instead of setting up as a grazier with a sheep station bought by his father, as he said he had planned – Gunn heaved a sigh of relief.

'But I'm afraid I've run meself a bit short,' said the young man with an unconscious pun. 'In fact, I'll have to borrow a bit more from you, old man, in order to get away by the winter. Say a hundred a fifty would do.'

'Sorry, I just don't have that sort of money to lend.'

'I just want you to arrange a loan; my father will repay it. If you will just stand security for me as I am not known in these parts.'

'Well . . .' A deep Scottish caution made Ronald hesitate. Yet if he didn't procure the money towards the fare, he would be stuck with Thomas Keir Short indefinitely. And that was likely to be expensive in the long run, as well as tedious. 'Well, I suppose I could arrange a bank draft and you give a draft on your father against its repayment.'

'Splendid! You are a friend in deed.'

Even then, armed with a letter of credit for £150, Short found this too small, and asked the broker's agent to guarantee a bill on a London firm for £178, with interest of 15 per cent to be paid half-yearly.

He left a few scientific books as a present, and sailed away in the *Guiana*.

Ronald's relief was short-lived. He began receiving complaints from local tradespeople whom Short had not paid; also bills for items he had booked up to Gunn's account. Finally even the washerwoman, to whom Short had given a worthless cheque, came to him in tears.

'His actions of swindling were carried out systematically,' Ronald told brother William indignantly. 'He's evidently an adept at the business. Yet he had such an innocent look!'

'My dear Ronald, haven't you learnt yet that the greatest rogues often have innocent-looking blue eyes? It's the stock-in-trade of the confidence man.'

'But he was my friend! Or I treated him as such. My kindness to him was unremitting. You know I'm naturally easy tempered, and said to be warm-hearted—'

'Yes, too easy and warm-hearted for your own good. You should have been suspicious when he first started borrowing money.'

'But he *seemed* like a man of wealth – and introduced by Hooker – and was always referring to his wealthy relatives in England – and he brought an expensive collection of luggage with him! And however he may have acted towards others, I at least thought *myself* safe – he had experienced my kindness and hospitality for months – he knew my circumstances, that I had five young children and was still deeply in debt from poor Eliza's habits . . .'

'More fool you, that you let him impose on you. How much does he owe you?'

'Two hundred pounds sterling, without interest.'

'I suggest you write to his relatives, or get Hooker to write, and point out that you probably saved the young man from a debtor's prison or worse.'

'Well, I'll try . . . Would you believe, he actually had the cheek to write to me from the ship wishing me "every happiness and fortune that I can wish myself in this world . . ." He's utterly unprincipled. And to think that Hooker—'

'You must remember that Hooker only sent a letter of introduction. He never expected that you would take the young man into your house and make a friend of him, and lend him money and give him free board and lodging. Your own judgement was at fault I'm afraid, my dear Ronnie.'

'I suppose so,' said Ronald miserably. 'But I always tend to trust people until I'm proved wrong.'

15

EARLY IN 1836 William Jackson Hooker was knighted
for his services to botany. As soon as news of the honour
came through in the London journals, Jorgensen took the
opportunity of writing to his former friend and congratulating him, adding that 'Nothing could afford me greater
gratification than receiving some few lines from you e'er
the grave closes either upon you or me . . . I heard from Mr
Gunn that you had not entirely forgotten me.'

He informed Sir William of the imminent departure of
Colonel Arthur, not a popular Governor but one under
whom the Colony had prospered in his more than twelve
years in office.

Ronald had become increasingly discontented with his
job, often having to try up to eighty cases a week. As he
told his brother, he had to work 'rather like a horse in a Mill
– round and round on the same spot, without rest'. Because
Launceston was a port, and a favourite place for 'jumping
ship' (even though the obligatory punishment was fifty
lashes), he had to deal with deserting seamen as well as
absconding or drunken servants.

Sometimes the offenders were mere boys, sometimes
they looked the part of a villain. Henry Geddes, aged
thirty, convict, fitted the description given on his convict
register: '. . . about five feet eight inches high, of a dark
complexion, black hair, large whiskers, several scars on his
face, and his voice very hoarse'. He admitted to being
guilty of neglect of duty – he had failed to make a mooring
cable taut, so that when a wind got up the ship banged

against the wharf – and being absent from his ship without permission. Gunn sentenced him to twenty-five lashes, the statutory number.

The offences of the women from the Female Factory were mostly trivial – talking at night, losing a cap, asking a Constable for tobacco, and even 'refusing to wash her face'. He sentenced them to work at the washtub, or three days on bread and water, or seven days' solitary confinement. Women who had been drinking were fined five shillings, or if they had no money were sentenced to go back to picking oakum.

The offences were boringly similar, he had heard all the standard excuses and he was tired of spending his days in such an occupation. He even thought of packing up and leaving Van Diemen's Land with its unhappy memories, and settling in the new territory across the Strait, the Port Phillip District of New South Wales, where there was no penal colony. He went across to look at possibilities, a hurried trip. A few pioneers were already opening up sheep country there. He collected a few mainland plants for Hooker, but the vegetation near the coast was very similar to that of Van Diemen's Land, except for the parastic mistletoe on the gum-trees.

In the last month there had been an upheaval in his household. He had begun to look with suspicion at the nursemaid's growing bulk, her inability to bend to pick up the baby and certain other signs. At last he challenged her: was she in the family way, and if so who was responsible?

Susanna looked sullen and hung her head. She did not reply.

'Come, my girl, you know you cannot conceal your condition forever,' he said impatiently. 'When is your child due?'

'Next monf.'

'Next month! Then this had been going on for almost a year! Who is the father?

'I'm not sayin'.'

'Won't he marry you?'

113

'Not 'im. E's got a wife in Hobart Town. Don't live with 'er or nothing. But she's up t' no good 'e says.'

'You realise I'll have to send you to the Female Factory?'

'Aw no, Mr Gunn, sir, not there! And Master Willum will miss me something cruel. You won't send me away?'

'Of course I must. I'm here to uphold the Law. Would you rather be transferred to the Factory in Hobart Town? I could arrange it.'

'Yus I would. But I'll miss little Willum, I will.'

'Well, you'll soon have another baby to worry about. Pack your things, and be ready to leave in a week's time.'

Several ex-convicts who had worked out their time had arrived in Launceston looking for work, and as one turned out to be an accomplished bird-skinner, Ronald employed him as gardener and house servant. Though he was not much of a shot, Ronald took his gun and proceeded to slaughter every small bird he saw, besides a pelican from the River Tamar and two herons. It was all in the name of science.

He packed the completed skins in new-washed wool, inside soldered tins to keep out any possible damp – 340 skins in all, comprising seventy-five different species – and shipped them to Hooker with a covering note. He included in one long box two Tasmanian emus, now almost extinct.

Then came the news which put all thought of Port Phillip out of his head. William Gunn had pulled a few strings before the departure of Colonel Arthur at the end of his term, and arranged for his brother to be transferred to the small settlement of Circular Head, more than a hundred miles to the westward of Launceston. Ronald was appointed Police Magistrate to the whole north-western part of the island, including the Hampshire and Surrey Hills, Emu Bay, Circular Head and Cape Grim: a Police District about a hundred miles long, but compared with Launceston his duties would be almost a sinecure. The salary was £300 a year.

Circular Head lay in the midst of the Van Diemen's Land Company's holdings, which extended along the north coast

114

as far as the north-west cape, Cape Grim. From the sea the headland, sometimes called The Nut, presented a strange aspect. It looked like a great stone Christmas cake. The vertical granite walls rose abruptly out of the sea; it was round, and flat on top, with an icing of green herbage. It could be climbed from the landward side, but from the sea the connecting isthmus could not be seen, and the jutting headland appeared to be an island. The only approach was by ship.

On each side was a curving, partly sheltered bay, so shallow that only ships of small draught could anchor there. Even at the end of the jetty there was barely four feet of water at low tide. Perhaps that was why it had never prospered, but remained a small community of fishermen, V.D.L. Company employees, and a few government officers such as the resident surgeon, Dr Hutchinson, and the Police Magistrate.

His area would be a huge one, Ronald explained to Hooker, but the population was scattered and fairly law-abiding. There was often no opportunity for drunkenness, for all supplies depended on the Company schooner *Edward* or the odd small ship which arrived from Launceston. There would be plenty of travelling involved, with a horse provided, and endless opportunities for botanising in a new district where he had not collected before, though he'd received plants from Dr Milligan and others. He was busy for weeks moving, sailing back and forth in the small schooner with his family, servants, and possessions.

A whole new field to explore! Hooker was just as delighted as he at the great opportunity for adding new botanical specimens from the coastal country and the north-western plains and hills – 'a glorious country!' commented Hooker ecstatically. Gunn wrote that he was now in a most interesting field, and could hardly be better placed for collecting.

Across the bay to the westward stood the imposing mansion of Highfield, built by Mr Edward Curr as headquarters for the Van Diemen's Land Company. Since a schooner belonging to the Company called regularly from Woolnorth, Mr Curr sometimes asked him to dinner at Highfield.

Young Lawrence had not liked Curr, yet Ronald found him congenial company in a place where only the local doctor was a 'conversible' acquaintance. Dr Hutchinson had once collected plants for Lawrence, but was in poor health and had not done any collecting for years. But Dr Milligan at the Hampshire Hills was still collecting for Ronald, who now would have a chance to meet his correspondent in the course of his official duties.

He was beginning to feel reasonably tranquil and happy in his new surroundings, and had just spent a pleasant few days at the Hampshire Hills V.D.L. Company's head-quarters, collecting plants in the adjoining countryside with young Dr Milligan, when a letter came from Ireland which destroyed his peace of mind. It was from his brother-in-law in Dublin. Eliza was dead. She had survived only a few months after her arrival in Ireland, and died soon after giving birth to a child that did not live. The letter was short and coldly expressed; it was evident that Eliza's brother blamed him for her condition.

Dead, after bearing their sixth child! He could not believe it. Eliza had never written, and he had not dreamed of such a consequence of that one farewell act . . . yet Eliza had always been fruitful. Ronald felt shattered. Helplessly he blamed himself. He should never have given in to her entreaties on the day of her departure; the doctor had said another pregnancy would be dangerous. He had sent her away 'for her own good'. Yet had he not done so, she perhaps would still be alive.

Might the move to Circular Head have reformed her? No, she would have hated this tiny settlement even more than Launceston. He argued back and forth with himself.

On a night of full moon, when the calm sea like a swathe of silver tissue lay sparkling behind the dark bluff, he woke with that well-remembered voice in his ears.

'Ronald!' It was her voice.

Was she calling him to join her in that other world? His hair rose on his scalp. He got up and looked out the window at the sweep of silvery sea, half-expecting to see a white shape outlined in the moonlight . . .

'Mamma!' A fretful whimper from the nursery, from little Isabella. Did she feel it too, that presence come from a grave halfway round the world, a grave he would never see?

'In sickness and in health . . . till death us do part.' Well, death had parted them with complete finality; some second sense had told him, when she sailed away a year ago, that the parting was forever.

He went to the nursery and turned Isabella's hot pillow over without her waking. Her dark hair was damp as he lifted it from her forehead with one finger. She had been dreaming, dreaming of the mother she could scarcely remember. William slept undisturbed in his cot, his bottom in the air, and Frances too slept on her face, her arms flung out on each side. The two older boys now had a room of their own.

It was long before he got back to sleep, the brilliant moonlight disturbing him, yet he was reluctant to pull the curtains and shut out that glittering sea. Full tide, and no sound of breaking waves . . . When he slept at last it was to dream of her, a vivid erotic dream which left him disturbed and shaken.

Then Thompson, his trusty plant-collector, 'memorialled' for a ticket-of-leave, the next step on to a conditional pardon. He could not in honesty refuse to recommend him, his behaviour had been exemplary. Except – for a moment the suspicion occurred to him: was Thompson the one who had got Susanna into trouble? He couldn't believe it. But then, when the ticket came through, Thompson announced that he was going to Hobart.

'You know Susanna has been sent to the Factory there?' Gunn asked sternly.

'Yes, yer honour.' The man looked sheepish. 'I'm sorry about that.'

'And you have a wife in Hobart Town?'

'It's true.'

'So, you are the father? She wouldn't tell me.'

'No, she's a great girl, is Susanna. She wus afraid you'd dismiss me, too.'

'Well, I'm not going to do anything about it now. You're free to go to Hobart Town and find work. But it's a pity you're not free to marry her. She has a little girl in the Orphan School, you know, and she's a natural mother. My youngest continues to miss her.'

'Who knows? My wife might die,' he said cheerfully.

'Indeed,' said Gunn. The pencil he was holding snapped in his tightened fingers. 'You may go,' he said coldly. The woman was punished, the man went scot-free. It was the system of society.

Meanwhile quite close to his new home he found plenty to keep him occupied. On a Sunday afternoon walk Isabella came to him clutching something in her sticky little hand – with a cry of delight he took it from her and gave her a big kiss.

'Pitty f'ower!' said Isabella.

'Yes, my darling, and a rare one – a new orchid!'

There were stands of paperbarks with their white papery trunks growing so closely round the small brackish lagoons behind the sandhills, their trunks no more than a foot apart, that the groves resembled picket fences. The traveller's joy, *Clematis blanda*, climbed almost to the top of the gum-trees, spilling its white stars in spring and later its feathery bearded seeds like a sprinkling of snow. In the poor sandy soil the boronia carpeted the ground with its bright pink blossoms.

He wrote enthusiastically to Hooker,

At Circular Head I find a considerable number of plants that I had not before seen growing – all the seaside plants were previously inacessible to me, or nearly so . . . My new collection is considerable, and contains about 150 new numbers – I am now in an interesting field . . .

He added that he was now a widower with five children at the age of twenty-eight:

I married her – love our only portion – at 18 years of age. I was very happy, never repented, until a few years ago she unaccountably became so attached to the bottle that all other considerations were forgot. My misery was complete – my ruin hung by a thread . . .

He could discuss with Hooker many subjects about natural history, subjects he would never mention to his personal acquaintances. Yet this man he had never met he felt to be a sympathetic friend:

I cannot tell you how delighted I was with your letters and the box of books per the *Elizabeth* . . . Your praise is most gratifying, and indeed incites me to go on – That my dried plants should please so veteran a Botanist as yourself is more than I could reasonably have expected – and now that you praise my Birds I hardly know what to think, unless that you lean with a kindly eye on a beginner.

My Botanical Collection for the past six months has been full of novelties . . . I am now arranging them as fast as I can.

Thank you for your kind intention of mentioning my name to our new Governor Sir John Franklin – I have not yet seen him, but hope to do so when I visit Hobart Town. There is little doubt that a man of his character will please, especially as he is a man of scientific interests.

16

'At Circular Head I have turned shell collector!' wrote Gunn to Hooker in 1837. He had rather looked down on shells, as worthy objects of collection only for children or ignorant non-botanists like Thomas Keir Short.

Now he had begun taking long walks on the beach with a compatible friend, a Mrs Ivy Grant Smith who had begun by offering to look after baby William. The boy was still unable to walk and rather sickly, perhaps as a result of his mother's poor health when he was born, though he was now more than eighteen months old.

Little William at once took to Ivy Smith, who became to him the mother figure he had so sadly missed since the departure of the wet-nurse and then Susanna. He almost at once began to eat more and before long was an active toddler, staggering between pieces of furniture or into his father's arms.

'I am inexpressibly grateful to you,' Ronald said, tossing William towards the ceiling of the Smith's living-room. 'You have made a different boy of him. And I know you're not very strong yourself.'

Mrs Smith's thin face, with large dark eyes which were its most noticeable feature, lit up at his praise.

'It is nothing. I love to have him, especially since I lost my own little one. He makes very little extra work; and I have a good, trustworthy maidservant.'

Mr Grant Smith was the Circular Head storekeeper, a man of some learning, with an aunt in Scotland who was a noted authoress. He said now approvingly, 'The doctor says fresh air and gentle exercise are good for my wife. Shell-collecting is getting her out in the open air – and I am cooped up in the store all day and cannot take her walking.'

It was Mrs Smith who found the best shells, as they walked – chaperoned by his younger children – on the sheltered beach behind Circular Head. There were beautiful ear shells, warty on the outside but lined with a pearly blue-green iridescence; scallop-shells and tiny fan-shells of translucent orange, so frail that it seemed impossible they could have withstood the power of the waves; and cockle-shells of sunset colours, palest pink and lilac.

'They are the flowers of the sea!' he said.

She showed him a small, unspectacular conical shell, no bigger than a finger-nail, which she explained was the one collected by the Aboriginal women for their pretty blue necklaces. Using the acid from a solution of vegetable matter, and then heating them in a fire, they removed the dull whitish coating of lime and revealed the sparkling nacreous blue beneath.

'How they discovered the colour beneath, or the means of removing the coating, no one knows,' she said. 'I suppose it is a skill handed down from mother to daughter for thousands of years. You know that only the women dived for shellfish? I shall try to find enough blue shells to make a bracelet for little William. Household vinegar works just as well.'

Ronald looked at her with admiration. She had such skills of observation, such snippets of fascinating observation, it was stimulating to be in her company. She was too thin, poor girl, with a tiny waist above the full, gathered skirt of her poplin day dress, but her complexion was beautiful: almost translucently pale, with two spots of rosy colour in the cheeks. Though he did not realise it, the colour was not a sign of health, but of the consumption which had been diagnosed a few months before. He knew she had been 'in delicate health', but thought it was the aftermath of her confinement, and the loss of her baby girl.

'Do you think,' she asked one day as they strolled on the beach, 'that Sir William is interested in sea-weeds? After all, they are plants too.'

'Why of course! Do you think you could collect some during the neap tides? The children will help, I'm sure. But mind you don't get wet or catch cold.'

She smiled and said she would be careful. He was beginning to feel protective towards her, and to look forward to the mornings when he could get away for an hour, and, carrying young William while the others darted here and there ahead of them, walk on the firm sands above the low tide mark. He had felt a little guilty at the time he was spending away from botany; with her; but now she had given a good reason for 'beachcombing'. He wrote defensively to Hooker:

> Do not be afraid that I shall neglect your favourite Botany. Birds, Shells, etc are useful in winter when the plants are not in flower – but in Summer – plants – plants – plants only. My Botanical collection for the last six months has been *immense* – yet I have left much undone . . . You need not think that you have yet received more than half the plants of Van Diemen's Land.

He had visited the Hampshire and Surrey Hills in February, and became almost delirious with the wealth of new plant life there unfolded: so many novelties, so many old friends – former species which he had never seen growing, but had received from James Backhouse, Dr Hutchinson or Dr Milligan. *Gunnia australis*, the genus of tree orchids named after himself, he found within five or six miles of Circular Head, growing on the dogwood or native pear in great abundance; a new hovea, the native lilac . . . He exhausted Dr Milligan's scant supplies of paper, and had to transport the rest of the new plants undried, packed in his pockets and his knapsack and even under his hat. His rambles had extended as far as the Middlesex Plains and over the Black Bluff, 4,000 feet high, where many new plants delighted him.

At Rocky Cape, a range of low hills falling down to the sea twenty miles to the eastward of Circular Head, he had found at Christmas time, in the boggy, poor soil of the small hollows between the hills, the beautiful blandfordia of Labillardière: great clumps of crimson bells edged with lips of gold, some in fruit; and the strange wooden fruit of *Banksia serrata*.

He felt quite pleased with himself when he enumerated the many novelties, including some new and beautiful orchids . . . besides many better examples of plants he had collected earlier.

'When you receive them, you will be delighted too,' he wrote, packing up a very large case of specimens.

In May of 1837 he sent off a collection of algae to Hooker, noting:

To a Mrs John Grant Smith you are indebted for the collection of Sea-weeds which are very prettily dried . . . Three fourths of the shells are also of her collecting. I was unable to inform her in what way the Algae were best preserved, but she has as it were naturally dried them so beautifully that I think she could hardly improve . . . She soaked them first for a night or so in fresh water. During the approaching winter it is probable Mrs Smith will add considerably to the number now sent. Some of what I suppose to be Corallines are very beautiful.

Ivy Grant Smith – and she was named after a plant! – had won his heart by her great and careful attention to his collections of plants while he was away at Woolnorth or the Hampshire Hills on his magisterial duties. Many would have been spoiled if she had not changed the paper every day when the pressed specimens were drying.

'I am under the greatest obligation to you, my dear lady,' he said sincerely after his return from a visit to Hobart Town in June. He had found her in the afternoon carefully transferring specimens, without the loss of a single bud or sepal. He thought briefly of Eliza, and how she had spitefully destroyed his work in one of her drunken bouts. If only he might have had a wife like Ivy Smith! Gentle, thoughtful, womanly, and with a feeling for natural history which made up for her lack of scientific study. His life seemed to have taken a great turn for the better. Only the continuing worry of wretched Thomas Short's so-far-unpaid bill marred his happiness.

'How did you find Sir John and his lady?' asked Mrs Smith.

'Oh, I was *much* pleased with them both. I had the pleasure of dining with them at Government House, with Captain Maconachie, a former Professor of Geography, who is Sir John's secretary, and Mrs Maconachie, a most estimable lady with a deep interest in botany! She had even heard of me, from Dr Lindley the orchid specialist.' He reflected that there was nothing gentle about the captain's vocal and forthright wife.

'That must have been wonderfully stimulating and interesting.'

'It was!' He was still glowing with the remembrance of that evening, the conversation, the wit, the wine – he scarcely tasted the food, he was so enjoying the company after his exile in the little settlement of Circular Head.

'And Lady Franklin, even more than her husband, is sincerely anxious to help the cause of natural history; they are to form a Natural History Society in Hobart Town, to meet every month at Government House . . . and they know Hooker, though of course I didn't mention my connection with him through collecting . . . By the way, I have something to show you.'

He led her to the study and opened his folder of letters from Sir William, the latest one on top. 'It came just before I left for Hobart Town: what think you of that?'

He held up a coloured plate of the mountain buttercup, glossy yellow flowers and fine green leaves: under it was the title, '*Ranunculus gunnianus*'.

'It was the very first Van Diemen's Land plant to be named after me. This letter has taken *two years* in transit!'

'It's beautiful. You must get it framed and hang it on your wall. Do you realise that you will be remembered, in a hundred years' time, not as the man who sentenced thousands of convicts to secondary punishment, but the one who discovered thousands of plants never before recorded?'

'Why yes, I suppose so . . . I'd never thought about it. But often I felt the deep contrast between the sordid facts of the court-room, the endless fines for drunkenness, the lash and the cells for more serious crimes – all that brutality and human degradation surrounding me, and then the innocent life of the plants. The delicate, fragile blue of the austral bluebell – and the sharp pink of correa, hanging its head in true fuchsia style, and the scented bells of *Lomatia* . . . I suppose in a way I murder them in order to dry them for my herbarium. On the other hand, many are flourishing in hot-houses in England from the seeds and bulbs I've sent over there.'

'And some would never have been seen or known but for your collections.'

'Yes. It's strange that such beauty should exist in wild, unvisited places – unvisited even by the Aborigines, I believe – with no eye to appreciate it. One wonders, why?'

'I read a poem of Thomas Gray's the other day;' she said.

'Full many a rose is born to blush unseen
And waste its sweetness on the desert air.'

He was standing close beside her while she bent above the colour-plate of the mountain buttercup, and looking at the vulnerable nape of her neck from which the curls had been gathered high in a Grecian style, he felt an overwhelming desire to take her in his arms and kiss the white skin above the edge of her gown.

Startled, even shocked at his own impulse, he stepped a yard away from her and muttered something about being tired after his journey and in need of a wash. She gave him a report on William, who was staying with her, and was 'flourishing', then she took her departure. Ronald, trembling with shock and unacknowledged desire, went to unpack his things, while his single manservant, who cooked, kept the house clean, and acted as a bird-skinner as well, prepared him a late meal.

In September his worst fears regarding Mr Short were realised. An account arrived for the £178 loan, with a 25 per cent re-exchange fee on the original bill, brokerage and other costs which brought the total up to more than £200. With interest, it would soon be even more; for he hadn't a hope of paying it. And Short had never returned his cash loans of £25 and £5.

He admitted to himself, and to William Hooker, that he had acted foolishly in guaranteeing so large a sum to a man who, he already knew, had little regard for the truth. Though in fact he had only agreed to lend £125, and Short, in his plausible way, had induced Mr Scott of Launceston to approve the larger amount before the mails could reach Circular Head for his assent. It was dearly-bought experience.

As he told Hooker, he had as little regard for money as any man might who had five children to provide for; but what hurt him and made him doubly indignant was that Thomas Short, not content with swindling his washerwoman (whom Gunn had paid out of his own pocket) for a small sum, had deliberately set out to fleece a man who had befriended him, for a large sum which he knew could be ill afforded. 'Your *kindness* has all but completed the ruin which my unfortunate wife began,' he wrote to Short, but tore the letter up and resolved not to answer any further communications from him, unless they contained a remittance. Short *did* write, in his cheeky, insouciant, ungrammatical style, completely ignoring the injury he had done. The man's impudence surpassed everything! There was not even a mention of the cash he had borrowed before going to New Zealand.

17

DURING THE winter and early spring, whenever he had a morning free, he snatched enough time to go shell and algae-collecting on the beach with Ivy Smith and the children. Sometimes all the children came; usually the older boys and Frances were in the schoolroom with their visiting tutor, an ex-convict who had been deported for forgery but had now received his pardon. William would be left with the new nursemaid at Mrs Smith's, and this left the adults more free to wander on the wide sandy flats above low tide, with only Isabella to accompany them, and sometimes a little friend of hers, daughter of the postmaster.

They walked on the firm sand near the water's edge, while the two little girls played at the foot of the low sandhills, finding driftwood in pale twisted shapes, and fragments of bleached bone among the sea-pinks and wild rosemary. The sea was calm and silvery. Sun lighted the green-grassed top of the Head and its dark granite walls.

At low tide the beach seemed to stretch forever, 'beyond the rim of the world', murmured Ivy. He had to bend his head to catch her soft words. Sometimes as he stooped beside her to examine a group of shells, their fingers touched. He felt a shock of delight go through him. Nearly two years since he had touched a woman, let alone slept with one. She was so pure, so sympathetic, so reciprocal – he felt he knew how she would be in bed. Then he tried not to think about it. Another man's wife! Sternly he fought down his feelings. She kept her head bent beneath her bonnet, he could not see her face.

They moved up towards the drier and softer sand, where strands of dried seaweed were caught in fingers of wave-worn wood. The two little girls were building a 'house' of driftwood sticks and seaweed, further along the beach.

As she bent to untangle a length of seaweed at the base of a grey-leaved bush, Ivy gave a cry of pain. A sharp stick had pierced the palm of her hand, which she put to her mouth in a childish gesture.

'You are hurt!' Concerned, he took the fine-boned hand in his, looking at the ooze of bright blood against the white skin. He lifted the palm to his mouth and licked it delicately. 'Now I have drunk your blood!' he said half-seriously. She raised her face to his. Her lips were smiling, a strained, serious smile which shook his heart. In a rush of feeling he took her in his arms and was kissing those lips, those dark eyes, as her bonnet fell back and she seemed to go into a swoon, or trance. 'Sit down,' he said tenderly, pulling her down on the edge of the dune.

'Papa!' He turned to see the two little girls trotting towards him, trailing strands of dried algae.

'I'm sorry – I didn't mean – ' he stammered.

'Don't be sorry.' Her hand touched his, briefly, and then the children were with them and he was admiring their 'specimens' of rather draggled weed.

After that morning he didn't care, he neglected botany to be with her. Sometimes she brought William over in the evening after minding him all day; sometimes they walked together, and the presence of the children gave a strange innocence and sweetness to their relationship. The sanctions which society and morality imposed were unimportant, because they were not alone, and did not have to guard against going too far; yet the small children left them free to communicate in low voices underlined by the voice of the waves as the tide turned. It was enough for him just to sit beside her on the sand, their hands resting lightly side by side, just touching, when he felt not desire but a great welling peace.

One afternoon when he went to collect William after

work, she beckoned him mysteriously into the kitchen. There, on a bench, was a long wooden box filled with soil and moss and a most beautiful collection of orchids, caladenia, thelmytra, the golden moth orchid and the nodding greenhood, the strange spider orchid and many others.

She had persuaded her husband to take her on a Sunday afternoon to the heathy plains behind the peninsula, where orchids thrived in the undisturbed, poor, wet, sandy soil.

He kissed the hand that had collected them so devotedly. She looked over her shoulder nervously. Her husband might come in at any moment from the adjoining store. But her thin face glowed with happiness at his pleasure in her gift.

He had been away, travelling with the Governor and Lady Franklin to Flinders Island – an opportunity he welcomed for the chance of botanising there. The trip was really to visit the Aboriginal establishment run by George Robinson, though Lady Franklin was anxious to see too the strange grass-trees, as well as the declining Aborigines. The two hundred men, women and children who had been taken there had been reduced to less than a hundred, and there were only ten children.

'They are an interesting race, and in my opinion the women particularly are far from the savages some have called them,' he said, walking on the deck of the schooner with the Franklins as they sailed out into Bass Strait.

'The great problem is, what is to become of them' said Sir John with a gusty sigh. 'At this rate, unless something is done, they will soon become extinct. The question is, what? By all accounts they are pining away.'

'Yet they now have food provided,' said Lady Franklin, 'the government has presented them with a flock of sheep for fresh mutton – and the benefits of a weatherproof home and of Christianity. I understand a church has been built, and there is a minister of religion and a catechist to look after the good of their souls.'

Gunn said nothing. His brother William was an Elder of the Presbyterian Church, but he himself would rather spend all of Sunday in the open air with his beloved plants. He had gradually shed his boyhood religion. The pointless death of young Lawrence and his own wife's tragic early end, the fact that charlatans like Thomas Keir Short thrived at the expense of those who sought only to do them good, the wickedness that came daily under his notice in the courts, the demons of drink and covetousness – his view of life had become cynical. Except when he thought of Ivy Grant Smith. Her goodness and sweetness reconciled him to much.

When they stepped on to the little wharf the Franklins were greeted by a boisterous welcome from the men, who danced a sort of impromptu corroboree in the shapeless clothing and knitted caps they had been provided with. One of the women, small and dark, came forward and offered Lady Franklin a necklace of the iridescent blue shells strung on kangaroo-sinew, which they had not forgotten how to make. Lady Franklin, a veteran traveller and collector of artefacts – feather capes from the Pacific islands, Egyptian mummy-heads, Russian wooden dolls – was delighted to accept.

She smiled graciously at little Mr Robinson, who was making a pompous speech of welcome, and inviting them to inspect the huts and dormitories 'where Mrs Robinson awaits with her older female charges'. As Mr Robinson became more platitudinous and polysyllabic, Ronald Gunn caught her eye. In that bright blue glance he saw an impish sense of humour which surprised him.

They found it difficult to get away from Mr Robinson's organised entertainments, which included verses from the psalms by the men, and a demonstration of basket-work by the women, but at last the three visitors found themselves walking briskly along a rough and hilly track, about four miles long, to the valley of the grass-trees. The low sun turned the stunted shrubs and small trees to an unwonted green, and suddenly Ronald Gunn started forward with a

130

cry of joy. A golden gleam on a twining stem halfway up the trunk of a small tree – the climbing guinea flower described by Mueller: *Hibbertia*, never seen by him in the wild till now!

Tenderly he collected a specimen of the flower and bud, and – yes, there was the fruit as well, like a pomegranate split into four, and full of orange-red seeds! Then he found a *Kunzea* in fruit, and a strange plant which the natives told him afterwards was called 'cone-bush'.

Sir John and Lady Franklin had walked on, she striding energetically through the tangle of sticks and prickly shrubs which caught her skirt; she took it all with a good humour that astonished and delighted Ronald Gunn. Who could ever imagine Colonel Arthur, and his large lady with her brood of twelve children, making such an excursion! He caught up with them, panting, and showed his treasures. By now all their clothes were somewhat torn, or had pulled threads. And then they were there, in the last of the sunset, walking over a low rise to be confronted by a plain filled with those strange 'trees'.

Against the lurid light of the sky, each held up a tall flower-spike – though not now in flower – above a shaggy mass of thin leaves at the top of a dark, misshapen trunk. They looked like a tribe of wild Aborigines, each standing on one leg brandishing a spear – especially when in silhouette against the sunset sky. As though they had been frozen into stillness while preparing for battle.

'If only one had the skill to sketch the scene,' murmured Jane Franklin. 'It is so picturesque, is it not? If only you could send a picture of this grove to Sir William Hooker.

For the Franklins knew now of Gunn's connection with the great botanist. Sir William had indeed written to Sir John in such glowing terms about his indefatigable plant collector, that they had determined to encourage him.

As they walked back over the track in the growing dusk, Lady Franklin outlined her plan for purchasing a piece of ground outside Hobart Town, out of her private income, to be given over to a collection of indigenous Tasmanian plants – 'for we prefer the names "Tasmania" and "Australia", though I know they're not official – and perhaps you could ask Sir William Hooker to recommend a sober, industrious man as gardener. I could offer him £40 a year, and a house, to keep up a garden of some two acres.'

'A wonderful idea, Lady Franklin! This is something that has long been needed. I shall come down to Hobart Town and select a suitable site for you, if you wish.'

'Excellent! And I hope you will dine with us while there; and your brother, whom we have met.'

Ronald Gunn was in a daze of happiness. As soon as he got back to Circular Head, he wrote to Hooker for a gardener for Lady Franklin.

'She is really a most amiable and estimable lady,' he told Ivy Smith. 'This garden will come entirely out of her own pocket, and when they leave she intends handing it over for the good of the Colony. What a difference from Colonel Arthur, who thought mostly of lining his own pockets, and grew nothing but cabbages for the table and carrots for his horses!'

When Ivy told him, the following month that she was going away, he could not, would not believe it. She and her husband were going back to Launceston. She was coughing a lot at night, and he wanted her under the care of a good doctor there, and near a hospital.

'What is wrong with Dr Hutchinson? Anyway I thought you were better!' he cried in despair.

'I was for a little while; but now . . . I think it's because . . . you see . . . I am to have another child.'

'What!' His face was white with suffering, he felt an angry, sharp jealousy that was like physical pain, and an absurd desire to cry like a child, as he had cried for his mother when she went away from him.

'After all he is my husband, Mr Gunn.'

The formality reproved him, denied all those snatched kisses and caresses which had meant so much to him. But not enough – never enough! Yes, Smith was her husband, she slept in his bed, she was carrying his child. Ronald

132

Gunn told himself he was a fool, all women were weak, what did he expect? He had expected that because she loved him, Ronald, she would not let her husband touch her.

She went on: 'William is quite old enough now to do without a substitute mother, though I shall miss him terribly. But then I'll have my own baby to care for, please God.'

She was pleased, she was looking forward to becoming a mother! 'And shall you miss me?' he asked bitterly.

'Of course I'll miss you, Ronald dear. In fact . . . it is best that I should go away. I was becoming . . . I was afraid I would reach the stage where I could not live without you . . . And yet I can't hurt John, he is so good to me, a good husband.'

'You mean – you mean you do love me? As much as I love you—'

'Oh, I do, I do. That's why I must go away. But I hope you may visit us in Launceston one day, it is not so far.'

'As far as I am concerned, you might as well be going to live on the moon.'

Leaving this earth! He felt the future stretching blankly ahead of him, without Ivy who had wound her tendrils around his heart, without the daily companionship which had meant so much to him, and the practical help and encouragement she had given to his botanical pursuits. He felt a pang, an intuitive knowledge that once she left, he would never see her again.

They walked for the last time to the western slopes of the town, at the base of the towering Head, to where the grassy cemetery lay above the sea, and a wide prospect of bay and further headland. The mansion and outbuildings of High-field caught the sun on the peak of the next headland, and surrounding it the green hedge of hawthorn which he had helped Mr Curr's gardeners to plant with cuttings sent out from England; he believed it was the first hedge of may to be planted in Van Diemen's Land.

The cemetery was Ivy's choice for a walk. 'To me,

cemeteries are peaceful rather than sad,' she said. (To the children, running and playing hide-and-seek among the gravestones and the long wind-flattened grasses, cemeteries were a good place for games.)

Ivy stared over the brilliant blue of Bass Strait, and sighed. He stared at her profile, her dark, well-marked brows, her pale face with its spots of bright colour, as if he would remember it for ever. She put her hand in his. 'If – if all does not go well, do not sorrow for me. This last year and a half, your company and conversation, the fun of collecting – it has all been wonderful, some of the best years of my life. I did not deserve your love as well.'

'You will have that always.'

'I hope you will find a new wife, a nice girl without attachments, and perhaps start another family.'

'I want only you.'

'And I belong to another.'

'Yes.'

'*No longer mourn for me when I am dead*
Than you shall hear the surly, sullen bell . . .'

'What are you saying? You are not going to die!'

She gave him a pale smile. 'No. Of course not. But should I do so, I would wish to lie in such a picturesque spot as this, within the sound of the sea.'

When she had left, little William cried for 'Aunty Smith', and Ronald felt like crying with him. There was no one he could confide in, except Hooker. All his suffering was compressed into a few lines:

This year's work has fallen entirely upon my own hands, except for the attention of my most estimable friend Mrs Smith to my Plants when absent, and for a splendid Collection of Orchideae and a new Collection of algae now sent. She has with her husband now left Circular Head permanently – and I am again alone. My youngest child was taken care of by her almost from his infancy,

134

and she was indeed a mother to him. Her loss to me on
his account is deeply felt – and indeed may prove fatal to
his health and wellbeing . . .

For little William, who had fretted when his mother left,
and now had lost his mother-substitute in Ivy Smith, began
to lose the weight which he had gained. He refused food,
and when he could be persuaded to eat any, it came straight
up again', violently, as if his body rejected all nourishment.
His little arms were like sticks covered in wrinkled skin,
and his eyes seemed to sink into his head; yet his stomach
was bloated.

'This child is suffering from malnutrition,' said Dr
Hutchinson after examining him. 'What does he eat?'

'Almost nothing. We can't persuade him to take his
meals, and when he does take anything, he vomits it
straight up again.'

'H'm. I'm afraid this is rather serious, my dear Gunn. If
we were in Launceston, or still better in Hobart, I'd suggest
putting him in hospital for observation. But he's so weak I
wouldn't advise such a long journey at present.'

'What can we do? I believe he's fretting for Mrs Smith,
who as you know is in delicate health herself and has left for
Launceston.'

'There's not much you can do. Give him gruel, beef tea,
anything nourishing which is easy to digest, bread and
butter, cream, and of course milk if he will take it.'

In desperation his father tried to force food down the
little boy's throat, but he set his mouth against it and very
little went down.

It broke Ronald's heart to see the pale, peaked face, the
mouth set in a straight line, and something patient and, yes,
old about the expression of the eyes – as though the child
were wise in the ways of suffering and accepted them
without a murmur. He did not cry, but was increasingly
listless and indifferent to those around him. Only Isabella,
who would lean over him and tickle his face with her dark
curls, could bring a wan smile to his pinched features. His

very quietness, as he lay in his cot or on a cushion on the floor, contrasted strangely with the boisterous racing round the house of his brothers and sisters. *They* had to be shushed into keeping quiet; he rarely made a sound.

After another two weeks it became evident that William was dying. Ronald felt a renewal of all his feelings of guilt about Eliza and her early death. If he had not separated him from his mother, might William have lived? And yet Eliza, in the state she was in when she left for Ireland, was no sort of mother for a sickly child. It did not occur to him that the baby was already an alcoholic when he was born, accustomed to sudden rises of alcohol in his blood.

The emaciated body of William Campbell Gunn in its small coffin was interred in the Circular Head cemetery above the sea, on a melancholy grey day. The waves broke and broke with a dull sound on the grey pebbles below, while Ronald Gunn stood bare-headed in the misty rain. It seemed as though he was attending the funeral of Eliza where he had not been present, not even been aware for another six months that she was dead.

Mr Edward Curr came over from Highfield to lend support and sympathy – he whose own baby girl had died so tragically a few years before, and was buried on the property.

Ronald had heard the story: how the little girl Juliana, less than three years old but full of adventurous spirit, used to drive a tiny dog-cart with a big collie-dog to pull it. One day the big dog had dashed beneath a fence and the wooden rail struck the little girl in the forehead, killing her instantly. But Mr and Mrs Curr had ten other children living.

After the boy's funeral Curr came back to the house for a drink. He was worried about the young man, with his shadowed eyes and set mouth. He did not want to lose him from the district – he was a good and fair administrator of justice and the V.D.L. company men he tried had no complaints about him. But Curr had the feeling that isolation, with his wife gone, was not good for him. And now his youngest son . . . He was too much alone.

As for Ronald, he wondered why Lawrence and so many others had found Curr arrogant and overbearing. He was a big man like William Gunn, with a sense of his own worth, but Ronald found the manager a kind and congenial neighbour.

He was often lonely. But there was one bright ray amid the gloom he felt. The Franklins had taken him up most warmly, and shown him the kindness and encouragement he valued far more than money. He admired Sir John for his exploits; he was a brave and famous explorer, though now putting on weight with increasing age. It was delightful to see his tenderness and concern for childless Lady Franklin.

Jane Franklin had been impressed with Gunn's devotion to science, and by his sensitive, suffering face in repose. She wrote to her sister Mary in London,

We find Mr Ronald Gunn, one of Hooker's most industrious collectors, a most congenial companion. He travelled with us recently to Flinders Island. While Sir John was below writing his report – and it could only be a sad duty, when the Aborigines seem inevitably doomed to extinction – I walked on the deck with young Mr Gunn, who told me something of his history. He was widowed at an early age and left with five young children; lost his great friend Lawrence who introduced him to Botany; and as he says, apart from his children now lives only for science. I wish we had him in Hobarton to foster our fledgling Natural History Society, and perhaps edit its Journal . . .

Gunn, overwhelmed by the encouragement he had so much wanted but never received from Colonel Arthur, wrote to Hooker that a new era had commenced with the arrival of Sir John and Lady Jane, and science was now receiving the attention it deserved in such a new and unknown field as Van Diemen's Land.

He was reconciled now to never seeing his money again

from Mr Short – with interest and his own cash loans the sum had now reached £250 – and felt a renewed interest in all the natural history productions of Van Diemen's Land. He began to feel that his work was not without worth, and that his children might even profit from his exertions after he was gone.

With new enthusiasm he set off on expeditions to west, east, and south, combining botany with business for the Crown. In less than a month of incessant activity, he walked or rode from Woolnorth in the far north-west of Van Diemen's Land to the Forth River, about 320 miles there and back, with eight river-mouths to cross and re-cross which were fordable only at low water, and even then dangerous.

The road, or rather track, ran much of the way along the indentations of the coast above high water. From Emu Bay he went inland twenty miles to the Hampshire Hills, another twenty miles to the Surrey Hills and the deserted V.D.L. Company's station at Burghley:

From Burghley I followed the road!!! which required a microscopic eye to find it, over the Leven River and from thence over the Black Bluff to the Vale of Belvoir and on to the Middlesex Plains, and penetrated a few miles towards the Forth's gateway, but was obliged to return.

On his next official visit to Emu Bay and the Hampshire Hills, riding through the dense humid forest, he found the long-looked-for *Dawsonia*, a genus of moss that had so far eluded him, in abundance; and on his way back found it in flower. He rolled the specimens in a parcel and carried them in his coat pockets, knowing how delighted Hooker would be; exotic mosses were one of his specialities. He was away only six days and travelled 160 miles; collecting on his way along the heathy coastal plain, the lovely little lilac bells of the George Town *Tetratheca*.

Then, just as things were looking up, life dealt him another blow. He heard with incredulity and despair, just

as the spring flowers were reaching their peak, that Ivy
Grant Smith was dead. He had hoped to see her soon,
however briefly, in Launceston. But her constitution had
been further weakened by childbirth. The infant survived
only an hour, and in a few weeks, on the eighth of October,
she had followed him to the grave. Five years, almost to the
day, since Robert Lawerence's death!

He wrote, with difficulty, to the bereaved husband,
feeling alienated, even angry, that he who loved her so
much had no right to be there at her death-bed, to press her
cold lips for the last time. His mind was filled with images of
corruption and decay. Had the winter rains reached down
to little William's body, accelerating the process? And Ivy –
and Eliza – lowered into the cold clay, to the inevitable
corruption of the once beautiful flesh:

> *And there the curious worm shall try*
> *That long-preserved virginity . . .*

Oh God! Was he going mad? He must fight off this
obsession with death . . . As usual, he confided in his most
distant friend, William Hooker:

> . . . And now another link in the chain which binds me to
> this world is broken. No doubt it is well ordered so – that
> when the time comes for our *own* removal, we may have
> as few links as possible to make us regret leaving this
> world.

He added a reference to Mrs Smith's 'beautifully preserved orchids' (while she herself decayed!) and con-
cluded:

> I am most unfortunate in my Botanical friendships – poor
> Robert Lawrence's loss has never been made up – the
> vacancy caused by his death still remains open – the
> wound unhealed.

When he wrote in this vein to his brother William, and added that he was making detailed maps of the places where he had made his botanical discoveries, 'so that should my career be, like poor Lawrence's, suddenly cut off other collectors may know where to find any rare species', William became alarmed.

As soon as he had an opportunity, he had a word with the Lieutenant-Governor. His brother Ronald, he said, was brooding on death again, and the probable suicide of his great friend almost exactly five years ago: 'I feel he should come away from that isolated station, sir, and live in the metropolis where I can keep an eye on him, and he will have more distractions and more congenial company . . . May I recommend him for a post as second Police Magistrate here? He seems to be in a state of deep depression.'

Sir John, busy but kindly disposed towards the young man whose brother was appealing to him, and knowing that Jane too took an interest in the young botanist, agreed at once.

'And I know Lady Franklin will be delighted to have an addition to our Natural History/Society meetings. There's a vacancy on the Assignment Board, by the way, if your brother would like to take it.'

'That would be very acceptable, Sir John. I know he is in some financial straits at present.'

'Yes. Well. That's settled then. We don't want your interesting brother buried in the Northwest forever. Quite the contrary.'

18

LADY FRANKLIN, ever seeking new adventures, was planning a visit by sea to the inaccessible far west coast, to Port Davey and Macquarie Harbour. Sir John could not get away from his official duties for so long, but Mr John Gould the noted ornithologist, with his wife, was staying at Government House and offered to escort her, and she invited Ronald Gunn to go along and botanise. Others in the party were her step-daughter Eleanor, and Captain Phillip Parker King, R.N. the naval surveyor, and Mrs King; besides Lady Franklin's indispensable personal maid and other servants, including John Gould's assistant bird-skinner.

The government schooner *Eliza* sailed from Hobart Town on December 10th. Ronald Gunn, on the rebound from his former depression, was in high spirits at the prospect of several weeks' holiday and some interesting botanical opportunities. He had long been anxious to see the Huon Pine growing, and he took ample means of preserving plants for any novelities he might find at Macquarie Harbour. Best of all, he would not have to walk and carry a pack with limited capacity, as all would be transported by sea; for the landlocked harbour penetrated deeply into the western forests.

Young Harry Elliott, Sir John's Private Secretary, came down to the wharf to see them off. He remarked in an aside to Ronald that Mr Gould seemed fully conscious of his importance as a 'lion' from London, a famous bird-gatherer. He came aboard bare-headed, in a natty double-breasted surtout which opened to reveal a floral waistcoat that his wife had embroidered in coloured silks on moss-green velvet. His forehead was high, broad, and smooth, his chin and mouth disproportionately small, and his black eyebrows were finely arched. Ronald thought that he had a slightly self-satisfied air, and did not think they would be inseparable friends at the end of the voyage.

The *Eliza* was a roomy and well-found vessel, a beautiful yacht-built schooner of 150 tons, with first-rate accommodation, excellent meals from the galley and an experienced crew. After a day's sailing in brilliant weather, and an excellent luncheon served under an awning on the after-deck, they reached the mouth of the picturesque D'Entrecasteaux Channel, with the low hills of Bruny Island beyond now gold with summer grasses. In the afternoon they anchored in mid-channel in the lee of the island.

Mr Gould set off in a boat rowed by his assistant, to look for a penguin rookery he had heard of on one of the small rocky islands. He did not ask Gunn to accompany him.

He came back without any eggs but with a live penguin still covered in down to show the passengers. He then proceeded to cut its throat on the deck with a penknife. The ladies, Mrs King and Lady Franklin and Eleanor, retired from the scene of blood. Gunn watched the grisly business as the bird-skinner flayed the body, tossing overboard the still-warm organs, the heart still visibly beating. The meat was kept as bait for crayfish.

Bad weather blew up from the southwest the first night. As they came out from the shelter of Bruny Island into the southerly swell, before entering the shelter of Recherche Bay, the weather was so rough that Lady Franklin's heavy table – she had brought with her her own iron bedstead, now cleated firmly to the floor of the cabin, and her cedar writing table – broke loose from its lashings and crashed against the wall. Water came through the part-secured porthole and poured over her books and papers. Snatchell, Lady Franklin's maid, came to ask Ronald Gunn's assistance in securing the table, muttering to herself that she would never come on such a voyage again, no never, she 'ated the sea and would probably die from sea-sickness before the voyage was over. She certainly looked rather green. There was no hope of proceeding in the teeth of the gale, so by 7.30 the next-morning they had anchored in the sheltered waters of Recherche Bay, named after the ship of La Billardière, the French botanist on the expedition with D'Entrecasteaux nearly fifty years before, and intensely interesting to Gunn for that reason.

He did not realise what opportunities he would have for collecting in the area, for they were to be weatherbound for nearly a month, and could not get to Macquarie Harbour at all. There was no hope of rounding South-East Cape while the winds blew from the south-west.

John Gould went out after sea-birds, and that night he wrote triumphantly to his wife:

> I have this day killed a rather extraordinary bird, you will remember the large Snow White Petrel which followed us nearly all the way from the Cape to Tasman's Head and which I was so desirous of procuring . . . I have also killed some beautiful albatrosses, petrels, small and large gulls etc.

For the time being the weather was clear, though the wind still blew hard from the south-west. Lady Franklin was not very well with toothache. Gunn had stayed on deck till a late hour the night before, admiring a moon of silvery brightness which paled the stars but made the waters of the channel gleam like quicksilver.

In the morning, with her Mamma still indisposed and plump Mrs King electing to stay on board in a comfortable deck-chair, Eleanor was inclined to trail after Ronald Gunn, the youngest male of the party.

'Look, Mr Gunn! I have found you something' she would call, holding up a plant which he had collected twice already. He felt rather sorry for her, she was at an awkward age and rather plain, with her father's round face and knobbly chin. She seemed not to get on very well with her stepmother, in fact to be rather in awe of her.

On some poor, sandy soil he suddenly saw a new boronia. He charged forward, almost knocking poor Eleanor down in his excitement. Tenderly he took a specimen of flower and leaf. It was, he felt sure, different from *Boronia Pilosa*, a new species.

While John Gould went birding, he and Captain King, whose father, Governor Phillip Gidley King, had established the first British colony on Norfolk Island, took a dinghy and rowed in the opposite direction, to the north end of the bay.

'I love exploring small islands,' said Captain King, who had been the first white child born on Norfolk Island, nearly fifty years before.

They found an island, its surface as white as a snowdrift with native mignonette. Gunn landed to pick some specimens, while Captain King held the boat in to shore. Then they landed on a bank of the inlet where the poor swampy land was scarlet with bunches of beautiful Christmas bells, the *Blandfordia punicea* of La Billardière.

After dinner, while it was still light, they persuaded the ladies to come rowing to the same place, under the overhang of some dark, wooded hills which turned purple in the evening light. They exclaimed at the beauty of the scene: the hills reflected in the calm water, the brilliant flowers painting the foreground. They could not resist landing on the bank to pick an armful of the gold-lipped beauties. Mrs King leaned on her husband's arm; she was rather short of breath. But they too wandered off, knee-deep in scarlet bells.

Lady Franklin, who had picked only a few magnificent specimens of blandfordia (while Eleanor was still busily plucking armfuls) was first back to the rowing boat.

'Mr Gunn,' she said hurriedly, 'there is a subject – a rather delicate subject – which I have long wanted to discuss with you. I tried to talk about it with Mr Forster, the Police Superintendent in Hobart, but I think he was embarrassed, or shocked . . . I am sure you will not be.'

She looked round to make sure Eleanor was still out of earshot, and took a deep breath, 'Mr Gunn, you must be aware that the Female Assignment system is a foul blot on our fair Colony! You know how often a female assigned servant becomes a mother of an illegitimate child fathered by her master, who should be her protector. She is conveyed to the Female Factory at Hobart or Launceston to have the child, and then nurses it, and is often selected from there as a wet-nurse to a private family, and perhaps becomes the family nursemaid.'

'That sometimes happens; yes.'

'And these women, their least crime perhaps that they were thieves, or women whose "trade" I have blushed to see recorded in the Surgeon-Superintendent's book – these women are the nurserymaids of our Colonial households, the earliest teachers of the infant generation, the waiting-maids of the grown-up daughters. It's not right, Mr Gunn! You must be well aware of it, from your position when in Launceston—'

'Yes indeed, Lady Franklin. When we first arrived in Van Diemen's Land, my own wife was horrified to find that the nursery maid had been transported for murder. But what can one do, when there are no other women available? In the Female Factory at present there are only five free women among four hundred inmates.'

'Even worse, the mothers, after the child is weaned, and after at most six months at picking oakum or working in the laundry, are sent back to the same masters, and the whole immoral situation begins again. I have written to Mrs Elizabeth Fry about it,' she said. 'No one here seems sufficiently upset by it.'

'Yes, I admit we have a problem; but it is not always the master of assigned women who are involved, especially if there are menservants in the household. I've just had to send away an otherwise excellent girl, who was good with the children, when her condition became obvious. My own manservant was involved.'

145

'Then I hope you sent him away too!'

'He has left, yes. But I blame the woman, as this is her second such offence.'

'Shocking! Perhaps if the authorities shaved off their hair— But no more of this now.' Eleanor was returning with a huge, carelessly-picked bunch of scarlet bells. Lady Franklin put her finger to her lips. 'But I am determined to do *something* about it.'

Mr Gould brought the nest of an emu-wren, and two beautiful dead parrots which he had not seen before. Gunn found a type of waratah, and that the boronia of La Billardière was also abundant.

After an abortive attempt in the next few days to proceed with the voyage to the west, they had to anchor again in Recherche Bay, the wind persisting with gale force from the southwest.

As soon as the weather improved a little they moved round to Mussel Bay, and celebrated with a dish of mussels and oysters for breakfast, fresh off the rocks. The next day, proceeding up the Catamaran River at high tide, they found much better soil, with fern trees, the myrtle-beech, and the celery-top pine.

By this time John Gould was getting impatient. He was not finding many new birds and felt he was wasting precious time. When the *Vansittart* arrived from Hobart Town with stores, he said he really must go back in her.

'I had intended to stop only a month in Van Diemen's Land, and how will I get through my work on the birds of New Holland if I go on in this way?' he asked.

'Oh, pray do not desert us, Mr Gould!' exclaimed Lady Franklin, who was feeling better and just beginning to enjoy the trip. They left him discontentedly pacing the deck while Eleanor and Lady Franklin went with Ronald Gunn in the boat to collect some petrified wood and coal, in a tidal inlet. The other bank was once more glowing with blandfordia; Ronald landed, and found among the crimson flowers a 'sport' of a warm orange colour but with the same yellow edge to the petals.

146

Lady Franklin, who found Gunn *simpatico*, had told him during one of their conversations while exploring how she dreaded the return to Government House and all its pin-pricking worries.

'Sir John never likes me to be away for long, but oh! the relief it is to live in cabins or tents after all the domestic entanglements at home! You have no conception how the running of such a large household wears my nerves!'

Now he realised that she was not worried about losing John Gould's company, but that if he returned early Sir John would see no reason for any of them to stay, and would demand their return also.

By a combination of charm and imperiousness, which Mr Gould for all his self-assurance could not resist, she made him on their return to the *Eliza* promise faithfully – giving his hand on it – that he would stay on and work a little longer.

They called at Pelican Island to pick up the milch goat who had been brought on board for fresh milk and landed there to get some green feed. Two rabbits had been placed there a year earlier, and had now increased to twenty-six. Returning to the schooner, they had to wait till after dark – and this on the longest day of the year, midsummer – for Mr Gould and his assistant to return from an expedition before they could sit down to dinner. Ronald found no interesting plants; all had been eaten by the rabbits or the goat. At last, on Christmas Eve, a fair wind sprang up from the north and east. They expected to set sail for the West Coast next morning at dawn; but by great ill fortune (as Lady Franklin felt) the *Vansittart* arrived that evening with letters from Sir John. They were summoned back to Hobart Town, though there was no chance they could get there in time to celebrate Christmas at home, since the wind was unfavourable to their return. It was New Year's Eve, 1839, before they anchored once more in the Derwent.

Such was the influence of the persuasive Jane Franklin, that Ronald Gunn's next letter to Hooker bore the address 'Hobarton, Tasmania', the lady's preferred nomenclature for Hobart Town and Van Diemen's Land. His next letters soon reverted to the official names, however. By then he had been appointed Private Secretary to Sir John in succession to Henry Elliot, and Mr John Price, now married to Sir John's niece, was to take over the post of Assistant Police Magistrate.

During his term as Magistrate, it rather shocked Ronald when a soldier of his own name, Private Thomas Gunn (no relation, of course) was brought up before him for secondary punishment. He had been transported for seven years on three charges of insubordination, including 'offering violence to a non-commissioned officer' (he had in fact knocked down a sergeant) and 'using disrespectful words against the Queen'.

Looking at the man's charge sheet before he was marched in, Ronald noted the medium height, five foot seven, brown hair and blue eyes, and a fresh complexion. Yes, he might have been a relative.

The present charge was 'insulting an overseer': no very heinous crime, for many of the overseers were only ticket-of-leave prisoners who had been advanced to take charge of their former mates. They were often bullies, and had got their positions through informing and toadying; they were generally disliked by the old-time convicts.

Superintendent Gunn was relieved, quite logically, to see that the prisoner bore no family resemblance to himself or William. He was a stocky, sturdy man with a complexion more red than 'fresh', his eyes looking the more vividly blue by contrast. He was clean-shaven, with a dark, bluish stubble on his knobbly chin, and his black hair stood up in a stiff brush. There was something aggressive, indomitable even in the way his hair grew.

'Convict Thomas Gunn. You have been charged with insulting an overseer. Read the charge, Sergeant.'

The Sergeant of the Court read out in a monotonous voice, '. . . did refuse to obey a direction, and give the overseer an insubordinate look before walking away with his back to 'im'.

'And what was the direction?'

'To remove a large stone from the road, which was thought 'ad been put there deliberately.'

'Have you anything to say in your defence?' asked Ronald Gunn formally of the prisoner.

'Well, it was like this, your Honour, I never heard 'im, see? They roughed me up a bit in the Army when I wuz arrested, and I copped a blow on the ear, and now I'm a bit deaf, like.'

'Only on one side, surely. And that doesn't explain the "insubordinate look" before you walked away.'

'No, sir. But he's alwus pickin' on me.'

The man gave him a look out of his blue eyes that said as clearly as words that he was guilty, and that he would do the same again tomorrow if he felt put upon. On an impulse, Gunn said, 'I see you have a large mark of vaccination on your arm, according to your dossier. Did you ever serve in the West Indies?'

'No, sir. Never.'

'H'm. Well, I must uphold discipline. Prisoner at the bar, I sentence you to one week's detention on bread and water in the Penitentiary.'

'Thank you, your Honour,' said the ex-soldier, with a gleam of real gratitude in his eye. No doubt the overseer had asked for him to be given thirty lashes. Seven days in the "Tench". It was nothing.

19

RONALD HAD been on a few excursions up Mount Wellington and collected some water-plants from the tidal Derwent River, besides a hurried trip to the Huon River to the south, but his duties on the Assignment Board as well as Magistrate had left him no time for arranging the new plants for transmission to England.

The Private Secretary's accommodation, a small villa in the grounds of Government House, was now so full of specimens that Gunn had to make time to send off a consignment. He had not yet even sent the *Dawsonia* gathered so gleefully in November 1838.

In excuse, he explained to Hooker that he was now the Secretary of the Tasmanian Natural History Society, and President of the Launceston Horticultural Society which he had established. Above all this, he had Lady Franklin's Botanic Garden at Ancanthe, Kangaroo Valley, to look after.

He had opened up a walk along the Brushy Creek, the wild rivulet along which it was placed, about four miles from town. There was a natural grove of fern trees, myrtle and dogwood along the creek; the setting was delightful, cool and with a natural slope which was not too steep. It was work he delighted in. He took the children there at weekends and the older ones helped him place stones to border the path. Lady Franklin simply provided the money. She was no gardener, nor particularly knowledge-able about plants, yet she saw the need for preserving the native species, near town, where development would soon remove the original bush.

Sometimes he walked from his house up through the grounds to take coffee at Government House after dinner; sometimes he was invited more formally to a meal. But the house was full of guests:

We are overwhelmed with Company, [Jane Franklin wrote to her sister in London]. We have the whole Montagu family in the house (they having vacated their own before leaving for London) besides the Goulds – she 'expecting'; – and in addition to this, a French ship of War *L'Artemise* of 50 guns, commanded by Capt. La Place, is in the harbour, and he (with some of his officers) dines here every day with company to meet them . . .

Lady Franklin was popular with the French Navy because of her fluent French, but nearly quarrelled with M. La Place over the French Navy's action in Tahiti. They had threatened to blow the biggest town to pieces if the Queen did not immediately salute the French flag with twenty-one guns, pay 2,000 dollars and write her apologies for having sent away from her island two French Catholic priests.

They got the money, though not the apology, and sailed for Sydney where, as Lady Franklin remarked indignantly, the ship *La Venus* was welcomed with civility.

'A more atrocious feat of the French was never heard of!' she said decidedly to her husband. 'Cannot you say something to the Captain of *L'Artemise*?'

'I have to be silent on the subject, my love, as I would be speaking for the Crown of England. It is for our Queen to censure them officially.'

'Well, I'm determined to let Captain La Place know *my* mind about it,' she said.

Accordingly she told him she was doubly glad to welcome him because he was not commander of *La Venus* who had carried out the raid. He had heard nothing of it; but admitted that he had the same instructions in his pocket. 'Well, I hope the matter will be taken up in England!' said she.

151

Lady Franklin called Gunn into the study, to admire the latest exquisite bird-paintings of Mrs Elizabeth Gould. Mrs Gould had a large bedroom upstairs with a good light where she worked, and two adjoining rooms for her maid and the nursemaid, and another as a nursery for her little boy John, and the expected new baby. Since Governor Arthur had had twelve children to accommodate, and the Franklins had only one, there was plenty of room.

Ronald gazed with pleasure mixed with envy at the delineation in most faithful detail of every feather, every nuance of colour in the gorgous parrots sent from New Holland by Mr Gould. Painted from dead skins or stuffed specimens, they yet seemed to glow with life. What a pity that flowers, unlike birds, immediately faded and lost most of their colour at death! And here were flowers, too, and gum-leaves painted so that you could almost pick them from the page.

'How I wish, Lady Franklin, that I had this facility with the pencil and brush . . . How often have I longed to paint some beautiful new specimen before its delicate colours faded! However, I've managed to preserve the fleshier flowers, like waxlip orchids, in pyroligenous acid. One day perhaps they may have a kind of machine which will preserve the images of plants on paper. Indeed, I have seen the outlines, or silhouettes, of leaves reproduced on light-sensitive paper, though without much detail.'

'But there could never be a machine capable of reproducing the subtleties of colour in Nature. Like these glorious birds, for instance,' she said, indicating the Paradise Parrot with its turquoise and pink.

'No; the artist will always be needed, I suppose.'

When the French ship had left, and the Montagus had departed for London with their family, Government House returned to normal. Lady Franklin set out on a new expedition to Port Phillip and overland to Sydney. She stayed away long enough to avoid giving a Ball for the Queen's Birthday; but her husband informed her in a letter that the people expected it, he had given a Public Notice about it, 'and I hope it will be as soon as practicable after your return'. He added, 'Mr Gunn dined alone with me yesterday . . . Eleanor and Miss Williamson are quite well but have not time to write.'

Ronald Gunn could see that Sir John was missing his wife and longing for her return. On June 20th she was still in New South Wales, exploring the beautiful Hawkesbury by boat, and 'I should like to have been home by the 28th, but it is now too late, as the *Eudora* has gone – and then the *Medway* presented herself and we could not hesitate to wait for her . . .' Sir John wrote to her that Mrs Gould and the new baby, named Franklin, were both doing well.

John Gould was still bird-collecting in New South Wales. In Hobart Town, Elizabeth Gould, who was missing her other children terribly, wrote bravely to her mother in England: 'I have quiet secluded apartments at one end of Government House . . . This climate is much finer than England's, so clear, so exceedingly pure in atmosphere.'

With Mrs Gould dining in her own apartment, Sir John sent an informal invitation to Gunn to dine with him. He felt it a great compliment to be asked to dine alone with the Governor. What a change since Arthur's day! He had a meal sometimes with brother William and his wife, and the two families met each Sunday at the Presbyterian Church.

At Christmas the Franklins went up to the Governor's Retreat at New Norfolk, a rather ancient cottage in a beautiful setting on the tranquil upper reaches of the Derwent. Ronald Gunn was asked to join them for the week after Christmas. Leaving the younger children with William's wife, he set off on foot instead of taking the steamer or the coach.

The day was clear and hot, and he wore a pith helmet to protect his face from the sun. With a knapsack on his back for specimens, he walked along the banks of the river wherever practicable. As he reached the end of the tidal influence, approaching New Norfolk, the banks became cliffs and he had perforce to walk on top of the bluffs, with a magnificent view of the wide, sweeping bends and the high blue hills enclosing them. He had been collecting on the way, examining the country closely for the whole twenty miles. Now his knapsack was bulging and the pockets of his bush-jacket were full. He had to carry a few flowers in his helmet, and some rather muddy water-plants with roots. But the sun was hot, so he placed the hat, complete with plants, carefully back on his head.

A mile out of New Norfolk, tired from his long ramble and thirsty in the December weather – for the river still retreated below steep banks – he came to some open gates and a driveway. On the gateposts were the words Glen Leith.

'Ah! The home of a Scot!' thought Ronald, for the Water of Leith flowed into the Forth near Edinburgh, his old home. He turned at the gates and walked up the shaded drive.

It was the height of summer, but the sun was now declining towards its setting and the air was a little cooler. As he rounded a bend in the drive he could see the homestead, a solid single-storeyed building of stone with a formal garden in front. Gathering flowers in a basket was a female, he could not tell her age at this distance, in a lilac poplin gown and a shady straw bonnet edged with the same soft colour. For some reason his heart beat more quickly as he drew near the figure, still unconscious of his approach.

Then she turned from her flower-gathering (lilac and pink and blue anemones, he noticed) and said, 'Good afternoon!'

She was tall and slim, with calm grey eyes and healthy pink cheeks – this was all he noticed as he lifted his hat from his head, muttering 'Good afternoon, madam, I—'

To his consternation she burst out laughing.

He drew nearer, looking puzzled. She pointed at him, still laughing merrily.

'Oh – I am sorry – but do look at your head!'

He reached up and found balanced there a heap of draggled plants.

'Oh dear! You see, I have been collecting – all the way from Hobart Town – and I ran out of containers for my specimens. My name is Ronald Campbell Gunn, and I am Private Secretary to His Excellency the Governor, who is just now in residence at New Norfolk—'

'Aye, we've been bidden to dinner a week today!'

'And you are a fellow Scot, I take it? I was not born in Scotland, but went to school there. My parents were from Edinburgh.'

'I was born there and lived there as a bairn; before my parents came to Van Diemen's Land. My name is Margaret Jamieson.'

'How do you do, Miss Jamieson. I must apologise for this intrusion.' He had dropped the plants into the crown of his helmet; now he took out a kerchief and wiped his hot face.

'But it is I must apologise, keeping ye here in the hot sun! Come in and we'll have some cool lemonade, or a cup of tea if ye'd prefer it.'

'Thank you, anything . . . I am rather thirsty. But also, I'm afraid, rather grimy. Perhaps if I could just sit on the veranda?'

'Of course, of course!'

She took her basket of flowers and went indoors, while he sat bemused and fanned himself with his handkerchief. That delightful Scottish burr! He had recognised it at once. She reminded him of his dead mother.

The notes of a piano sounded from the drawing-room, where the windows were open on to the veranda. A plaintive, rather cracked tenor voice accompanied the piano.

> 'Ye banks and braes o' bonnie Doone
> How can ye bloom sae fresh and fair?
> How can ye chaunt, ye little birds,
> And I sae weary, full of care . . .'

155

Margaret Jamieson came back, bearing a tray with two cool crystal glasses of lemonade. She had removed the bonnet. Her hair was fair and smooth, braided high at the back – not a single fashionable curl to be seen!

'Robert Burns!' said Ronald, indicating the open window.

'It's my father,' said Margaret, who never called her parent 'Papa'. Her mother was dead, and as the only daughter she ran the house for him. 'He's having one of his sorrowful days today. I dinna care to disturb him with a visitor—'

'No, no. I must go in a minute, anyway. I've trespassed on your hospitality long enough, and must get to the Governor's Retreat before dark.'

He drank the refreshing lemonade, rose and thanked her. 'Goodbye, and thank you, Miss Jamieson. Or rather, *au revoir*. I shall look forward to our meeting next week.'

And so shall I, thought Margaret, watching the back of his tall, spare figure disappearing down the steps.

The dinner at the Governor's Retreat was a great success. In the long twilight the guests sat looking over the beautiful, tranquil reach of the Derwent among its wooded hills. Away from the formality of Government House and the critical eyes of Hobarton matrons, Lady Franklin relaxed and enjoyed being hostess as they consumed fresh fish from the river and tender roast lamb. She was wearing her loose-fitting red silk dress from Malta, which had caused such raised eyebrows at a Government House reception. 'It's only a peasant dress, not a proper gown at all,' one scandalised guest had been heard to remark. But the vivid colour suited her dark hair, and made her rather pallid complexion glow.

'Come, Mr Gunn, I have seated you next to Miss Jamieson, as I believe she is a little botanically inclined,' said the lady, indicating their chairs. Ronald flashed her a grateful look. He had hoped not to be seated next to young

Eleanor, with her earnest and somewhat pious conversation. He had undemanding Mrs King on his left, and she was seated next to Sir John at the head of the table. At each place was a little bouquet of local wildflowers, everlasting daisies and austral bluebells.

This made an opening for conversation with Miss Jamieson. He was pleased to see her again in different circumstances, for he was conscious that when they had last met he'd been hot, sweaty and rather grubby from his twenty-mile walk. She smiled at him and he noted that her teeth were good, while her braided pale-gold hair shone in the lamplight.

She wore a simple white gown of *broderie anglaise* with a blue sash, and a small sapphire brooch at the neckline. It was, indeed, her only formal gown, which she had had made for her brother's wedding; she rarely went out and they did not entertain at Glen Leith these days.

'May I do that for you?' he asked as she attempted to pin the wildflowers to the front of her gown.

He struggled with the rather stiff pin of the brooch, very conscious of the warm flesh of her young bosom beneath the eyelet-embroidered material. 'There! That looks charming. *Wahlenbergia billardieri*,' he said, touching the delicate sky-blue bells on their fragile stems. 'It is quite different from the English "bluebell", which is of the hyacinth family; and more like the Scottish bluebell, which is a campanula.'

'Which of course derives from the Latin for a bell.'

'That is so.' They continued to talk flowers, while Lady Franklin, who had planned the whole thing – Mr Gunn certainly needed to marry again! – watched with a gleam of happy amusement in her blue eyes.

After dinner, she strolled with her arm through the girl's on the long veranda overlooking the river. When they were round the far end of the veranda, out of earshot of the other guests, she said, 'Mr Gunn tells me you have met before?'

'Indeed yes, Lady Franklin; he called in at Glen Leith for a drink on his walk up from Hobart.'

157

'Hobarton. He is a delightful young man, but has had a sad life. Sir John and I find him very congenial.

Indeed my friendship with Mr Gunn has been one of the consolations of this rather demanding post. For you realise that *I* am on duty too, can never relax but must be on my best behaviour, except when travelling, or in this idyllic spot.' She added, 'New Norfolk is a beautiful place, but isolated for you, my dear Miss Jamieson.'

For she was aware that Margaret rarely went out or met any young men, and that any who came were discouraged because she felt her father needed her.

'I like the country,' said Margaret, 'and the bonnie river and all.'

'Yes, but you should get *out* more, my dear girl. You must come and stay with us at Government House, we have plenty of room.'

'That is very kind of you, Lady Franklin. But my father is not so well at present. It's more in his mind, you understand?'

'Yes, I understand,' sighed Jane Franklin. She sometimes suffered from that sort of malaise herself.

20

FOR RONALD the incessant official drudgery, both as Private Secretary and as a member of the Assignment Board – though he was no longer a magistrate – had 'almost knocked Botany out of my head', as he wrote to Hooker. He did not mention his growing attachment to Miss Jamieson, and the time spent journeying to New Norfolk. Mr David Jamieson had asked him to come and 'botanise' whenever he liked.

To his delight he found Margaret Jamieson was not only interested in botany, but had a 'wee collection' of pressed wildflowers. She knew all the best areas for finding them near her home. Ronald was enchanted. Besides, he liked her father, a tall, bony Scot whose knobbly wrists stuck out from his jacket sleeves, and whose bright blue glance from under his white eyebrows was alert and penetrating. He felt himself being assessed, and believed he had not been found wanting.

Jamieson told him that he had Scottish bluebells growing in his garden, 'Aye, and the bonnie thistle too, the national flower o' Scotland.'

They talked about the acclimatisation of plants, from roses to apples, willows to weeds. Ronald told him that he had reservations about imports which could spread their seeds by wind-dispersal like the thistle, and which might later take over whole tracts of country and spoil them for pasture.

'Na, na, yon thistle's a bonnie plant, it'll no' become a threat to the land.'

'Well – we'll see. But the trouble is, if an introduced plant becomes established away from its natural enemies, it is likely to become very hard to eradicate.'

'Eradicate! I should hope they'll ne'er eradicate the thistle.'

After his second visit to Glen Leith, which he spent rambling through the bush with Miss Jamieson (who wore sensible boots and did not make a fuss about walking through prickly undergrowth and boggy paddocks), he wrote to thank her and express his admiration. But he made no declaration. He felt that his heart was partly buried with Ivy Smith, that his emotions had become dried up. And after his experiences he feared another marriage which might go wrong . . . Anyway, the young lady might not want him, he told himself modestly.

A new interest was to prevent him visiting New Norfolk again in the next few months. The Antarctic ships, *Erebus* and *Terror*, under the command of James Ross, were expected, and on board the *Erebus* as ship's surgeon was none other than Joseph Dalton Hooker. Sir William had written to say that his son was looking forward to meeting 'Van Diemen's Land's leading Botanist. He hopes to see much of you.'

But the first to arrive were the French exploration ships under Captain d'Urville. When they sailed again they left behind a French lieutenant who was a first-class cook, but as Lady Franklin complained, he spent most of his time making advances to her maid. 'My household is in a most disorganised state,' she wrote in January to Elizabeth Gould (now in New South Wales with her husband). 'First my little housekeeper going away to Norfolk Island with the Maconachies, the Butler leaving, the old Cook gone, and my own maid only detained by the attentions of the Frenchman . . .'

She wrote enviously of their living in tents on the Hunter: 'How I should like to be travelling with you!' and invited Mrs Gould to come back to stay. 'As long as you are over here, your home is with us. Besides,' she added

160

half-seriously, 'I miss the sweet little face of my Franklin whom I think you should make over to me! Come, what say you to such an arrangement?'

Lady Franklin liked children and had adopted an Aboriginal girl, and then a little boy, Adolphus, from the orphan school, who was proving rather a handful. John Gould had taken him on collecting sorties in Tasmania, and found him a great help, with 'an eye like a hawk, and throws the spear and the waddy with the utmost dexterity – extremely useful in the Bush'.

The Natural History Society now met at Government House after dinner every fortnight, when Ronald Gunn read the minutes and sometimes a scientific paper. But it was not his activities with the Society, nor his rather half-hearted courting of Margaret Jamieson, which stopped him writing one letter to Sir William in the next months. It was the arrival in person of Hooker's son Joseph: it was, in some way, like meeting his old correspondent in the flesh, made miraculously young.

Ronald had waited in a state of nervous excitement for the ships to berth. A whole contingent from Government House was waiting at Sullivan's Cove, only a short walk from the Government Domain: the Governor himself, his Private Secretary, his aide-de-camp and two footmen to carry any bags that might need transporting from the ships. The officers would live on board, but would dine every night at Government House during their stay of nearly three months.

Down the gangway came an erect, firmly stepping figure in white breeches and gold-frogged blue coat: dark curly hair, and deep-set, brilliant black eyes, a long, inquiring nose – Ronald stared, his heart thumping in his chest. Could this be – ? He had expected someone more scholarly-looking in Hooker's son. Then a second tall figure appeared behind the first – a thin young man with a sensitive, humorous expression, and shoulders rather stooped as from bending over a desk. This was he! He knew it at once. The other had been Captain Ross.

It was almost as if Robert Lawrence had come back. Young Hooker was only twenty-three, the same age as Lawrence when they first met. Like Lawrence, Joseph Hooker was dark and thin, rather tall, with that suppressed nervous energy which had made Lawrence such a vital companion. Hooker wore steel-rimmed spectacles, for his eyes were weak, though for close work his vision was excellent; and large bushy eyebrows gave strength and character to his long, thin, thoughtful face.

Sturdy Captain Crozier joined them from the sister ship, and Ross's first officer, FitzJames. Then there were handshakes and back-slappings all round – if it had been the French Navy, reflected Ronald wryly, kisses would have been exchanged – Sir John beaming at James Ross, nephew of his old friend and fellow Arctic explorer Sir John Ross.

Gunn was introduced to young Hooker, and their hands met and gripped. 'I've been so looking forward to this meeting, my dear Gunn,' he said.

'I too—'

'My father has sent all sorts of messages of good will and gratitude for your sterling work here.'

'Sir William is a kind and generous correspondent.'

In the next weeks he was as in a dream. Joseph Hooker was a real, qualified botanist, who could teach him much; yet he always deferred to Gunn as the local expert. He said he felt almost stunned by the verdure and variety all round him, as they sat beneath the shade of a fern tree glade drinking locally brewed Tasmanian beer. Joseph pulled a piece of moss and studied it in his palm.

'You know, I thought I wasn't going to reach here, after all,' he said thoughtfully.

'How so?'

'Well on our way here, as you know, we called at Desolation, or Kerguelen, Island and I wandered off – my collector's enthusiasm overcame my caution – and I found myself lost among some rocky vales, no sight of the sea. The sun was completely veiled by low cloud, and mist.

'I had nothing with which to make a fire, and I knew that

162

even if a search party set out from the ship it might take them days to find me. It was intensely cold. After panicking a bit, stumbling around and falling over, I took myself in hand. I sat down on a rock and stared at a bright green moss.

'If God can look after that little plant in these desolate wastes, surely he will look after me,' I thought. I got up, put a piece of the moss in my pocket, and walked straight to the coast, not far from our ships. It was like a miracle.'

Together the two men rambled on foot or on horseback, always collecting, arguing amicably over the allocation of species, poring at night in Ronald's study over the books of their great predecessors, La Billardière and Robert Brown.

'I never cease to be amazed at Brown's *Prodromus*,' said Ronald. 'He was so accurate, so early! What a pity he didn't continue his work, and conclude it.'

'Never mind, *I* shall do so one day,' said Joseph half-jokingly. 'With your help and my father's, we'll bring out a definitive *Flora Tasmaniae*. My father is an excellent draughtsman. I wish I'd inheritied his talent.'

'Well, you've inherited his talent for botany, that's certain. It's so wonderful to have someone who knows and understands to talk and argue with – you've no conception how lonely I've been for this sort of congenial company, my dear Hooker! I hope your ships return next winter, after your voyage to the south.'

'If talent is "the wish to do well" as someone said, then I think I have it,' said Joseph. 'My father always fostered my aspirations to become a traveller and a botanist. I chose medicine because I thought with a degree I could more easily get an appointment on such an expedition as this.'

'Tell me about Sir William,' said Ronald when they were seated after dinner in his study beside a fire of blue-gum logs. 'I feel that I know your father already, although I've never met him. I can tell, for instance, that he's basically a *kind* person, who cares about people as well as plants.'

'That is true; and I don't believe he has an enemy in the

163

world. For utter absence of self-esteem and genuine kindness, I have never known anyone like him.'

'I wish I could afford to travel to Scotland again, and meet him in person. But having you here is the next best thing.'

'I know he esteems *you* highly, my dear Gunn. "The best and most indefatigable collector in Van Diemen's Land", he told me. He says you were born to be a naturalist: you have an unerring eye for the differences in species, for the details that are important in classifying and comparing.'

'I often regret my lack of knowledge and formal training in botany,' said Gunn. 'But my knowledge is improving all the time, thanks to the splendid library your father has helped me to build up. He's a marvellous correspondent, and extremely generous. And he illustrates his letters with charming little drawings, and accurate sketches of the anatomy of plants – I know he has illustrated his own books.'

'Yes, I sometimes wonder how he keeps up with his correspondents all over the world,' said Hooker, sipping his port. 'Of course he's always up early and rarely leaves his study before midnight. He has a single-minded devotion to science. He's also a religious man, far more so than I am. I was lucky growing up in a botanical environment. When my father was Professor at Glasgow, he would take us boys, about seven and eight years old, to his early-morning lecture at eight o'clock, walking all the way to the University. We'd get back for breakfast about half-past nine, as hungry as young hawks. I've often known him to walk forty miles in a day.'

'Do you look like him?'

'Not really. I'm thinner and more ascetic-looking,' Joseph laughed. 'My father is tall, but sturdier, and with warm brown eyes and a most frank, genial manner, though he doesn't socialise much; he just hasn't the time. I have a much longer face, and I think I'm more reserved.'

'You remind me very much of my much-lamented friend, Robert Lawrence – he who started me in my interest in

164

botany. He was tall and dark and thin, and full of energy like you; and was much more knowledgable than I. I've never got over his loss. But having you here – a botanist and the son of a great botanist – I can't tell you what it means to me.'

Joseph Hooker was never to forget those idyllic days in Tasmania in the spring of 1840. Captain Ross, too, fell in love with the green and blue setting of Hobart with its magnificent harbour below the bastion of Mount Wellington. Both Ross and Hooker were overcome by the beauty of the climate and picturesque countryside, the wooded hills and mountains which made an extraordinary contrast to their last port of call, the uninhabited Desolation Island. For Hooker there was the added charm of seeing flowers and plants in all their vigour of life and beauty, where he had before seen them only as dried specimens.

Years later he was to write nostalgically to Ronald, of the time 'when he walked, galloped and jawed in "Tasmania", my spirits equal to another bottle of ale on Grass-tree hill or Tree-fern valley. Happy days there, old Gunn – I should like well to see you again!'

When he couldn't get away from his duties to accompany Hooker, Ronald sent his servant Brownlow whom he had trained as a plant collector, to accompany Joseph and help carry back his specimens.

'I think I shall make Mr Robert Brown arbitrator between us,' Ronald wrote to Hooker senior. He and Joseph had had some amusing and engrossing arguments over whether *Ranunculus vestitis* was a distinct species, and whether *Tetratheca glandulosa* and *pilosa* were also distinct. He was impressed by young Joseph's sound reasoning and grasp of the subject, and promised to help him with his proposed monograph on the eucalypts.

He took Joseph on a Sunday afternoon to the Ancanthe native garden he had prepared for Lady Franklin. Hot from the walk, they flung themselves down in the cool mosses by the Brushy Creek.

'Lady Franklin didn't like my going out collecting on

Sunday!' said Joseph with a laugh. 'But after all, I did go to church first, and listened to boring old Bedford without falling asleep. I really can't bear to waste one of these glorious spring days indoors.'

'Me neither. Sunday has often been the *only* day in the week I could get away from official duties and go collecting. And even then I felt guilty at not spending the time with my children.'

'They're lovely children. I hope to have a large family one day, but there is much work and travel to be done first.'

A few miles away they could see Sullivan's Cove, with the masts of ships reflected like bare trees in the silky calm of the water. Above and behind them towered the bulky shape of Mount Wellington, its basalt columns glowing in the sun, its caves and hollows cobalt blue with shadow. On the very summit lay a streak of white, unmelted snow from the past winter.

'You know this was entirely her idea,' said Ronald, waving an arm at the native trees and shrubs surrounding them. 'She's a remarkable woman.'

'Lady F. Yes, but a mite imperious, I find.'

'Well, she's used to getting her own way. Sir John can be obstinate as a mule, but *she* has a will of iron, and of course he adores her and nearly always gives in to her. She simply wears down opposition by a mixture of charm and determination.'

'Is she really going to build a museum here, out in the wilds of Kangaroo Valley?'

'She speaks of it; and I believe she'll do it, too. She wants a sort of Greek temple to the arts and sciences, built of stone – there are plenty of good stonemasons in the country, fortunately. It will cost the earth, but she apparently has thousands to spend of her own. It will hold a library of Van Diemen's Land books, and scientific journals, as well as natural history specimens.'

'Good! I shall donate the first volume of my *Flora Tasmaniae* to it. And the foreword will contain a tribute to my great friend and collaborator, Ronald Campbell Gunn.'

'And I shall drink its health in the cider of the cider tree, *Eucalyptus gunnii*.'

He had sent a bottle of this cider, fermented from the sap of a gum-tree which grew in the mountains behind Launceston, to William Hooker. He had followed the Aboriginal method of making incisions in the bark in late spring when the sweet sap was running freely. The Aborigines, having few water-tight utensils, would gather the sap in holes in the ground lined with impermeable clay, then they would cover it with bark and leave it to ferment.

Knowing that Sir William Hooker was corresponding with Ronald Gunn, and had made inquiries about him of Lieutenant William Gunn, the Danish adventurer Jorgen Jorgensen once more approached Ronald for a handout, spinning hard-luck tales. Only when he was three-parts drunk could he summon up courage to approach the Governor himself, asking Sir John for a little money 'for an old shipmate' – usually with success, since he had once held a commission in the Royal Navy.

He then wrote to the Police Magistrate at Hobart Town, requesting the incarceration of one Norah Corbett Jorgensen in the Women's Factory where she could not get drink, for a period of six weeks. He could not, he wrote, personally swear evidence against her in court, for fear of future violence . . .

Thus the author of five books in two languages was reduced to using his education to write despairing letters to the authorities. He was afraid of his Irish wife, a former laundress and quite illiterate. In her drunken rages she used to chase him down the street, screaming abuse. Jorgensen was now in a bad state, often up before the Magistrate himself for being drunk; a shabby and pathetic figure with unkempt hair and soiled clothes, rheumy eyes and dirty fingernails.

Having heard that young Joseph Hooker, son of his former friend, was visiting Hobart with the *Erebus*, Jorgensen determined to see him. He introduced himself on the docks one day. Joseph Hooker felt both surprise and pity for the old man: no tall, fair Viking as he had supposed, but a small shrunken figure whose wild dark hair was streaked with grey, and whose brown face was deeply seamed with the ravages of time, weather and dissipation. His tattered clothes looked as if they had been slept in. Yet he spoke an educated English, almost without an accent, as he grasped Joseph's hand and cried, 'My dear sir! It gives me unspeakable satisfaction to behold the son of one who in former, happier days was my friend . . . How *is* Sir William? He has never replied to my letters, though I know he still takes an interest, and inquires after me. Alas! I have lost the friendship of many good men, of Sir Joseph Banks himself, through my own folly.'

And he began to weep maudlin tears, much to Hooker's embarrassment. He pressed some silver into the old man's hand, and managed to get away while he was counting it.

Jorgensen wrote to Sir William:

I endeavoured once or twice afterwards to see Mr Hooker, but he dedicated the whole of his time to look for plants, etc . . . I am now advanced to that time of life, sixty-one years, when I cannot much longer expect to linger in this world, and I am desirous, in case of final departure, that some memorial be left of me. I have been so careless as not even to keep one copy of each of my publications . . .

He died in hospital the next year, and was buried in a pauper's grave. The once uncrowned king of Iceland had gone on his last adventure.

When the two ships *Erebus* and *Terror* sailed off on their dangerous mission to try to reach the South Magnetic Pole, life seemed suddenly as empty as after Lawrence's death. But Joseph Hooker was not dead; he would, all being well, be returning the following autumn; and in him Ronald felt he had a friend for life. Meanwhile, though the ships bearing the news had not yet arrived in Tasmania, an important advancement had come to his friend and correspondent, Sir William Hooker. He had been appointed Director of the Royal Botanical Gardens at Kew, a position he had long hoped for.

Feeling ashamed of his neglect, Ronald went on a boat up the Derwent to New Norfolk to call on Miss Jamieson, with the excuse that the Franklins wanted him to have a look at the Government Cottage there which was falling into disrepair. Lady Franklin had a pet scheme for establishing the new Boys' College there; for which the Reverend J. P. Gell had arrived as potential headmaster.

Ronald believed that Margaret Jamieson liked him, and he thought she would make a most suitable mother for his children; he liked her merry, brisk, no-nonsense manner and her candid grey eyes and smooth fair hair, caught up with combs in a rather severe style to the top of her head. But he had resisted 'falling in love' after the bitter experiences of the last eight years.

He had hesitated for another reason. He'd written to William Hooker at the time of Ivy Smith's death, 'I am unlucky in my Botanical friendships'. He had a superstitious fear that if he once let himself love anyone, she would be taken away by death – perhaps at her first confinement, like poor young Mrs Lawrence.

But now Joseph Hooker's visit, his frank friendship and the letters he had sent back since leaving, convinced Ronald that his luck had changed. After all, he loved his children, too, and they were healthy and flourishing in this wonderful climate. And he longed for a woman's touch, not just in bed, but in his everyday life: to sit with her over breakfast, to show her his new discoveries, to enlist her help as a collector.

Margaret greeted him gravely, accepting his explanations of how busy he had been, with Hooker's visit and the Ancanthe garden. But she was pleased to see him again, no doubt of that.

They went on many rambles together over the estate and along the high banks of the river which Glen Leith house overlooked. He found himself telling how his unfortunate wife had nearly ruined him, then left him a widow with five young children; and of that other, deeper loss of his never-forgotten and ever-mourned friend Robert Lawrence. She was a good listener, interjecting an occasional interested exclamation. He did not, though, mention Ivy Grant Smith whose death was indirectly responsible for his leaving Circular Head and coming south to live.

'Aye, I see now why your face is a sad one,' she said softly. 'But – but you are young enough yet to start a new life and find happiness once more.'

'You mean marry again? I had not thought of it until I met you. Miss Jamieson! Margaret! Would you consider me as a husband?' He took both her hands in his, looking into her face.

'I didna mean – I canna say – ' She became more broad in her accent with agitation. The pink in her healthy cheeks deepened.

'And with a family of four ready-made?'

Margaret Jamieson laughed. 'So long as I may have four more of my own!'

Margaret was not sure how David Jamieson would take the news; she was his only daughter and he did not want to part with her. But she was twenty-three, no longer young, and he would have to make up his mind to it soon, 'or have me on his hands for ever more!' she said merrily.

Ronald felt diffident about approaching Mr Jamieson, for he could not be called a brilliant catch – with four children to support and a job which could not last beyond the present Governor's term of office. His small house in

170

the Government House grounds was already over-full. But when he made a formal request to Mr Jamieson, he was more warmly accepted than he had hoped.

'Ye're a Scot, laddie, and a man after my own heart!' said David Jamieson, clapping him on the shoulder and bringing out the Scotch whisky.

Ronald had not told him that he was actually born in the West Indies; but his parents had both been Scottish, and he had been educated in Edinburgh.

Mr Jamieson was saying genially, 'Drink up, drink up laddie! That was just a wee dram . . . Ye have the look o' my son Thomas – ye ken I lost him awhiles back?'

'Yes. I am very sorry, sir. Miss Jamieson told me her eldest brother had died . . . You have other sons?'

'Aye, but one's away to Port Phillip District. And the other at school in Scotland. And it seems that now I must lose my only daughter.'

'And, I hope, gain a son. My own father died years ago. But I have a brother in Hobart Town.'

'Lieutenant Gunn. Aye, he is well spoken of.'

Since speaking of his loss, Mr Jamieson had slumped in his chair, and two deep-grooved lines appeared beside his downturned mouth. 'My daughter had an education, too,' he said almost challengingly. 'The gel has a good head on her shoulders. Aye – Margaret has her own life, I'll no' stand in her way.' He sat up, downed another glass of whisky, and declaimed:

'"Come back, come back!" He cried in woe
Across the stormy water
"And I'll forgi'e your Hie'land Chief,
My daughter, oh my daughter!"
– But the waters wild went o'er his child,
And he was left lamenting.'

Tears glittered in his blue eyes. Margaret Jamieson came in, looked anxiously at her parent's flushed cheeks, and quitely removed the bottle to the sideboard.

'Come, Father,' she said gently, 'there is coffee waiting in the drawing-room.' Ronald helped him get rather unsteadily to his feet.

The wedding was to be held at Glen Leith in December. Then, just before Christmas 1840, an answer to Ronald's problems presented itself. Old Mr Lawrence's health was failing; and he wrote to Ronald, with whom he had kept in touch, to ask if he would consider taking over the management of his extensive estates, 'as soon as possible'. The salary named was generous, a house would be provided near Launceston, a roomy brick mansion, and there was also a country house at George Town, near the mouth of the Tamar.

It was arranged for young Henslowe to come from Sydney to take over as Private Secretary, and as soon as Ronald had initiated him into his duties, he would be free to retire and return to Launceston, his old home. He could not believe the good fortune that had come all at once. He was to take up residence in what was really his favourite part of Van Diemen's Land, or 'Tasmania' as it was beginning to be called locally. He would have plenty of travelling over the countryside and opportunities for collecting, and in the acres he had once intended to turn into a Botanic Garden he would be able to indulge in the hobby of gardening once more.

Life had suddenly expanded and opened up before him, with endless possibilities. It was as though he had been toiling up the side of a steep hill, his eyes on the ground in front, when suddenly a fresh breeze buffeted him, he raised his eyes, and there he was at the top – with a vast new prospect of sunlit vales and hills, mysterious rivers and distant mountains all awaiting his discovery.

21

DURING HIS period in Hobart, William Gunn had persuaded Ronald to have his portrait painted. Among the convicts was an excellent portrait painter named Wainewright, who had been transported for forgery. He was now a ticket-of-leave man, working in the Colonial Hospital at Hobart Town as a wardsman. He had painted several sensitive portraits of the family of Dr Nuttall, and William Gunn had given him a commission to paint a portrait of his wife. William said that whatever his crimes – and it was openly hinted that he had been guilty of poisoning his sister-in-law – Wainewright appeared to be a gentleman; and he was much pleased with Frances's likeness.

Ronald was in his early thirties when the portrait, a fine watercolour drawing, was done. William declared that it was a speaking likeness, the eyes were particularly good. 'and he has even caught your slightly worried look, my dear chap'.

Ronald Gunn, though not given to vanity, was not sure he liked the portrait; he thought perhaps he had been made to look rather effeminate, with his soft brown hair and clean-shaven chin, in spite of the neat side-whiskers. Later on he might send it to Sir William Hooker.

Mr Lawrence died in 1841, and named Ronald Gunn one of the executors of his will. He had vast estates, which he wanted managed on behalf of his children. So Ronald Gunn, as resident manager, settled in at Penquite, near Launceston, with his children and his new bride. Ronnie, the eldest, was to remain at boarding-school in Hobart. To his father's disappointment he was not interested in botany: He wanted to be a doctor. But then, Ronald reminded himself, Joseph Hooker was a doctor of medicine. Most of the naturalists on exploring ships were also physicians.

Once more a married man, Ronald was content as he had not been for years. The wedding had been held at Glen Leith, when a small quantity of champagne and a large quantity of whisky had been consumed. The guests who came up from Hobart Town were put up at the Bush Inn at New Norfolk, and the married pair stayed a few days in Margaret's old home. Her father became rather tearful after the ceremony and a certain amount of whisky, and went to bed early, but not before he had rendered 'The Keel Row' on the piano with great spirit.

In the room her father used to share with his wife, Margaret waited in the big double bed in some trepidation to be initiated into the mysteries of married life. At least, she thought vaguely, Ronald had been married before and would know what to do.

As for Ronald, he felt like an ecstatic bee – no, a humming-bird like the ones he remembered – probing the delicate petals of an intricately folded rose, the pink flower of her virginity. He hoped, afterwards, that he hadn't frightened her. It had been so wonderful, after the long drought, to bathe in a pool of sensuality.

But Margaret was not Eliza with her healthy, almost animal enjoyment of sex. He could not call his new wife prudish, but she had to be wooed and won each time, only gradually warming to him. And she had been horrified at the blood. She'd had no mother to instruct her, no sister to talk to, and the whole thing must have been rather a shock.

He waited for her to get over her maidenly feelings, too grateful to her to be impatient. It was wonderful to have a woman in his bed again. She was, besides, a dear companion in his walks and his arranging of specimens.

Ronnie had come to the wedding and got on well with his stepmother. Frances was a little more guarded; young

Robbie was openly hostile. When his father told the children, 'This is your new Mamma,' Robbie gave Margaret a scowl, and said distinctly, 'She's not my Mamma!'

'Go to your room, sir!' said Ronald instantly. But Margaret persuaded him not to give the boy a whipping for his surliness, as it could only make him dislike her more.

However, in the school holidays he and his elder brother were both in hot water, for going exploring together up the gorge of the South Esk river, and not getting home till after dinner when their father was preparing to go in search of them. He whipped Ronnie as the ringleader, and being old enough to know the worry they would cause.

Their next trangression was more serious.

Ronald had employed an old ex-convict as a gardener to work on his acreage at West Launceston, which he was now cultivating both with acclimatised orchard plants and vegetables for the household. The boys sometimes helped by pulling carrots or picking young peas. The surly old fellow would be digging and weeding nearby. He had the cramped gait of one who had spent a long time in the chain-gang, and his jaw was grimly set.

Ronnie and Robbie noticed that he never took his shirt off, even on the hottest day in summer. They wondered aloud if he slept in it, and if he ever had a bath. He was known in the town, perhaps because of his peculiar aroma, as 'Old Possum'.

'I suspect,' said Ronnie to his young brother, 'that the old fellow has the marks of the "Cat" on his back, and that's why he won't let anyone see him without his shirt.'

Their curiosity was aroused. They discussed ways of making Old Possum take off his shirt: if they accidentally spilt water on him – or still better, tea with sugar in it?

'He still wouldn't take it off,' said Ronnie.

'I know, let's get up very early, and hide in the tool-shed. He might come outside for a wash, without his shirt.' For the old fellow occupied a cottage in the grounds.

'You've got it, little'un. We'll try it tomorrow.'

So they told their parents with conscious virtue that they

intended to rise early and work before it got too hot, as the peas were setting fast. Next morning they crept out of the house, before even the servants were stirring, and made their way across Launceston to the garden. Venus hung in the sky like a great lamp, which paled as the sky lightened before the coming sun. The top of Ben Lomond was veiled in mist.

They crept into the tool-shed, leaving the door ajar. As the sun cleared the eastern hills, gilding the old weathered boards of the cottage to something like beauty, a curl of smoke came from the chimney and rose straight in the still air. Ronald nudged Robbie. 'See! he's awake.'

Outside the door, beside the tankstand, was a tin basin in a stand. Old Possum emerged, a kettle of hot water in his hand. His grey beard was ruffled, and he wore only a wrinkled pair of cotton dungarees low on his hips. He stood looking up at the sky, as if judging the weather. Holding their breaths, the boys watched him go to the tap on the tankstand and half-fill the basin. Then he turned so that the early sun picked up the terrible ridges and scars on his brown back, like the surface of a weather-gullied hillside.

Young Robbie gave a whoop. 'Look at his back!' he cried, before Ronnie could get his hand over his mouth.

Old Possum turned, scowling, his mouth set in an uglier line. He stared straight at the tool-shed. He looked dangerous.

Ronnie decided it was best not to wait to be discovered; each grabbing a hoe, they came out as if that was the reason for their presence in the shed. The old man backed through his door and emerged again wearing an unbuttoned shirt.

'Hallo there, we just came to do some gardening before it gets too hot,' said Ronnie with false heartiness. 'Come on, Rob, look lively,' he said, giving his young brother a push forward. The young idiot was grinning at the shirt. Ronnie was beginning to feel a bit ashamed of their exploit. He saw the old fellow's hands trembling as he fumbled at the buttons.

'I knows why you come,' he growled. 'And now youse

a'seen what you come to see, you can get. Go on, get off home!' And he made as if to fling the kettle of hot water over them.

Robbie backed behind his big brother, looking scared. The joke of catching out the old man no longer seemed funny. The boys walked back along the ridge between the two arms of the Esk, feeling uncomfortable, and turned up at Penquite in time for breakfast. To inquiries about their early return, they replied sheepishly that the peas weren't quite ready yet.

In the summer of 1841 Lady Franklin made one of her expeditions to the mainland, to stay with the Henty brothers at Portland Bay – the first successful pastoral enterprise in the Port Phillip District. They had brought Merino sheep from England, and transferred them in their own vessel from Van Diemen's Land as early as 1834. The Hentys were the first permanent settlers on Victorian soil.

They had built a substantial homestead of twelve rooms with a long veranda overlooking the blue waters of the bay. It was the nucleus of a village of six cottages for stockmen and servants, sheds, huts, barns, a dairy, store, stables and workshop, as well as boatsheds for whaleboats and whaling gear. When the little township was surveyed in 1840, the population consisted of less than a hundred persons.

Lady Franklin had met Mr and Mrs William Henty, as passengers on the *Fairlie* when she and Sir John first came out to Hobart Town; Mrs Henty had lost her baby boy who was buried at sea. William had remained in Tasmania, while Edward, John Frank and Stephen developed the Portland Bay property and squatted on wide acres of grazing land. Stephen Henty invited Lady Franklin for a visit, and she asked Mr and Mrs Gunn to accompany her party in the *Breeze*, which called at Georgetown to pick them up. Ronald was delighted to have a chance of visiting this part of Victoria's coast, as he had so far seen only the plants from round Port Phillip Bay. And for Margaret it was a long-delayed honeymoon trip, for there never seemed time for them to get away before.

They managed to get a respectable Irish girl, a daughter of free settlers – for even the children of convicts were regarded as 'contaminated' by their parents – as a nurse-maid, and with the trustworthy manservant Brownlow they felt free to leave the younger children in Launceston for a week. Frances was now a big girl and able to supervise the others, while Ronnie was on holiday from school. And Ronald still had an acting manager at Penquite from whom he was learning the ropes, and who would carry on while he was away.

The weather was hot and clear, with a sea-breeze every afternoon which dispersed the heat and made afternoon tea on the veranda very pleasant.

'I sat writing my journal on the veranda,' wrote Lady Franklin, 'while Mr and Mrs Gunn botanised among the sandhills.' The Hentys' little son Richmond, not quite three, followed her about and climbed on her knee whenever he could. He was the first child born in Western Victoria.

Ronald and Margaret Gunn had no children as yet, after a year of marriage. He felt that it was because she had not responded to him fully, though she never denied him but was shyly anxious to please. He tried not to make comparisons, knowing she must feel some diffidence as a second wife.

In the new surrounding and holiday atmosphere of the Hentys' comfortable home, she began to relax. One hot morning they wandered far long the shore, finding many species which were similar to the Tasmanian ones across the Strait – not only similar, but astonishingly like, and yet different in some particulars.

'It's very interesting to me,' he said, picking a fruiting capsule of *Ricinocarpus*, 'as showing the variation between the flora of Van Diemen's Land and that of New Holland. Sir William Hooker has remarked that botanical geography is yet in its infancy, and much remains to be known.'

Dense thickets of tea-tree covered the frontal dunes with rounded green outlines and dark trunks bent to fantastic forms by the sea-winds.

'Banks used the little pointy leaves as a substitute for tea,' he said, picking some and holding them to his nostrils. He had not brought a big enough knapsack, and had already filled his hat with fruit and flowers, blue berries of *Scaevola*, and orange seeds of *Hibbertia*.

'A pity you're not wearing a shawl, my love, with which we could make a package. I know! Give me one of your petticoats, and I'll knot it into a bundle.'

'Ronald!' said Margaret, scandalised.

'Come on. I bet you've got two or three on under that skirt.'

He reached out to lift up the lilac poplin – it was the garden dress she had been wearing the day they first met – but she twitched it away from him and ran, stumbling, into the next hollow.

'Oh!' She tripped over a trailing rope of silvery dune grass, and fell full-length in the sand.

'Now I've got you!'

Laughing, he pushed up her skirts and unlaced a petticoat and began pulling it down, while she resisted. He felt his own growing excitement, and began to kiss her. At first she struggled, exciting him further, then suddenly she flung her arms round his neck. Her cheeks were glowing pink, her eyes were bright, so different from her pale, determined face when she lay in bed at night in her high-necked nightgown, letting him do as he would.

Murmuring endearments, he struggled with their frustrating clothes, and only half-succeeded in penetrating past her many voluminous undergarments before it was all over. She smiled at him dreamily, there among the shell-shaped hollows of white sand, her bonnet fallen back, lying in the tea-trees' dark-blue shade. He kissed her fiercely, gratefully, but she pushed him away and sat up, pulling down her skirts. 'Oh, Ronald, for shame!' Her cheeks were flaming, but there was a smile lurking in her eyes. She helped him tie the petticoat to make a bundle for the specimens, which he had dropped as he ran after her.

What had come over him! he thought, rather amazed at himself. One of the whalers might have come upon them, anyone, though it seemed as deserted as a beach on an uninhabited isle. But he felt a great glowing contentment. He knew what it was. This was the consummation he had longed for with Ivy Grant Smith, among the sandhills at Circular Head. Now all his love turned towards his wife, and she felt it and responded. The ghosts of Ivy Smith and Eliza Ireland had been laid to rest for ever.

22

LITTLE MARY ANN was born the following year and baptised in Launceston a few months later. Margaret had been scandalised to find that only Robbie of all Ronald's children had been baptised. So they made a mass baptism of it; the baby Mary Ann in her mother's arms in a long-skirted, lace-edged christening robe, the girls Isabella and Frances in white dresses and straw bonnets. St John's Launceston was filled with flowers, and friends of Ronald's from the Public Service – it was almost like a wedding.

Isabella was the beauty of the family, with her black hair and blue eyes. Frances at fourteen, almost ready to put her hair up and let down her skirts to her instep – at present her rather thick ankles in white ribbed stockings were allowed to be seen – was fair like her mother, but had not inherited Eliza's bright curls. Fate, or inheritance, had blindly given a red-gold mop to Ronnie, who did not appreciate his luck. The baby Mary Ann still had only a soft down on her head, while Robbie took after his father.

For this reason if no other Margaret tried to like him, indeed to love him as if he were her own – but it was difficult when the boy was so unresponsive, receiving caresses with indifference and kindly remarks with a suspicious stare. He stated his position quite clearly, when Margaret announced brightly to the children, 'Mamma is going to take you on a picnic to the Punchbowl, shall you like that?' Robbie was heard to mutter – though not in the hearing of his father – '*You* are not our Mamma. Our Mamma is dead.'

Margaret would have liked to slap him. With an effort

she kept her temper and ignored the remark, leaving it to Frances to reprove him for his rudeness to 'our new Mamma'.

She helped Ronald whenever she could with his plant-drying and annotating. His assistant, Brownlow, had returned to Hobart, which limited his work in the field. 'I am entirely without a Botanical assistant,' he wrote to William Hooker, 'however Mrs Gunn helps me a good deal, though she has plenty to do with a rising family without bothering herself with my hobbies.'

He used to stuff his hat and pockets with any novelties he found while riding round the different Lawrence properties, scattered over seventy miles.

'I dare not carry *visibly* the means of collecting plants, or the good people at the farms would think I was neglecting work and only culling flowers,' he told Margaret.

'You shouldn't worry about what they think, Ronald. Besides, they know fine that you're a good manager.'

'Still, I feel happier hiding them under my hat.'

'Like you did the day we first met! How I laughed when you lifted your hat, looking so correct and polite, and there was a great heap of muddy plants on top of your head!'

'That was a happy day for me.' He drew her tall figure towards him – no longer slim for the second of her 'four of her own' was on the way – and gave her a kiss. 'Dear wife!' he said.

He had a big black gelding named Rajah, who took him untiringly on his rounds with his comfortable amble. He seemed a sure-footed beast, and the accident, Ronald admitted afterwards, had been his own fault.

A heavy rainstorm came on as he was returning home, while still some way out of Launceston. Instead of sheltering under a tree or a rock till it had passed, he pressed on, wanting to reach Penquite before dark. Coming out in the open paddock that sloped towards the house and garden enclosure, he gave Rajah his head. The horse, smelling home, hay and warm dry stable, began to gallop. Ronald knew it was dangerous to gallop downhill on wet grass, but he and the horse were seized with the same impulse to race for home.

Then somehow Rajah missed his footing and came down. He went slithering down the slope on his near side, with Ronald's left leg, still in the stirrup, pinned beneath him.

Rajah recovered himself and stood up, fortunately freeing the foot in the stirrup as he did so. But that movement was such agony that Ronald knew his leg was badly broken. He explored with one hand and felt the splintered bone protruding through the flesh. The rain continued to fall. He turned his face up to it, struggling to retain consciousness. He would have to call for help, and trust some of the men working outside would hear him.

But Rajah, unhurt, trotted home with his empty saddle. The alarm was raised, and two servants come out to search, to find their master lying in the grass with his leg at a strange angle.

One of them went back to get a stretcher, and to tell Mrs Gunn that he was found. Margaret came running, bareheaded in the rain, and flung herself down beside him in the wet grass.

'Oh, Ronald! Are ye all right? Is it just your leg is hurt?'

'You shouldn't be . . . out here . . . in your condition,' he managed. And then, 'The horse . . . Rajah . . . there are valuable specimens in the saddle-bags – a new species of . . .' and he fainted.

They lifted him and carried him back to the house. 'Thank God it happened close to home,' Margaret said to the doctor, as he administered chloroform while the bone was set.

'Yes, it's a very nasty fracture,' he said. 'But he is young enough for it to heal perfectly, given sufficient time.'

'He's no' going to like being close confined to the house, even for a wee while.'

'Well, he's just going to have to get used to it. And I'm afraid it will be for a long while.'

For a time he and Margaret were both confined to bed; for their son John Jamieson Gunn was born before he was on his feet again.

It was not just the being confined to the house – it was winter, anyway, and not a good time for collecting – but he worried about the farms and estate business, while a deputy manager carried on. The doctor said it would be at least six months before he would be on his feet. But it had been a bad break, a comminuted fracture which took almost nine months to heal. During that time he could not ride a horse nor even hobble any distance. What he dreaded was that he would never be able to walk again, or at least to climb mountains and ramble over rivers and plains. It would be like death to be restricted to the house and garden for the rest of his life.

He did not speak of his fears to Margaret, but to his confidant at Kew Gardens: 'Whether I shall ever be able to clamber the Hills as I used to do is a question I cannot answer . . .'

On top of it all, the Franklins were planning an overland trip of some danger, to Macquarie Harbour on the west coast; but his broken leg would not allow him to go, though they had invited him to accompany them. It seemed he was fated never to see those gloomy shores where the Huon pine flourished. At the thought of all the unexplored territory the party would be travelling, he almost gnashed his teeth in frustration. He'd have to depend on Joseph Milligan to collect for him, but Dr Milligan was rather lazy when it came to botany as geology was his first interest.

The next year would have to be spent in gaining a thorough knowledge of his duties as estate manager, his learning having been cut short by the accident. As much of the land he was supposed to inspect had no roads and was inaccessible except on foot or horseback, there had been nothing he could do but wait with what patience he could muster, spending a lot of time with his books and his last

184

collections. The one in the saddle-bag he had been so anxious about was *Agastachys*, the rare white waratah.

By the time the *Erebus* and *Terror* returned from their furthest south, Ronald Gunn was still confined to bed with his broken leg, while Joseph Hooker kept on board in Hobart with a bad cold, so they did not do any collecting together, though they wrote regularly.

Sir William had been worried about his son's health and the dangers of the voyage, and wrote to Sir John Franklin for reassurance. Sir John assured him that young Hooker, according to Captain Ross, was always well at sea, and that he was much pleased with the young naturalist's energy and zeal in collecting.

'Though it's not easy in Antarctic conditions, sir,' Joseph Hooker told Sir John. 'Many of my best little lichens were gathered by hammering out the frozen tufts, or sitting on them till they thawed.'

'Good gracious! No wonder you caught cold,' said Sir John.

In late March the expedition to the West Coast set out, a kind of track having been blazed through the bush by the Government Surveyor, Calder, and his men. The country between Macquarie Harbour and the settled districts for about eighty or ninety miles was covered in impenetrable forests, rugged mountains, impetuous rivers, deep gorges, and swampy buttongrass plains. Macquarie Harbour was now abandoned as a penal settlement. During Colonel Arthur's time only a handful of prisoners had ever managed to escape overland, and they were on the point of death from starvation when they gave themselves up.

Poor Calder had a hard time of it. Once across the headwaters of the Derwent, which his party crossed by means of a large fallen tree, the track was made nearly impassable by large stones. Then there were ten miles of swamp, a vast morass of reeds and buttongrass, with a few islands of trees on higher ground. In a million acres of plain they found scarcely a blade of grass, or any useful herbage that would feed a horse. Even the forest ground was sterile, producing only moss and lichens.

Leaving the swamps, the track wound up to the summit of a high hill which Calder named Fatigue Hill. From the summit there was a fine view of Frenchman's Cap and its surrounding peaks to the west, and of the black and boundless forest to the north.

Descending the long slopes of Fatigue Hill, they crossed the small plain Sir John was later to name Wombat Glen, and came through a dense myrtle forest upon the banks of the Franklin river. When forty miles nearer to Marquarie Harbour, it was no longer possible to avoid crossing this rapid river. Before they did so, in the midst of a small plain, they found some old bark shelters left by the last of the Tasmanian Aborigines; and on the bark were drawings in charcoal of animals and birds.

For the last fourteen miles to Marquarie Harbour the surface was extremely rugged and rocky.

'Indeed, it is particularly unsuitable for travelling,' Calder told Sir John and Lady Franklin, hoping to dissuade them from this mad plan. 'Macquarie Harbour is a very unapproachable place from the land, travel it as you may. You see, Sir John, there's this great peak of Frenchman's Cap exactly in the way, and by whatever route we attempt to reach the Harbour, we have to cross one of its great spurs. Besides which there is often a dense and almost impenetrable jungle to be negotiated. I don't think her ladyship—'

'Dear Mr Calder, don't worry about *me*', said Jane Franklin firmly. 'Where you can make a track, there I can follow.'

Sir John looked rather worried, but he knew better by now than to argue with Jane. Calder, however, had not learned his lesson.

'And then, Lady Franklin, there is the dark and densely wooded glen, which my men gave the name of Glow-worm Forest, from the luminous fungi there. Now nothing can be

186

worse for the traveller, and especially for a female, than this part of the track. It is always unpleasant, frequently precipitous, and generally muddy and slippery. Then the walls of the valley close in, leaving no level surface beside the stream which flows in the bottom, and which I have called the Acheron, and which has to be crossed several times by temporary bridges. So you can see—'

'I can see that we may look forward to a most interesting journey, Mr Calder. I cannot wait to see this Stygian vale with its eerie lights in the depths of the dark and gloomy forest. Can you, Sir John?'

'No indeed, it sounds most enticing. And we must see this beautiful river you described earlier, the Franklin, which you named after me. Perhaps we can find a tributary stream and name it the "Jane".'

'It *is* a beautiful river,' said Calder reflectively. 'And so is the Gordon, which is even larger. Where we cross it the banks are low; but they are mostly high, and often perpendicular, and overhung with many fine Huon pines, whose green branches droop to the surface like those of the willow. They add much to the beauty of the stream, but I was chiefly pleased to find them because I had to build a raft, and most of the dense and sodden wood in the western forests won't float, but sinks like a stone.'

Aware that the lady was following his description with intense interest, and was being encouraged rather than put off by it, he added, 'Er-hum! yes; and if there should be heavy rain in the mountains (which occurs at all seasons of the year) the river may prove uncrossable. And *then* where would you be?'

'Why, on the Hobart side, and we could simply retrace our steps.'

Big, bearded Calder gave a heavy sigh. 'Yes, your lady-ship, but the provisions will all be aboard the *Breeze*, waiting for you in Macquarie Harbour. My men cannot carry provisions for so large a party to travel in *both* directions.'

'Why then, we must pray for fine weather,' said Lady Franklin imperturbably.

187

As it happened, the Franklin party did find itself cut off from the Harbour and the food supplies on the ship, by a flooded Franklin river flowing seventy yards wide, until at last a kind of canoe was built and warped across the stream. Before the viceregal party crossed the river, they wrote letters to send back with the returning group: Lady Franklin to her sister in London, Dr Milligan to his friend Gunn:

> We are now on the east bank of the Franklin, only fifteen miles from Macquarie Harbour . . . Lady Franklin asked me just now if I have said anything kind from her to you, and I was scolded when I said – No. This speaks volumes for the admiration which Her Ladyship holds for you.

Yes, but what about *plants*? thought Ronald Gunn impatiently. What about *Dacrydium*, the Huon pine, which grows along the banks of the Franklin and trails its fronds in the water? No one had as yet brought back a living seedling or a fruiting cone. Oh, this cursed leg! If only I could have been there . . .

Though the Franklins managed to get to the shore and aboard the *Breeze*, she was weatherbound in Macquarie Harbour and unable to join the government schooner *Eliza* which was to take the party back to Hobart. Great excitement prevailed in the town, and the newspapers argued whether the viceregal party had perished by starvation or by drowning. However, they returned safely after a somewhat perilous journey, and Joseph Milligan sent his collections of plants to Ronald Gunn.

'Dr Milligan did not collect *any* specimens of the Huon Pine, strange to say,' he wrote to William Hooker. Indeed he could not believe it. Such wasted opportunity!

Milligan had collected a few novelties, but Gunn had found most of his plants previously. Once more he cursed his broken leg, but by now he was getting almost as strong as ever, and had managed a walk of ten miles. His worst fears were unfounded.

188

With all these disturbances he had not written to Kew Gardens for a year, having no specimens to send; yet William Hooker had written warmly, 'This mode of intercourse is *very delightful* to me, and your letters I prize very highly; so that I hope to hear from you very often, whether you have specimens to send or not.'

He had been corresponding instead with Joseph Hooker, who had written him three letters from Sydney since the expedition returned from a visit to South Africa, where the ships had put in at Cape Town for repairs after being sadly battered in the ice. They had run foul of each other among the icebergs, and for almost ten minutes had their masts and shrouds tangled together, and were in imminent danger of capsizing.

Captain Ross had left £350 with Lady Franklin for the purchase of some land in Tasmania, and she managed to buy him 400 acres of Crown Land at well under the usual price of £1 per acre. She sent down a surveyor to mark it out in 100- and 50-acre allotments, which she suggested letting on a twenty-one years' lease, nothing being paid in the first five years, and 10/- per acre in the remaining sixteen.

She had let her own adjoining land on similar terms, and had built a wooden chapel for the farmers in the Huon Valley, and a ship, the *Lady Franklin*, to carry their produce to market. She collected some specimens of the soil for Captain Ross, and of its wildflowers. 'A specimen of wattle from his own "Tasmanian" estate will I think be acceptable to him,' she wrote to Ronald Gunn referring to Ross's custom during his stay in Hobart of always wearing a sprig of wattle blossom in his buttonhole. Ronald continued to be on the best of terms with the Franklins, and as he told Margaret, 'I must go over to Hobart Town some time next summer to see them. Their kindness to me has been unceasing.'

But the recall of Sir John Franklin, long rumoured by the gutter press of Hobart Town, was soon to be a fact. Before this happened, Lady Franklin had completed her pet project of building a 'temple to the arts and sciences' or, more mundanely, a Tasmanian Museum at the entrance to her Kangaroo Valley property. In keeping with 'this Island of Grecian climate and Grecian beauty', as Dr Gell called it, she had had it designed with the perfect proportions of a miniature Greek temple, its fluted columns echoing the tall straight columns of the blue gums in the bush.

On a beautiful, sunny day in March the foundation stone had been laid, and now the Museum itself was opened, and furnished with geological and natural history specimens from Lady Franklin's own collections, and with all the books she could obtain dealing with Tasmania or written by Tasmanians. If there were few of the latter, the lady was sure that this would be remedied over the years, and that Tasmania would export apples from the Huon, grain from the Midlands, and works of poetry and natural history, to the mainland. The Museum's Committee of Management consisted of Ronald Gunn, Bishop Nixon, J. E. Bicheno, J. P. Gell and T. J. Ewing. All were members of the Tasmanian Society to whose care it was entrusted.

A picnic was held at Ancanthe on opening day, A libation was poured of local wine which had been brought by ship from South Australia. The ladies, like exotic bright birds in their coloured silks and parasols, perched on folding chairs or arranged themselves on cushions on the ground. It was, Margaret and Ronald Gunn agreed, a most delightful day.

In 1834 Sir Eardley-Wilmot arrived, unexpectedly early, to take over the position of Governor from Sir John.

The Franklins left for a visit to the Port Phillip District, before sailing to England. Ronald had hoped to sail over and take leave of them there, but it was a busy time of the year and he could not get away. However Mr Wedge, MP, whose daughter had been married to Robert Lawrence, and Mr Thomas Henty had arranged to hire a small steamer to go up to George Town and bid farewell to the viceregal party as they sailed through Bass Strait in the *Rajah*; so he went with them.

Sir John heartily shook his hand. 'The best proof of the continued confidence I have in you, my dear Gunn,' he said, 'is to make you my agent in the Colonies, where my wife has bought me several thousand pounds' worth of property. D'ye mind taking it on? I'll send you the papers.'

'I should be honoured, Sir John.'

Lady Franklin took his hand and pressed it long. 'I am so glad to see you happily married again,' she said softly. 'And you will look after my Huon tenants, as well as the Ancanthe garden and Museum?'

'Thank you, Lady Franklin. I can't say how much I shall miss you both; your unvarying kindness, your interest in the natural science of this fascinating island.' His lips trembled with emotion.

'There, there,' said Lady Franklin, patting his hand. 'I have had to say goodbye to many a distant island in my life, Mr Gunn, and have become philosophical about it.'

She smiled and turned to Mr Wedge. Ahead, the great bluff of Circular Head glowed in the westering sun; that too was an island, an island within an island, to which he had said farewell . . .

Soon the three climbed down into their small steamer, and the *Rajah* set sail to the westward, on her way back to England and Home.

'Well, we are going to miss our Governor; he is certainly a good man,' said Gunn. 'His motives were always of the best, however unpopular or unwise some of his decisions. I fear Sir Eardley-Wilmot will be a sad change for the worse.'

23

His words had been prophetic. The new Governor became automatically President of the Tasmanian Society. He called a meeting at the Mechanics' Institute in Hobart Town to discuss the formation of a new society, a 'Royal Society of Van Diemen's Land for Horticulture, Botany, and for the Advancement of Science', as it was to be grandiloquently called.

Members of the old-established and well-regarded Tasmanian Society asked for time to consider his proposals.

'I see no need for any delay,' said Sir Eardley in his arrogant way. 'The proposals are clear enough; either take 'em or leave 'em. If you *don't* amalgamate, I'll form the Royal Society without you.'

The members of the Tasmanian Society, which had already published some important scientific papers in its monthly Journal, looked at each other in disbelief. There was a short conference, then they got up in a body and marched out.

Ronald Gunn, in Launceston, heard with dismay of these developments, but he felt sure the old Society would survive. He wrote to Joseph Hooker an account of the 'takeover', adding 'The "Royal Botanical Society etc." will go to the devil.'

Now that his leg was healed he resumed his collecting with new enthusiasm. The widely scattered Lawrence Estate properties gave him plenty of opportunity. Besides Penquite and Lawrence Vale on the North Esk river, and Vermont thirty miles away, there was a large sheep run near George Town at the mouth of the Tamar, Danbury Park near Cormiston, Formosa below the Western Tiers, and the high sheep-run of Billopp.

He usually took a gun with him, slung across his shoulder as he rode. On a trip to Billopp, the most distant of the properties under his management, dusk was falling as he made his way over the high stony plateau on the last stage of his journey. He dismounted to pick a sample of a new fern growing against a rocky outcrop – for the whole plateau was covered with these stony eminences which in the half-light resembled ruined castles – when he had a strong impression that he was being watched. There were no Aborigines left on the main island, he knew, yet his spine went cold. He stood, his back against the rock, and looked carefully round him, while unslinging his gun and cocking it.

Then a faint movement caught his eye, in the opening of a cleft between two rocks. He looked again, and saw the outline of a sharp muzzle, two glaring, slanting eyes – it was a 'hyena', the Tasmanian Wolf, or Tiger as it was sometimes called, watching from its lair. Quietly he brought the gun up to his shoulder, and fired.

There was a coughing bark, the animal began to run, then fell. He approached it cautiously, but it was dead. The pointed wolf-like jaws were open, revealing the long sharp, canine teeth for grasping and killing its prey. The dark tiger-like stripes showed on its back and the base of its tail. There was no pouch, although this was a marsupial; it was a male. Elated – for the creatures were becoming rare, and the British Museum would appreciate it – he slung the heavy body over the saddle, and walked the horse to his destination where he skinned the animal he had shot.

Later he forwarded it in a very long case to the British Museum, together with the skins of two specimens of the nearly extinct Tasmanian emu. But he was disappointed, as he told William Hooker, that the Museum authorities had not seen fit to remunerate him in any way.

193

It is rather unfair,' he said, 'because with a large family to support I yet spend every spare shilling for the advancement of science – and look for no return but that of books or similar things.

He added forlornly,

From Mr Short I have never heard. I don't expect now that I ever shall. I am in debt £300 on his account, with charges and interest, which I must pay off as soon as I can gather the amount.

On a visit to the George Town property, he took the whole family (the older boys being home from school for the long summer holidays) to his house on the beach. It was a wonderful holiday for Margaret, who rarely got to the seaside. She tucked up her long skirts over bare legs, and joined him in collecting seaweeds of which there were many varieties just inside the estuary. Since their visit to Portland Bay she had become less prim, much to his content. Next he chartered a steamboat for a day's cruise to the Hebe Reef about seven miles from George Town, to gather algae from the rocks. There was an unusually low tide and the day was beautiful, with scarcely a breeze stirring until the afternoon. The boys swam off the boat when it was anchored close to the reef, with a great sense of daring at being so far from shore.

On the way back, after waiting for the tide to turn, they anchored again on a point of land where there were many more seaweeds growing about a foot below the water, among them the beautiful *Claudia elegans*.

Margaret preserved the new specimens herself, and showed him the results with pride. He was pleased to see that, though she used a different method, without soaking in fresh water, her algae were almost as beautifully dried as those of Ivy Grant Smith.

'*Claudia elegans*,' murmured Margaret. 'How very apt some botanical names are, are they not? It is a most elegant weed.'

'All botanical names strive to be descriptive, or else to commemorate their discoverer,' said her husband.

'Aye, you have so many named after you, the botany textbooks of the next generation will be full of Gunn. Even a whole genus, *Gunnia*, bears your name.'

'Yes, and a bandicoot too, what's more!'

The third of his new family was on the way, after Margaret had presented him with a son and a daughter in the first three years of marriage. Like his first wife, she had no complications in her pregnancies and came through each birth without danger.

Dr Joseph Milligan had been appointed Commandant of Flinders Island, to look after the remnant of the Tasmanian Aborigines now that Robinson was gone to the mainland as Protector in the Port Phillip District. Milligan would have a fine field for collecting, but Ronald feared he would do little there.

Following the collapse of the land boom across the Strait in the early 1840s, land and stock prices in both Van Diemen's Land and Port Phillip fell disastrously, and many speculators became insolvent. Seeing land so cheap, Gunn was tempted to borrow money and buy some, but his debt to Short's creditors deterred him. At least, not being wealthy, he had nothing to lose.

He responded enthusiastically to the news that Sir William Hooker planned to publish a combined Plants of Van Diemen's Land, New Zealand, and the Antarctic Islands.

'I'm really anxious that our Tasmanian natural history should be well known,' he said to Margaret as he packed a box of bottles containing orchids in pyroligenous acid, among bottles of preserved snakes, frogs, birds, molluscs and crustaceans. 'And if I can be the humble means of collecting the specimens, I shall be satisfied.' The second case contained a very large collection of the smaller algae dried on paper, and plenty of large specimens of *Claudia elegans* and some of the beautiful corallines.

'These are almost entirely the labour of my *Womankind*

as the Antiquary has it', he wrote on a note inside. Another parcel contained some of the larger algae collected from the reef, including *Zostera marina* and others. They were to form the basis of the fifth volume of the botanist W. J. Harvey's *Phycologa Australica*, a volume dedicated to Ronald Campbell Gunn, 'from whom came to me the earliest collections of Australian algae through Sir W. J. Hooker. Many new specimens are of his discovery; to him is also due the re-discovery of Claudia elegans.'

Even the great Robert Brown, Gunn's hero, wrote in person from London to thank him for *Dawsonia* and other mosses received through Hooker: 'This moss is very interesting to me . . . Among algae of V.D. Land I find you have lately detected Claudia elegans, a highly interesting discovery . . . European Botanists will be delighted in this *very beautiful plant.*'

A recent invention was to revolutionise the transferring of plants from one side of the globe to the other. Mr N. B. Ward wrote to W. J. Hooker's 'Companion to the Botanical Magazine' that he had placed living plants in a strongly made box containing moist earth. The glazed lid, shaped like a hip roof, was sealed and clamped down, and the box could be placed in sunlight on the deck of a ship. Barring accidents to the glass, the survival rate was relatively high. When he heard that such a 'Ward's Case' was on its way to Hobart from Kew Gardens, Ronald Gunn was excited. Why hadn't he thought of such a thing himself? He wrote at once and arranged for the large box to be sent round by sea to Launceston, and asked Sir William in a letter to send him two more. When he unpacked the first he found that more than half the English plants had survived the journey out.

As the small bush orchids were now in flower he filled the case as soon as it arrived, almost exclusively with *Orchideae*.

'You will I think receive many of them alive,' he wrote contentedly.

And what riches there were! Such strange and delicate flowers, like insects, like birds, like nothing on earth – their common names were gnat orchid and ant orchid, blue fairy orchid and onion orchid, spider orchid and golden moth, baby-in-the-cradle and parson-in-the-pulpit, and all of such soft and delicate colours, the nodding greenhood having a pale green flower . . .

He could imagine Sir William's delight as he unpacked the case. The plants were in the balls of natural earth in which they were dug out of the soil, and should survive. He added some native violas and bluebells, blue pincushions and brachycome, the Tasmanian daisy, till the box looked like a spring garden. There were even some seedlings of pencil pine and of *Fagus cunninghamii*, the myrtle-beech.

Joseph Hooker had been fascinated to find the *Fagus*, in Tasmania and Southern Victoria, almost identical to that in Tierra del Fuego in South America, which gave him ideas about the distribution of plants on islands. Now Ronald Gunn gave him another clue: he had found a strange parasite called orange-ball fungus, on the Tasmanian beech, very similar to the *Cyttarium darwinii*, first discovered by Charles Darwin parasitic on the Antarctic beech of Tierra del Fuego. If not the same, it was certainly closely allied.

'It shows how interestingly many plants are distributed and associated,' he added thoughtfully.

Joseph had been discussing with his friend Charles Darwin a theory towards which they were both groping, a new and revolutionary theory about the origin of different species – Darwin being more interested in animals, Hooker in plants. Now Ronald Gunn had provided them with another small piece of the jigsaw, which was gradually taking form in a definite pattern. So an amateur botanist on a distant island helped, almost unwittingly, to lay the foundations of an 'Origin of Species' and a new idea of man's place in the universe.

Ronald had 'a botch of a carpenter' on the home-farm build him a Ward's Case, and sent Joseph Hooker some seedlings he had grown of myrtle-beech and various conifers and cypresses. But eight months later he had a disappointed letter from Joseph: they had nearly all, he wrote, arrived dead in the 'Ward's Coffin'. Ronald felt sure it was because of faulty construction, the case not being airtight.

He was busier than ever, as he had taken over the Secretaryship of the Tasmanian Society, its headquarters now removed to Launceston.

The Society had become almost moribund in Hobart until its removal to Launceston, where its monthly Journal was printed, supervised by Ronald Gunn. Apart from being secretary, he acted as editor, collecting material for publication, visiting the printer with illustrations, and correcting proofs.

He was determined to make the journey to the far West Coast which he had missed because of his broken leg. In February 1845 he set off, with two men and a packhorse – which could be taken for only half the way – over the high plateau to the headwaters of the Derwent and the picturesque Lake St Clair; thence through uninhabited country to the Gordon and Franklin rivers, which they would have to ford.

It was the hottest month of summer, and bushfires burning in the hills to the southeast filled the sky with haze and reddened the sun. It seemed ridiculous that their knapsacks and the pack-pony were burdened with warm woollens and waterproofs, yet from the Franklins' overland expedition and his own experience, Ronald knew how capricious the Van Demonian weather could be in the high country.

Calder's party with Sir John and Lady Franklin had left a little later, in March, in beautiful dry weather, but were confined in their tents under Frenchman's Cap for a week by torrential rain and snow, and then found the Franklin river in flood and almost impossible to cross.

By the time Gunn's small party had reached Lake St Clair, the weather was still fine. They had had to leave the packhorse, and now he and his two men carried all their provisions and bedding and spare clothing on their backs.

They camped by the crossing of the Upper Derwent, where the smoke of their camp fire rose straight in the still air. Dark blue Mount Olympus was reflected in perfect outline in the calm waters of the lake, held in its ring of hills. Ronald went off looking for new ferns and waterplants. Gazing into the glassy calm of the lake, he had almost a feeling of vertigo: all was so perfect in reflection, he lost the sense of 'up' and 'down' and seemed to be suspended in some weightless region between two skies. Then a sudden marring of the surface, by an insect falling or a small fish jumping, established the line of the water's surface.

He clambered down to the bank, and pounced with a cry of joy. *Hymenophyllum* – the Filmy fern, in a new variant, it seemed! Putting all his weight on the left leg, he realised that it had entirely recovered – and he'd thought once that he would never be able to go for long walks again!

By the time they returned they had covered twice 150 miles, much of it unexplored bush, though they were able to use the track blazed by Calder and his men, and by the later party that went looking for the supposedly lost Franklins. It was already starting to be overgrown. The men were uneasy in the dank south-western forests, everything dripping with moisture or bearded with moss and lichen, and fungus glowing eerily in the darkest gullies. Although it was colder, they preferred the cold west winds in the more open country beyond the Franklin, where their master began with almost demented eagerness the task of digging up seedling Huon pines, the *Dacrydium* he had long been seeking.

'Do you realise, men,' he panted as he rested on his spade which had been carried on men's backs all the way from Derwent Bridge, 'that these are some of the oldest trees in the world? Those big ones there may be a thousand years old; they're very slow-growing, and take hundreds of years to reach maturity. And it's a fine and durable timber, floats easily – ' He tossed a piece of a branch into the stream.

But the men were more interested in collecting pieces of

firewood, whatever its botanical name might be, and lighting a fire to boil their billy of tea.

Safely home with his precious specimens, and happy in the expedition's results, though tired and hungry – for they'd run out of tea and flour, and had been unable to shoot any game in the last two nights on the plateau – he found Margaret tearful and distraught. His heart sank. Was his life going to follow the same pattern as before? Would his bonnie Scots lassie turn into a shrew or a drunkard?

But as soon as the children were in bed, she explained. Her father was seriously ill, probably dying; the doctor gave him no more than a week or two. Her married brother was with him, but he was asking for Margaret.

'I couldna well leave before your return,' she wept. 'But I must away home now. My poor father!'

'Of course, my darling. I'd drive you over myself, but I'm "ower weary" just now. Could you take the Launceston – Hobart coach tomorrow, stay a day with William, and then go up to Glen Leith from there? The New Norfolk coach goes every day, and the steamer every day but Wednesday.'

'Yes, you look tired out, and you've lost some weight. I'll away tomorrow, if you'll drive me to the coach, and take Baby to see him. He's been so lonely since my brother Thomas died.'

David Jamieson died on April 4th, and Ronald went down for the funeral, and to support his wife. He had not previously met Margaret's younger brother John, who crossed from Port Phillip for the funeral. The youngest boy, Walter, was still in Scotland.

When the lawyer came up from Hobart and the Will was read, it turned out that Mr Jamieson's property was left to John Cundell Jamieson, who decided to return to Van Diemen's Land. He was four years younger than Margaret and still unmarried. There was also a handsome bequest to the youngest brother, and to Margaret and her son, John Jamieson Gunn.

Ronald had not given a thought to Margaret being an

heiress, but with only three children surviving her father had been able to provide well for them all.

As soon as he'd returned from the far west coast, and before Margaret had come back from her father's, Ronald wrote off to Joseph Hooker a delighted account of all he had seen. Now he packed up a Ward's Case with treasures: Huon and celery-top pines, the new filmy fern and the myrtle-beech; white- and red-flowering waratahs; the mountain raspberry and the forest iris; and a specimen of the strange horizontal scrub which had so impeded their walking. It was a species of tangled bush which grew sideways, and as it died sank down to make an impenetrable tangled mass below the living layers. Once a man fell into it, he needed a lot of help in getting out. There was even a Port Arthur plum, though without the fruit, and a new lily-like bulb.

'Many of these are very rare plants,' he wrote, 'they are all very young and love a humid atmosphere. All the moss which is about them was brought all the way from the Franklin with them . . . The Huon pine grows in moss saturated at all times with water.'

He was vexed to see that the Huon pines which had been in the box some time looked sickly. He hoped and prayed that some might survive.

'After carrying plants on a man's back in a knapsack over rugged country for about 150 miles and then sending them by sea 15,000 miles – well, they ought to have some little interest,' he muttered.

He added a case of living ferns for Sir William containing some species not previously sent, including the beautiful filmy fern, and some splendid fronds of *Alsophila*, the tree-fern. They went off together on the deck of the sailing ship *Dawsons*; and this time most of them survived.

Dr Milligan, who had been sent round to Macquarie Harbour on Government business in the schooner *Eliza*, brought back at this time an example of the curious lily-like plant from Macquarie Harbour which Gunn had sent in the latest Ward's Case of plants; but Milligan's specimen was in flower. Sir William Hooker named it *Milligania longifolia*, and it was to become known as the Gordon lily.

Milligan had retired from Flinders Island, which had nothing but unhappy memories for him. His young wife, a sister of the late Robert Lawrence, had died there at the age of only nineteen, two days after her first confinement. The baby survived, but Eliza Milligan suffered a massive haemorrhage which nothing could stop. He held her marble-white body in his arms and was swept by a terrible guilt: not only was he responsible for her pregnancy, but he had been her doctor as well! She had refused to leave him to go back to Launceston for the confinement, and in his professional arrogance he thought she could not be in better hands than his.

Now, as he wrote to Ronald Gunn, he felt doubly to blame. The placenta had failed to detach after the birth, and an unstanchable haemorrhage followed, though he had raised the foot of the bed and packed her with cold cloths. He had had to watch her life slowly ebbing away. Perhaps an operation might have saved her, but the first flood had been so copious that she was already too weak to survive the shock.

He buried her in the island graveyard, not far from the proliferating graves of the doomed Tasmanians, who were still steadily dying out. He recommended to the Government that the remainder should be taken back to the main island – for which they were still homesick. There were fewer than fifty left in the world. Like the Tasmanian Emu and the Tasmanian tiger, they must soon become extinct.

Ronald Gunn, receiving his friend's agonised letter, was sharply reminded of the deaths of Elizabeth and Robert Lawrence. But though his expression of grief was extravagant, he dimly felt that Joseph Milligan was a more resilient character than young Lawrence, and the same tragic result was not to be feared.

By 1846 Ronald's financial troubles were at an end. He

had paid off the debt of the wretched Thomas Keir Short, and was able to develop his original forty acres, where he had once begun a botanic garden, as an orchard. He also acquired 107 acres on the eastern side of Launceston and the town side of Penquite between High Street and the North Esk river.

His visits to the summer sheep-run of W.E. Lawrence at Arthur's Lakes persuaded him to lease some land there himself, to give him more excuse for travelling 'on business' to that high, cold, rocky plateau, where he usually managed to find something new for the Hookers.

William Archer, who now collected orchids for Sir William Hooker, and also was an accomplished botanical draughtsman, came over sometimes from Chestnut near Deloraine under the northern, or Launceston, side of the Western Tiers. Gunn had made Archer's home a base for several collecting trips to the high plateau in his company. Archer, whose father was a local landowner, had studied architecture and drawing in England; he was still a young man of only twenty-six.

Penquite House, with Margaret Gunn as chatelaine, became a place almost of pilgrimage for visiting botanists, who were entertained and shown around the extensive gardens by their host. The house (which really belonged to the Lawrence Estate) was set in a formal garden, where Margaret grew her roses and he cultivated the more showy native plants, surrounded by a park where the native forest had been enclosed but not disturbed beyond a little judicious clearing. Wildflowers still grew there, and there were stands of fine native trees, and a romantic rocky glen (now the Punch Bowl) with masses of vertical basaltic rock weathered into battlements and ramparts. Here grew the tough and scrubby shrub, prickly and uninviting, but with small purple flowers, which was called either tree violet or thorn bush by the locals. Anything less like a 'violet by a mossy stone, Half-hidden from the eye' would be hard to imagine; yet botany classed it among the violets. He had found it first on Pig Island in the upper Tamar river.

The buttercups were like their English counterparts, but even more enamelled and glossy, gilding the damp hollows, while the clematis twined up trees and around fences, drooping its starry white clusters which turned afterwards to filmy seeds of 'old man's beard'. The children were recruited as collectors, and one rare ground orchid, which showed only a pale spike of flowers on a fleshy stem without any leaves, had been discovered by three-year-old Charlotte Claudia Amelia, who had been named after that elegant seaweed. The little girl liked to hold a yellow buttercup under her brother's chin till the sunlight reflected the colour there. 'Do you like butter?' she would ask, and ''Ess, he likes butter, Papa.'

24

'DON'T FORGET I asked you for some roses', Ronald wrote familiarly to Sir William. Asking for some live cuttings to be sent in the next Ward's Case, he had explained that they were 'for Mrs Gunn, as I garden far less than formerly'.

His brother William had come to live in Launceston, which was a great source of contentment to Ronald. William had settled on a large property he named Glen Dhu, and here, rather to Ronald's surprise, had begun to lay out extensive gardens.

The occasion of his leaving Hobart had not been a happy one. In 1846 a Dr John Hampton, a former surgeon-superintendent of convict transports, was appointed Comptroller-General of the whole Convict Department in Van Diemen's Land. He was not a popular official and his attempts at being a 'new broom' were not appreciated. William Gunn opposed plans to alter the internal adminis-tration of the Penitentiary, giving more power to convict constables. Also there were rumours that the new Comptroller was using convict labour unofficially on his properties, for personal profit. Hampton reacted by trans-ferring Lieutenant Gunn to Launceston. Hobart citizens, to whom Gunn's huge stature, heroic deeds and known integrity had made him a popular figure, got up a petition to have his service retained, but Hampton was adamant. So William came to Launceston as Superintendent and visiting Magistrate of the convict establishments there, the same post which Ronald had held years before.

He called with a proposal for the whole family to come

over for the day as soon as they were settled, so that the cousins could meet each other once more – he now had five children, William, Margaret, Louisa, Ronald, and baby Elizabeth. When Margaret had brought him tea, and they sat drinking it in the sunny drawing-room at Penquite, he suddenly set his empty cup down and cleared his throat.

'Ronald if I could just have a word with you in private – ' He looked apologetically at Margaret. He liked his sister-in-law, and the last thing he wished was to hurt her feelings.

'Of course!' Margaret jumped up. 'I want to go and look at the rose-bed the gardener is preparing for me . . . You two sit and have a talk. It will be lovely for Ronald, having you so much closer, and for the children too. They always like to see their Uncle William.'

William, uncharacteristically nervous, picked up his empty cup and affected to drain it. Ronald offered to refill it from the pot.

'No, no. It's just – I've had rather a shock, you see. Not the transfer, I don't really mind that, though I did regard Hobart as my home. No, it's – it's about Frances.'

'Willy! Is she not well? I always thought of you two as being most happily married.'

'We were – we are! It's just something she told me recently. You wondered why I didn't fight Hampton over this transfer, or at least fight harder, take it to the Colonial Office in London? The reason was – Well Frances had a very bad time after Elizabeth was born, believed she was going to die. She called me to her bedside and said she had something she wanted to tell me, it had worried her for years. It then came out that she had known for a long time, certainly since before we were married, that her grand-father Surgeon Arndell's wife was a convict! Transported for stealing four linen handkerchiefs. She was his second wife, married in New South Wales; but that woman brought up Frances's father.'

'Well, it's a long way back, probably not generally known.'

'She said most people in New South Wales would know.

It's why her father settled in Van Diemen's Land rather than the older Colony when he left Norfolk Island. He didn't want to acknowledge a convict stepmother.'

'I wouldn't worry about it. Even if it were known, Frances is only related by marriage, she is not a *descendant*. And the next generation, your children, need never know. It seems important to us, because we've been so involved with convicts and convict women. But in a hundred years' time, who will care?'

'But if it got out now, it could affect my authority with the convicts. It's very much a "them and us" attitude with them. Frances says she was frightened to tell me in case I refused to marry her.'

'But you would have done so.'

'Yes. I suppose I would have . . . But still, a common thief!' Ronald, already detached from the System in his new job, did not take the news as seriously as William, though he knew the stigma attached to convict birth, the prejudice against emancipists. One judge had refused to work in the courts with men he called 'convict lawyers'.

But recalling the day of William's wedding, and that snobbish sister-in-law sitting opposite when Eliza had so embarrassed him, he could not help a secret satisfaction. Connected to a ducal family she might be, but on the other side to a convicted felon! William asked him not to tell his wife. Margaret was kept busy with her garden and with her four children; John Jamieson now four years old, and the girls Mary Anne, Claudia and the new baby Agnes Jane. Margaret would drive into town with them all in the pony-phaeton; she was good with the reins and had strong wrists and was fearless with horses. Sometimes Isabella and Frances came too, each sitting one of the little ones on her knee. It was handy to have a ready-made family of 'little mothers', Margaret thought contentedly. Only Robbie remained obstinately unco-operative with the new family, but he was mostly away at boarding school.

They did not always get to church on Sundays – though William was now Elder of the Kirk in Launceston – but had

207

family prayers morning and evening, while the chidren had to learn some verses of scripture each week. In Circular Head, Ronald's first family had been allowed to grow up 'little heathens', according to Margaret. She had inaugurated a system of Sunday School, with Bible reading and drawing pictures of holy subjects, and supervised their bedtime prayers.

They had a family Christmas at Penquite, with William's children and his wife Frances, who was expecting again. Ronald's eldest son Ronnie was now studying medicine in Edinburgh, spending his vacations with his Uncle Robert. He wrote that Sir John Franklin had sailed from the north of Scotland with the *Erebus* and *Terror* to find the Northwest Passage – in his fifty-ninth year.

In a letter from Lady Franklin about the Tasmanian estates written soon after the departure of the ships, she wrote,

> After the humiliation of *our recall*, I dreaded the effect on Sir John's mind of being without honourable and immediate employment; and it was this which enabled me to support the idea of parting with him on a service of some difficulty and danger, better than I other wise should.

The children woke to an Australian Christmas: the sun well above the horizon at five a.m., in a blue sky streaked with fine films of white, 'mares' tails', which promised a hot day. The younger ones each had a pillow-case of good things attached to the foot of their beds, and as soon as it was light there were whisperings and giggles and the rustle of brown paper being impatiently unwrapped or torn aside.

Agnes Jane was sleeping in her parents' room, so they did not have to worry about waking Baby. John, only four, had to be helped by his half-brother Robbie.

Soon they were tooting trumpets, bowling balls, dressing and undressing new dolls – Louisa and Mary Ann each had

208

a wax-faced beauty – and racing from room to room to compare their treasures.

Frances pretended to be too grown up to take part in all this excitement, though she had received a beautiful pair of soft yellow leather gloves, and had to be dissuaded from wearing them at breakfast. Isabella had been given a box of watercolour paints.

'Come on, children,' called Frances to the boys, who were now outside playing on the sunburnt lawn. 'Breakfast!'

'Don't want breakfast!' said Robbie cheekily. 'I'm saving up for Christmas dinner.'

'No breakfast, no dinner,' said Frances firmly. 'And don't make such a noise, Mamma and Papa are still asleep.'

'Urk, powidge!' said John Jamieson disgustedly in the breakfast room. 'Powidge on Christmas Day!'

'You know Mamma likes you to start the day with porridge. Then you can each have a slice of ham.'

The wood stove was alight, warming the already hot kitchen, the trussed turkey standing ready under a muslin cloth to receive its stuffing, the great plum pudding which Margaret had prepared tied in its white cloth for boiling. The servants usually rose at six and got the stove alight, but on holidays they were allowed to sleep half an hour longer. There would be fourteen sitting down to dinner in the big dining-room with its high ceiling and tall windows, which remained cool – while the upstairs rooms grew hotter – on the warmest days.

'Couldn't we just have cold chicken and ham, it's always such a hot time of year?' Ronald had asked when they were first married, but Margaret was scandalised. Christmas was Christmas, even in the Antipodes. She hung the hall and draped around pictures with bunches of green gum-leaves and decorative blue-gum, and boughs of cypress pine, so that the scents of pine and eucalyptus cooled the air. There was even some real holly to put on the pudding – though no red berries in the middle of summer – from the exotic tree Ronald had planted in the drive.

'Strange to think that Ronnie may be having a white Christmas over there, with snow,' he said to Margaret as he got up and looked out at the hard blue and marble-white of the summer sky, at the parched lawns that were so crisp and dry that they crunched underfoot, for there had been no rain to speak of since early November.

'Has he called upon Sir William Hooker at Kew Gardens yet?'

'I fear not. I hope he hasn't forgotten.'

'Ah, I see you have picked some *Callitris oblonga*,' he said approvingly later, as he looked at the decorations.

'Why can you not call it "native cypress" like everyone else?' she laughed.

Once the family Christmas was over, and leaving Margaret busy with the children, Ronald set off in the New Year for a journey which would be less arduous, but he hoped no less interesting in its results, than the trip to the far West Coast. The brief time spent at Lake St Clair on the way to and from Macquarie Harbour had been tantalising. He knew there must be riches there. This time he planned to ascend the summits of the mountains surrounding the lake.

On his return he wrote off to the younger Hooker that he had sent

a noble lot of Tasmanian plants [though he still headed his letters Van Diemen's Land]. You will soon have the best collection of Flora Tasmaniae in the world; and when the Magnum Opus comes out we shall see the results. Among the *new* plants that I sent you was a new Fagus! very like one of the Fuegian ones; a new fern from Mt Olympus – and a new Clematis and a new aquatic Ranunculus with fine thread-like leaves. . .

The new *Fagus* was the deciduous beech, peculiar to the south-western and western highlands, and the country's only deciduous tree. Gunn did not see it in its autumn colours of rich gold, so unusual in the evergreen Australian bush.

210

He had arranged an ingenious system by which Sir William and Joseph Hooker would not have to pay for his botanical and other books out of their own pockets. He still received large parcels of most welcome volumes, so valuable that he protested:

> Your last *immense* consignment of books has left me dumbfounded, to use a Scots expression. . .
> For your son's Flora Tasmaniae I have still many new things which he shall have in due course.

He now included with each consignment of living plants or box of seeds and wooden fruit, fossils and skins, a kind of blank cheque on Kew Gardens.

> 'Pay the sum of . . . Pounds to Joseph D. Hooker, in account of a case of rare Tasmanian Plants shipped by me per . . . to the Royal Gardens at Kew.'

He wanted no money himself, just the books and botanical journals which gave him so much pleasure and helped him with his work. He was flattered when the next number of the *London Journal of Botany*, edited by Sir William, contained his account of his 'Excursion to Mount Olympus', with the note, 'Mr Gunn's name is familiar to our readers as the most active and intelligent Botanist in Van Diemen's Land.'

The article described how he had made the trip on foot, climbing first over the Western Tiers where there were acres and acres of 'green cushions' – thought at first to be a moss, but it had a tiny flower like a daisy. The bright green plants grew closely, round as stones, and became slippery as they were crushed underfoot, each mass extending for yards. Arrived at Lake St Clair he found an old leaky boat left by someone, and was forced to make it watertight by grilling some wallaby chops and using the cold fat as a caulk. Camped at the foot of Mount Olympus West where it came down to the water, he found it very steep and covered with *Fagus cunninghamii*.

At 7.30 a.m. he made a start to scale the waterfalls and precipices to the top.

At the base of some perpendicular basaltic cliffs, I found a new *Fagus*! It formed dense, almost impenetrable thickets from four to six feet high . . .

[Here Hooker had interposed, 'I propose naming this most interesting addition to the Tasmanian Flora, *Fagus Gunnii*, after its indefatigable discoverer.']

As I ascended, a dense mass of clouds with rain began to form; it was bitterly cold; and I was complelled by prudence to commence my descent, and returned safe to the boat.

Richea Pandaniflora, a pandanus-like palm, was abundant up to 2,000 feet.

Ronald also wrote reports of journeys and discoveries for the Tasmanian Society's journal, which only his enthusiasm had kept functioning. One interesting observation he made was that the peculiar character of the Van Diemen's Land vegetation – from its general resemblance to much that was characteristic of the Carboniferous era – led him to infer that that period millions of years ago in England need not have been so much warmer than the *present* climate, as geologists inferred.

It has struck me for a long time [he wrote] that if our vegetation was found in a fossil state people would assuredly infer that our three species of Fern Tree, our Richea Pandanifolia with leaves like those of a palm, and Athrotaxis like the extinct Lepidodendron, et cetera, would characterize a warmer climate than the cold bleak region of the South West of Van Diemen's Land, with a mean temperature for the year below some parts of Britain, and much below many parts of France.

In the spring of 1848 he made a business visit to the Arthur's Lake region on top of the high, rocky, lake-studded dolerite plateau, between 3,000 and 4,000 feet above sea-level, and carrying stunted alpine plants and the curious, bright green cushion plants resembling round, moss-covered rocks. There were still plenty of small kangaroos or Brush Wallabies about, but the big Forester kangaroos, which Robinson had seen bounding in front of his party 'like troops of soldiers' in 1830, had almost disappeared.

The sweet-scented *Lomatia* was everywhere in flower and *Carperdontus lucida*, the leatherwood, with the little native bees busy about its apple-blossom clusters. He took a bunch home for Margaret; there were no novelties for him to collect, except for a new Cruciferous plant, small and insignificant to look at.

At least he could get away for more frequent exursions now. His first family was almost grown up, Ronnie away in Edinburgh, and Margaret busy and happy with her four 'bairns'. Since the troubles in Ireland in 1847 there were free Irish girls emigrating and the maids no longer had to be drawn from the ranks of assigned servants or emancipated convicts.

After returning from Arthur's Lakes, Ronald set off again, first riding past Mount Barrow to the Diddleum Plains along the stock track which led to his grazing property there. He followed the Valentine Rivulet to the headwaters of the Ringarooma River; and from there till he came out on the coastal sandy plain, he walked for several days through a dark myrtle forest interspersed with giant eucalypts. The stringy gums were sometimes as tall as 300 feet, and one, which he measured five feet above the ground, with the tape measure pulled tightly round it, was forty-nine feet in circumference.

This area to the north-east of Launceston, between it and the coast, had still not been explored. Even the natives had avoided it, with its dense, grassless, tangled forests, everything covered in moss and lichens in the sunless, shadowed understory.

Nothing grew beneath the trees but moss and cathead

and water ferns. Dead logs, trunks of trees, even the ground itself, were covered with mosses and liverworts, and small ferns were parasitic on the tree-trunks. No grass, no shrubs, no flowers, no birds – it was an eerie place in which to be travelling alone. It was as though the plant world alone existed, the primitive plant world before the time of flowers and nectar, of butterflies and bees. He might have been the first man, black or white, ever to penetrate there. And he felt he was an alien, an intruder.

It was with a sense of relief that he came out on the sandy, undulating plains near Bridport on the north coast. At once the vegetation changed. He welcomed his old acquaintances of Circular Head and its environs: the heathy, stunted scrub, and the bridal bush, now covered in its starry white flowers. The acres of white-blossoming shrubs, after the darkness of the *Fagus* forest, had never seemed so beautiful. It occurred all along the north coast east of Port Dalrymple, and he had seen it also growing on the coast in the Port Phillip District. Girls about to be married in September or October used to send their friends out to gather the faintly-scented blossom, which was the nearest thing to orange blossom they could find, and so it got its name of bridal bush or wedding bush.

But when he got back from this journey it was not a celebration of a wedding that greeted him, but the news of a funeral. Little Agnes Jane was no more.

Margaret, who usually welcomed him with open arms, greeted him with tears, and for once with reproaches for being away when she needed him most.

Agnes Jane had died quite suddenly and unexpectedly – she seemed well when she went to sleep, but woke in the night with a terrible attack of croup. Before the servants could get the doctor she had gasped her life away, choking for air as the false membrane closed the back of her throat. Margaret could not, would not believe it at first, but kept begging the doctor to do something, to revive her, to make her breathe again! Until at last he had turned on her and said, 'Mrs Gunn, I am not God, and I cannot work miracles. I'm afraid you must accept the fact that your baby will never breathe again.'

Poor Margaret had never lost a child, though Ronald had. She took it very hard, and was no longer happy to let him go on his long exploring expeditions.

'I never know what will happen while ye're away. Suppose little Johnnie should be taken, and I all on my lonesome with just the gels to support me. And the funeral arrangements and all! You must bide at home now, Ronald, till I recover my spirits.'

'But dearest, you know I have to travel in my work, quite apart from botany. We shall have another baby, another wee girl for you to love – '

'I'm not so sure I want another bairn,' she said darkly.

Margaret bitterly opposed his next journey. She had not got over little Agnes's death, and the shock of having to cope with the funeral arrangements on her own. Ronald was more philosophical about it, having five daughters, and year-old babies did not have the same appeal to him as little ones who could talk and understand what was said to them. At the table he liked to ask them questions on geography and natural history, or give the younger ones simple sums in mental arithmetic. He loved to teach.

In early April he returned to find to his disappointment that no Ward's Cases had arrived from Kew Gardens, though he had an immense collection from lake St Clair, growing in a nursery and waiting to be shipped. There was celery-top pine and King Billy pine, and a strange prostrate conifer with a cone that was soft and red like a raspberry.

Though he had kept up a regular correspondence with Joseph, he had not heard from Sir William for some time. When a letter did come he was away, and on his return there had been all the domestic upset of little Agnes Jane's death; perhaps he felt guilty, for he did not reply for months to his old friend. Margaret certainly made him feel an outcast. She would go to bed early and curl herself up with her back to him, all shut away and hostile, even as she pretended to sleep. She might as well, he thought, have been an echidna, the Antipodean form of the hedgehog, with prickles all over her back.

His latest collecting trip had been over the northern and highest parts of the Western Tiers, climbing nearly 3000 feet up the precipitous cliffs to reach the vast plateau above, about forty miles square, and sloping gradually to the south. The tableland consisted of long narrow grassy plains running into one another, and divided by narrow rocky ridges, the whole formation of greenstone; he was reminded of a heavy sea off the Cape of Good Hope suddenly arrested into stillness – the waves forming the rocky hills.

He descended by way of the gorge cut by the Meander river, and below the Meander Falls found the King Billy pine growing in the bed of loose rocks and stones fallen from above.

It had not been a good season to get any plant in flower, and though it was still early autumn he was caught in a snow storm which covered everything from sight. After the snow came sharp frost – the thermometer fell to two degrees below freezing. This gave him hope for the survival in the open our many plants he had sent to Kew Gardens.

'Our Mountain plants ought to be able to stand any vicissitudes to which they can be exposed in Britain,' he noted.

He wrote at last to 'My Dear Sir William (instead of the formal 'My dear sir' – they were now old friends):

From some not easily to be explained cause I have permitted your kind and most welcome letter of 10 January 1848 to remain unanswered . . . I assure you I was indeed rejoiced to see once more your old familiar writing, and although I do not possess the advantage of being personally known to you, yet I always look upon you as one of my oldest and most valued friends . . . and I acknowledge the pleasure which your letters always afford to a poor Botanist like myself at the Antipodes . . . I have almost abandoned all hope of ever being better

216

than a mere culler of weeds and wildflowers for you. My Zeal remains but alas! my time is sadly trenched upon.

He made up for it with a very long and interesting letter, page after page describing his 'rambles' over the countryside, his new discoveries and his thoughts on them. He ended this letter with a personal note. 'My eldest son Ronald has passed as a Surgeon and MD at Home. I have begged him to call at Kew ere he returns to this Colony and shall be glad if you can induce him to collect for you too.'

Margaret was very happy with her gift of rose-cuttings from England. One was a beautiful Gloire de Dijon, a splendid climber, and one a pale single dog-rose, also a climber. Ronald helped her plant them against a trellis, and after a day spent companionably digging and planting the other new plants – for Margaret loved her garden – the ice which she had felt about her heart since the baby's death melted at last. It was spring, and it was full moon. That night she did not shrink away to the edge of the bed with her back to him, but turned to him gladly. Ronald was so relieved at her forgiveness that he cried a little on her shoulder.

When a daughter was born the following February, he asked if they might call her Jane Franklin, after the late Governor's charming wife, and in memory of little Agnes Jane who was lost.

25

RONALD GUNN, aged twenty-three, was travelling from Scotland down to London for the second time in his young life. The last time he had been only two-and-a-half, and he and his parents were going to join the ship *Greenock* for Van Diemen's Land. He could vaguely remember the ship and its arrival, and being swung off the deck by a big, jolly uncle with one arm.

Now he was returning to London as a qualified doctor and surgeon, one who would perhaps be responsible for removing a man's arm one day in order to save his life. He gazed through the window at a sunny landscape that gave an illusion of warmth – but out there, he knew, the air was still frosty, and the footwarmers were in use in the compartment.

He had loved the city of Edinburgh and felt at home there at once, its steep streets reminding him of Hobart when he was a child, but instead of Mount Wellington there stood the romantic castle on its towering rock, and instead of the Derwent Estuary, the Firth of Forth gleamed bluely along the horizon. He had celebrated Hogmanay with his young cousins at Uncle Robert's home, and heard the wild bells ring out under a frosty, star-spangled sky to welcome the new year of 1849.

He would be going back to practise in Australia, but he was glad he'd had this experience of the Old World, so different from the brash new Colonies. He was exhilarated by the speed of the steam train, faster than he'd ever travelled before, the smell of coal smoke and the rhythmic click of the wheels over joints in the track. And he was on the way to London, the greatest city in the world, hub of the great Empire which was ever growing under the rule of young Queen Victoria.

Berwick-on-Tweed – there was the border, where so many ships were built which sailed round the world to Sydney and Hobart Town. The Tweed and the Till . . . He remembered a Scottish rhyme his stepmother used to tell the younger ones:

> Says Tweed to Till,
> What gars ye rin sae still?
> Says Till to Tweed,
> Although ye rin wi' speed,
> And I rin slaw,
> For aye mon that ye droon
> I droon twa.

Grim! But the children had loved it.

He was not going to Ireland to see his own mother's people. He had been old enough to remember those frightening scenes before she went away; unlike Robbie he had never cried for 'Mamma'. Since her death fifteen years ago the families-in-law had not kept in touch. He always called Margaret 'Mamma', and regarded her now as his mother.

Durham and York, the great cathedral cities, went by, then they were through the Yorkshire moors and the dark industrial air of the north, and travelling southwards through an incredibly green and smooth landscape, divided by neat hedgerows into a patchwork quilt of varying shades of green and of dark rich ploughland, smoke rising lazily from farmhouse chimneys, brindled cows in a field, white may-blossom in the hedgerows. . .

By the time the rain reached London it was already dusk; the pie-sellers and chestnut-roasters were calling their wares outside the station. If it hadn't been for his bags, he'd have gone walking off to explore the streets, to find the

Thames at once. Instead he took a cab to his lodgings, (arranged by letter by Uncle Robert) in Bayswater. It had been a long journey, and suddenly he was very tired. He would leave exploring till tomorrow.

In the morning he was up early, and after a good English breakfast of two eggs, bacon, and toast and marmalade, and well wrapped up in a woollen ulster and a long muffler against the cold, sallied forth into an English spring. He walked down to Hyde Park, and then through the park eastward to Green Park and St James's. Everywhere he looked, flowering bulbs greeted his eyes. His father would be delirious at the sight! All the flowers that were grown carefully as imported garden specimens at home, here seemed to grow wild. Daffodils, bluebells, hyacinths, in unbelievable profusion; flowering cherries dropping their petals in drifts of pink, hawthorns covered in snowy white.

He walked on beneath great elms just coming into leaf, and past pussy-willows bearing their soft fur-like catkins – no doubt his father had some polysyllabic Latin name for them! – to where people were braving the cold on wooden seats in St James's Park, and feeding the ducks. And just up there was Piccadilly, and here was Birdcage Walk, and Whitehall where Charles I was beheaded . . . He was walking on stones steeped in history.

But it was the River Thames he wanted to see, above everything, and he pushed on, south and east, till he came to the river. And there, leaning on a wall, he looked down at the muddy, swirling, tidal waters of Father Thames.

The river curved round towards the noble dome of St Paul's, London Bridge, and the Tower of London. He had seen it so often in print and woodcut, the scene was familiar and yet strange: was he really here, in London, twelve thousand miles from home? He could not remember his birthplace in the West Indies, there was only a vague memory of kindly brown faces and hands, and often a sound of singing . . . he had been only two when they left. Yet his father, who had been born in Cape Town and gone to school in Scotland, still hankered for the tropical fruit,

220

pineapples and mangoes and pawpaws, that he remembered from *his* childhood in Réunion. Ironical, when he grew the most delicious apples and pears in his orchard in Launceston. Now that steamships were coming in, perhaps they could be shipped fresh to England.

A haze from thousands of coal fires hung over the river, and the buildings were dingy. There was none of that sharp, clear light of the Tasmanian spring and summer – except when bushfires were raging – even though the day was sunny.

He decided to make a steamer excursion up the river to Kew Gardens, feeling a curiosity to see the Australian House where so many of his father's discoveries in the plant world were now housed; but he felt diffident about calling on Sir William Hooker, the Director, though Papa had made him promise that he would before he returned to Launceston. No, he would write a letter, and judge by the reply whether such a visit would be welcome to such a busy man.

Walking up from the steamer-landing to the imposing iron gates, he wondered if he would be disappointed. But at the entrance he was already beginning to be impressed. A magnificent magnolia in full bloom stood just beyond, and as he walked up the wide path he came upon great walls of lilac, in different shades but all shedding perfume; a lime-tree whose drooping fronds were plumed with sweet-scented blossom; and everywhere in the grass clumps of bluebells and daffodils, seeming to grow wild in their profusion.

He did not know the direction of the Australian House, but seeing some tall, exotic-looking pines he pressed on, keeping parallel with the high brick wall covered in ivy and flowering creepers, stopping to read the name on many a strange tree as he passed along the wide, gravelled path where visitors were walking or pausing to sit on the wooden seats and admire a vast bed of Dutch tulips in red and yellow – a brilliant display, but they were gaudy flowers that did not appeal to him as much as a bed of modest

221

English pansies. He had, of course, seen these growing at home, for nearly every settler brought a few seeds or cuttings or cherished seedlings with him round the Cape.

And there, over to the right, was the Australian House! Its glass roof and walls let in the sunlight, but the doors were kept closed and a perpetual micro-climate degrees above the sharply cold English weather outside was maintained. The first thing he saw was a clump of tree-ferns from Tasmania; then a *Eucalyptus globulus* and *Eucalyptus gunnii*, and a variety of wattle trees – among them *Acacia gunnii*. He was suddenly overwhelmed by homesickness; it must be the scent of the hard-leafed, aromatic plants that surrounded him. Surreptitiously he broke off a small gum-leaf and crushed it, holding it to his nose and even chewing a little of the bitter, eucalyptus-scented leaf. He felt a certain pride that his father had contributed so many of these plants, and that so many bore his name. He had not yet visited the orchid-house, where no doubt *Gunnia*, the whole genus named after Ronald Campbell Gunn, would be growing as a parasite tree orchid. There was even a Bunya-Bunya pine from Queensland, named after Bidwell though Cunningham had sent the first specimens of its huge fruiting cones to England where they sold for £10 each at Covent Garden. No doubt it would have to be moved outside soon, it would be far too large to be enclosed even under this lofty glass and metal roof.

He began to feel too hot in his outdoor clothes, and rather claustrophobic; and walking back by a different route that took him past the back of the administrative buildings, he saw an important-looking group of ladies and gentlemen. One large lady in a flounced gown and magnificent feathered bonnet was holding forth with emphatic gestures, while beside her a tall, sturdy man, bareheaded and with dark hair going grey, listened with bent head while scuffing in the path with the toe of his boot. He appeared diffident, embarrassed. Could this be the great Sir William Hooker, Director of the Gardens? Ronald felt sure it was.

He decided to write the next day and ask for an appointment.

'So you are Ronald Gunn's eldest son! Tell me, are you like him? No, I think not.' He indicated the watercolour portrait by Wainewright which hung on the wall of his office, and which Gunn had sent him years ago. And the question was the very same which Ronald Gunn had asked *his* son, when he and Joseph first met in Hobart Town.

'No, I'm afraid not, sir. I must have taken after my Irish mother.' He indicated the reddish curls which he kept short and well-brushed, but which refused to lie down. 'I don't have that long Scottish jaw, either, nor have I inherited my father's love of botany.'

'But you studied medicine, just as my son Joseph did. But not my eldest son. William' (a shadow crossed his face) 'died recently in Bermuda; he was always interested in birds and insects.'

'I am sorry to hear it. But you must be very proud of Dr Hooker and his achievements.'

'I am, I am. He and your father became friends at once, you know, and still correspond regularly. Your father asked me to try to persuade you to do some collecting for Kew Gardens.' A warm smile lighted his bright brown eyes, as he shook his head ruefully. 'But I feel sure that if it were possible to persuade you, he would have managed it before this himself. You're a lost cause, aren't you?'

Ronald laughed. 'I'm afraid so, sir. As a child I used to help a little, but I was always more interested in the anatomy of insects and animals. And with a busy medical practice, as I hope to have, there won't be much spare time for botany.

He knew that Sir William's own Herbarium collection (which he had transferred from Glasgow on his appointment to Kew) was the largest and most valuable private collection in the world.

Sir William showed him a little of the North American

collection, which included specimens brought back by Sir John Franklin's overland journeys to the Polar Sea, and sent by Douglas from Oregon and the Rocky Mountains, and by many officers of the Hudson's Bay Company in Canada.

'We saw much of the Franklins in Hobart,' said young Gunn, 'and Sir John and Lady Franklin were always extremely kind to my father, and encouraged his botanical work. Has anything been heard of the Arctic Expedition under Sir John? If not, surely all hope must be lost by now.'

'Lady Franklin has not given up. She has amazing spirit, and has defied the Admiralty's wish to give her a widow's pension. She is outfitting yet another search vessel at her own expense, I believe.'

'It does seem incredible that a hundred and twenty nine men could disappear almost without trace, and without leaving any record.'

'Unless the ships were suddenly crushed, and sank beneath the ice. Thank God *Erebus* and *Terror* returned safely from their South Polar journey, when Joseph was on board. I feel for Lady Franklin. The *not knowing* must be the worst.'

He pushed the tall sliding panel back into place.

'I think I saw you in the Gardens the other day, with a visiting party of important persons,' said Gunn.

'Was there a large lady in a feathered hat?'

'There was.'

Sir William sighed. 'She is, I fear, a thorn in my flesh. The Duchess of Cambridge. Her house adjoins the Royal Gardens, and she insists that I plant more garden borders full of annuals! Of no *botanical* interest whatever, but she likes the Gardens to look 'pretty'. Oh dear. The time spent by my gardeners over a bed of violas and pansies could be far better spent in propagating rare ferns and orchids and even mosses, which are beneath her notice.'

'But you are the Director!'

Sir William sighed. 'Yes, indeed. But of a public amenity which spends public money. So my hands are greatly tied.'

224

He insisted that young Gunn should walk with him to his home, West Park, nearby, with a detour across Kew Green to see the picturesque old church and the huge flowering lime-tree there. They walked under an avenue of horse-chestnuts, their boughs bedecked like those of Christmas trees with branching candles of white and pink flowers. The damp green grass beneath was strewn with fallen blossom.

'What a beautiful, tranquil place!' said Gunn.

'Yes. I plan to be buried here, in the churchyard. *Not* in a vault, but where flowers can grow on my grave.'

26

ABOUT THE time his son was visiting Sir William Hooker
in London, Ronald Campbell Gunn was writing to Sir
William about getting a cross-section from one of the giant
eucalyptus trees for the proposed Kew Gardens museum.
He pointed out that the largest cross-cut saws had blades
of only six to seven feet in length, whereas the trees could
be up to twenty feet in diameter; trees over fifty feet in
circumference and more than 300 feet tall could be met
with.

He asked about 'a Daguerreotype apparatus' to make
portraits of some of the trees, and the fern tree glens and
types of callitris and casuarina.

He now had a copy of Gould's magnificent book on
Australian birds – it had been bought too by nearly every
well-to-do family in the Colony, mainly so that they could
display it on a table.

'I wonder if the *Flora Tasmaniae* will be as popular?' he
said to Margaret.

'Do you not think ordinary, non-scientific people are
more interested in birds? They notice them more than
plants; birds are so bright and bonnie.'

'So you wish I'd taken up ornithology rather than
botany?'

'No, no; I never like to see you shoot the wee creatures,
the wrens, and the beautiful parrots and cockatoos. There
was a flock of sulphur-crested white cockatoos I saw once in
a tree at Glen Leith. They looked like great white flowers.
Very noisy, though.'

'So are the black cockatoos, in a different way. The farmers say, if you see more than three black cockatoos in a flock, it will rain within three days.'

'Aye . . . so they say.' She stroked the feathers of a White Hawk, which he had shot and had stuffed and mounted in his study. It perched realistically on a piece of dead timber, its yellow glass eyes glaring fiercely. It was not an albino, which would have had pink eyes, but a true white species.

'*Astur Novae-hollandiae*', said Ronald.

'Eh? Where's an aster?'

'No, the hawk – that's his Latin name.'

'Oh, aye?'

She still teased him because he would never refer to a buttercup as anything but a 'ranunculus,' and daisies were 'compositae'. 'I suppose ye'd have the children sing,

"Ranunculi and compositae,
O the pretty flowers . . ."

It doesna sound quite the same to me as "Buttercups and daisies".'

'Common names are all right for children,' he said loftily, 'but one should always give the correct botanical name where possible. Robert Lawrence taught me that. Otherwise you have the same name given to entirely different plants in different Colonies – Christmas bush, for instance. Backhouse always said it was better to give a wrong name to a plant than leave it without one, but I find that wrong names have a habit of sticking, and mixing up the records.'

'And as for your namesake, yon "Gunn's Striped Bandicoot" – I wish you'd instruct it not to eat my bulbs. Two whole beds of ixias are entirely eaten, the crocuses were dug up before they showed a leaf.'

'Destructive little beasts!'

Their home was now a Mecca for botanists from the Old Country. Dr Harvey of Dublin University wrote of his 'projected algocological tour' of Australia and Tasmania; he who had been so delighted at the re-discovery of *Claudia elegans*. He had written ecstatically:

227

Claudia elegans: This is a rare and beautiful plant – there are not half a dozen specimens in all the cabinets of Europe – no-one in England had it except Robert Brown, and he only one specimen. With its red lace-like 'leaves', this is one of the Network algae; they are the Orchideae of the Marine plants . . .

After a visit to Launceston and a trip with Gunn to the mouth of the Tamar estuary, and a stay at Penquite House, Harvey wrote warmly from Sydney enclosing samples of dried seaweeds collected around Newcastle.

He sent kind remembrances to Mrs Gunn, and gave the news that the first sheets of the 'Flora Tasmanica' were in the Press, and added that he had a copy of his *Nereus Australis* put aside for Gunn – 'only a *fragment* of a book however; It abruptly stops at the 50th plate.'

Spurred on by Dr Harvey's praise (though he said it was really due to Margaret), Ronald organised a family holiday at the house at Low Head, north of George Town on the east bank of the Tamar, inside the last headland before the open sea. The Tamar was very wide here, but because of the obstruction of Hebe Reef the tides swirled rapidly in and out twice a day.

While he and Margaret and the younger girls would be able to do some collecting of algae, the boys could go swimming on the sheltered, sandy beach, edged with smooth grey pebbles, across the road from the house. The low sandhills which backed it, covered in a dense growth of banksia and acacia, kept the seawinds from the house but blocked out the view of the sea.

The weather in January was perfect. The boys spent hours on the beach, building a 'smuggler's hide' of branches to shade them from the midday sun, and tumbling in and out of the canoe that Robbie had got for Christmas.

'You must never allow young John to go out in the canoe on his own,' his father warned. 'Although our beach is sheltered, there's a tremendous tide race further out at times, and he could never paddle against it.'

'Yes, Papa. I won't let him.'

'Promise me.'

'I promise . . .'

Fanny was staying with her fiancé in New Norfolk for Christmas. She had become engaged to John Cundell Jamieson, Margaret's younger brother now back from Port Phillip and living at Glen Leith. He was no blood relation, though when they married he would be not only Ronald's son-in-law, but his brother-in-law as well. Margaret was overjoyed at this development, so unexpected. She was fond of Fanny, and now her old home would be 'in the family' in a double sense. The younger children would be able to visit their uncle who was also their half-sister's husband. John was ten years older than Fanny, but that was no drawback; Ronald was ten years her senior and they were very happy.

Margaret was expecting a baby in a few months, but did not allow her pregnancy to hamper her exursions after seaweeds, though she found bending awkward. Isabella, who seemed to have less energy than the others, spent her time lying in a hammock or sketching in watercolours, while the little girls Mary Ann and Claudia Amelia played on the sand. Though not allowed to swim, they had the unusual freedom of leaving off their boots and long stockings to run barefoot on the beach or paddle in the shallows – always wearing shady straw hats to protect their complexions from the sun. Though Isabella and John were dark, most of the children took after their fair Celtic mothers, whether Scots or Irish.

One afternoon when Margaret was resting in her room, and the boys, having been made to wait an hour for their lunch to settle, were over at the beach, and baby Jane Franklin slept, and the girls declared it was too hot to go out, there was a sudden commotion on the veranda: a barking dog, and loud sobs and cries.

Ronald put down his *Icones Plantarum* and went out to investigate. He found young Johnnie in a hysterical state, unable to speak.

229

'Stop that!' he said sternly, suspecting a quarrel over use of the canoe. 'Be quiet, and don't wake Mamma and Baby. Now stop crying and tell me.'

But Johnnie, pointing wildly towards the sandhills, continued to gasp and sob. At last he managed, 'R-Robbie . . .'

'What about Robbie?' Ronald gave him a shake. 'Calm down now.'

'R-Robbie. He's g-gone!'

'*What*?'

'He, he lost the paddle – and the canoe drifted, so fast – '

'Oh my God!' He grasped the little boy's wrist and almost dragged him across the road and over the track through the sandhills to the beach.

'Now, show me,' he said grimly, pointing towards the Strait. 'Robbie has been swept out to sea?'

'No.' The child shook his head, and pointed in the opposite direction towards Launceston.

Of course, the tide was coming in. Thank God! 'Did you see where the canoe drifted to?' It could go aground on the west shore, anywhere, or on one of the points of land towards George Town . . .

'I c-called out to him, I'd go and get help, but he-he'

'*Yes*?'

'He jumped over and tried to swim back to the beach. But the tide was carryin' him backwards. I saw his head getting smaller 'n smaller.' Johnnie burst into sobs again. 'And now – now he won't never come back, will he?'

'Of course he will,' said his father briskly, but he felt cold with dread. 'You wait here on the highest sandhill, and keep watching, while I run and get the telescope.'

Ronald raced back to the house, tripping over the tufty grasses, and grabbed the telescope from the mantelpiece. Isabella met him at the door as he went out again.

'What is it, Papa? I heard – '

'Nothing. It's nothing. They've lost the canoe, that's all. Don't worry Mamma now, will you?'

He raced away again, and from the highest sandhill swept the grey-blue waters with the glass. Empty – there

230

was no sign of the canoe, even, and no dark spot of a swimming head. The tide swirled up the estuary, encroached on the beach.

'Now, Johnnie, I want you to be brave. I have to go and get a fisherman to help me look for Robbie. You mustn't tell Mamma that you saw him swimming, just that he was swept upstream in the canoe. Mamma's not very well and any shock would be bad for her.'

Johnnie looked disbelieving. Mamma had looked perfectly well at lunch-time, and ate a good meal. 'I'll try, Papa.' He was only six years old and loved and admired his big half-brother, who was ten years older. He sniffed and gulped and polished his nose with the sleeve of his shirt.

Robbie was a strong lad and a good swimmer, Ronald kept reassuring himself. They went downstream in the fisherman's small steam launch, making good time with the tide, but stopping to investigate every cove and inlet. They found nothing, not even the canoe. After two hours, as the sun was setting and the tide was turning, they gave up and turned back.

There followed three days of deferred hope, of sleepless nights and days spent searching the beaches. The police had organised a search of the western shores, and had found the canoe washed up on rocks and damaged. But of Robbie there was no sign.

In a chastened mood the family packed up and returned to Launceston. Margaret wept for the young life lost. But in her heart she thought, 'Thank God! Thank God it was the other. Not my son.' Ronald felt numbed with shock and grief, blaming himself for the gift of the canoe and for not having supervised its use. But Robert was a big boy of nearly seventeen and used to the water. If only he had stayed with the canoe, instead of trying to swim against the tide, he would probably have been all right.

The worst time came when he had to identify the body. It had been found far up the river, almost half-way to Launceston, where the banks narrowed and formed Whirlpool Reach. As soon as he saw the body at the mortuary on its marble slab, he knew it was his son. He recognised the straight dark hair, the sturdy shoulders, the navy-blue bathing suit with a white stripe at the edge of the neck and sleeves. He lay stretched out as though asleep, but the fish had been at the most vulnerable parts, the eyes, eyelids and lips. A wisp of seaweed was caught in one rigid hand. *Zostera marina*, Ronald noted automatically. He had been down to the bottom of the river, then. A wave of horror swept over him and he felt he was going to faint.

For Ronald's sake, Margaret hoped against hope that the coming baby would be a boy. He was far more affected than when little Agnes Jane was taken, she realised. This was the second son he had lost. But when the baby was born in March 1851, it was a girl. They named her Margaret after her mother – though that was Isabella's second name too – and her first given name was Louisa. She looked rather like Isabella, as her hair was straight and dark like her father's.

Lieutenant-Governor La Trobe of the newly formed Colony of Victoria (no longer just 'the Port Phillip District of New South Wales', of which he had been administrator for years) sent a sympathetic letter of condolence for Robbie's death, when the news of the tragedy appeared in the Melbourne papers, Gunn being such a well-known figure in Launceston society. The Gunn family and the family of Charles Joseph La Trobe had become great friends. La Trobe was a cultivated and travelled man who had written several travel books and was interested in botany and natural history; he was an amateur of music and art and could sketch and paint. He had stayed with them on a visit to Launceston, and sent a specimen of what was supposed to be the skull of a Bunyip, the legendary water-creature of the mainland Aborigines, to Ronald Gunn for the Tasmanian Society. In return Ronald sent to Government House, Melbourne, boxes of fresh fruit, and sent roses from the garden, whenever a steam-ship was going direct to Port Phillip.

It was about this time that Ronald suddenly felt that he had become an expert – he, Ronald Campbell Gunn, the

232

diffident young amateur, the 'mere culler of weeds and wildflowers'. It was as though he had been studying an unknown landscape through the eyepiece of a telescope that was not quite in focus; then, at a slight adjustment, all that had been blurred and ill-defined took on the sharp outlines of hills, trees, valleys, and distant shorelines. He could *see*.

He was emboldened to point out to Sir William what appeared to him an error in his pamphlet 'Species Filicum'. He added, 'Since I last wrote I have enquired and satisfied myself that *Athrotaxis laxifolia* is a true species . . .' He wrote with authority. At last he knew what he was talking about. And almost all his knowledge had come from books. Apart from Robert Lawrence and James Backhouse, and more recently William Archer, he'd had no one to compare notes with; and the only true botanist he had met was Joseph Hooker.

Upon young Ronnie's return from London, he had questioned him eagerly about Kew Gardens and its famous director, his correspondent now for more than twenty years. How he longed to go there and see for himself the Australian Pavilion and the great fern-house! But there was no question of being able to afford either the time or the money. With a growing family to feed, clothe and educate, and the cost of Ronnie's fare back and buying into a practice for him in the new Colony of Victoria, (now a thriving community of squatters and merchants, with already 18,000 people and five million sheep), there was no prospect of travelling Home himself.

In a belated attempt to get some help from the Government on the grounds of having been a pioneer settler, he asked Calder, the Surveyor-General, for help. Fearing a rebuff from the new Governor, Sir Henry Fox Young, he did not apply directly but asked Calder to sound out the possibilities before he made his official application.

'You see, I neither like to be refused – nor to ask for anything which might be considered unfair,' he explained. 'Under the new Land Regulations I can only obtain *one* section of land, and that for myself. My family consists principally of daughters, who are not entitled to any land; my eldest son is at Port Phillip and my only other two boys are very young.

'I emigrated in 1830 and I never got a grant although I possessed a note from the Secretary of State that I could obtain one; but I was too poor to show capital, and too honest to claim that I had . . . as was often done at the time, as you know.'

'True,' said Calder.

'So, I wondered would it perhaps be possible to get a grant in the names of my elder daughters?'

'Well – '

'I wouldn't have asked, but nine children press heavily on the exchequer.'

Calder was not hopeful. 'I advise you to apply for a grant in your own name, as being a pioneer settler. The Government is getting short of Crown land for grants. You might get a lease.'

Ronald had already bought 107 acres of land near Launceston, with a frontage to the North Esk river, for a future home. He now applied for a grant of land on the St Patrick's river to the north-east. He was granted a pastoral lease of 17,000 acres, with a small section of freehold for a head station.

Now his own opinion of his new ability in botany was confirmed. On Sir William Hooker's recommendation he was elected a Fellow of the Linnaean Society of London, a great honour. He had sent that year a living specimen of Thylacine, the Tasmanian Tiger, to Mr Gray of the British Museum.

27

RONALD KEPT a staff permanently at Low Head, and regularly received laboriously-written accounts from his man there, mostly for feed for the turkeys and hens. The housekeeper, Mary Lochrie, was a Scottish convict woman who was now a 'passholder of the second class' on a ticket-of-leave.

When, on a routine visit to the Lawrence estate property at George Town, he called in to his own house (empty for the winter) and grounds, he found the housekeeper in her full, striped apron and grey dress inclined to hide behind the open door of her cottage. Suspicious, he asked her for a glass of milk – for the man milked each day, and supplied them with fresh milk during the holidays.

As she walked to the food-safe and produced a jug, he watched her shrewdly – her heavy gait, leaning back slightly to balance the weight in front . . .

He accepted a cup of milk and thanked her, then looking her in the face sternly, he asked, 'Mary Lochrie, are you in the family way?'

Miss Lochrie turned and looked out the window.

'Aye . . . and what if I am?'

'If you are, it is my duty to send you to the Female Factory for the birth. It will have to be the Cascades in Hobart, since the Launceston Factory has closed.'

'Hobart! No no, sir, dinna send me to there!'

'You know I have no choice. It is the law. Do you know who is the father?'

She flashed him an angry look. 'Aye. I ken weel, but I'm no' tellin'.'

As she still had almost three months to go (or so she told him) Ronald agreed for her to stay on for the present. She was fairly literate, and a good housekeeper. Margaret would be sorry to see her go.

Mary Lochrie must have had the same idea, for when he returned to Launceston a letter arrived for Margaret from the housekeeper. She gave, as required, her name, status, and the name of the ship in which she had been transported. It was the '*Margaret*'.

She wrote, in a cramped hand,

Dear Mrs Gunn

I hope you will beg Master to keep me to George Town instead of to Hobart Town as my time is going on and I think it very hard that I am sent to the Factory I shall be glad of a little tea and sugar as I have bin very ill.

Mary Lochrie.
I will be much abliged.

'Well, Ronald?' said Margaret, showing him the letter. 'Poor Mary, it does seem very hard. Couldn't she have the baby in the north?'

'But she must be sent away, if only for the child's sake. And the law says – '

'I know what the law says. What about the man who is responsible? Babies don't make themselves. The Factory is no more than a prison. Why isn't the man sent to the Penitentiary?'

'We don't know who he is, for a start. And it isn't possible to prove paternity if he should deny it.'

'It isn't fair that the woman should be punished. She has as well all the pain of the birth, and the responsibility of bringing a new life into the world.'

'They don't have any sense of responsibility, these women; that's the trouble. Otherwise they wouldn't get into trouble.'

'Och, I have no patience with you!' cried Margaret, with heightened colour in her pink cheeks. 'Mary Lochrie is no' a loose woman. If the man willna marry her, she'll bring up the bairn on her own. Better than the Orphanage for the poor wee mite.'

She kept on at him in this strain until at last he agreed not to banish the housekeeper to Hobart and the Factory; while Margaret parcelled up some tea and sugar and some used baby-clothes for the woman.

His friend the orchid specialist, William Archer, asked Gunn to accompany him on a visit to the North-Western division where Archer was campaigning for a seat in the first elected Legislative Council of Tasmania, though they were on opposite sides on the question beginning to divide the community, that of the cessation of transportation, Gunn had been asked to make a report for the British Government on the affairs of the Van Diemen's Land Company so he went along too.

At Circular Head he wandered round his old haunts with memories crowding in on him, thoughts of mortality and mutability uppermost in his mind. Edward Curr had now left the Company and settled in the Port Phillip District. Ronald remembered the children of his first family when they were little, his walks on the beach with Ivy Grant Smith, their last farewell. He walked to the graveyard above the sea where she had told him not to mourn for her if she should die. He sought out the small headstone of little William Gunn, and among the grey memorials, some with their inscriptions already worn away by the salt winds, he came on another name he knew: 'Hinks Hutchinson, Surgeon, died May 1839, aged forty-two'. Dr Hutchinson, who had done some collecting for Robert Lawrence, and who had helped in little William's last illness . . . He placed some sprays of white heath he had gathered on the two graves.

The small waves broke against the shallow stony shore with a melancholy sound, and the wind soughed through a lone cypress that someone had planted. Beyond the shallow bay the mansion of Highfield caught the sun on the next headland.

Tears stung his eyes and were dried on his cheeks by the seawind. He thought of his first wife Eliza – only twenty-six when she died; Robert and his young wife, Elizabeth Wedge; Elizabeth Gould, worn-out with childbearing, dead in England at thirty-seven; and Eliza Milligan, a sister of Robert Lawrence, dead in childbirth at only nineteen and buried on lonely Flinders Island. The doomed Aborigines had been moved again, to Oyster Bay on the main island, while anthropologists and doctors interested in 'crania' dug up their bodies from the old graveyard and removed the skulls. In their decline they had suddenly become valuable, even dead ones, for their rarity value. Everyone knew, though the Government did not admit, that the Tasmanian pure-bred race must soon become extinct.

In spite of the efforts of Ronald Gunn and other influential landholders, and their petition to the Queen and the British Government, transportation to Tasmania ceased in 1853. The huge unwieldy bureaucracy which had administered the System brought to perfection by Colonel George Arthur, was dismantled; and as convicts on seven-and fourteen-year sentences of transportation finished their terms, they were freed into and absorbed by the community. Not all convicts were of the servant class. There were artists, too, like W. B. Gould, the flower-and-fruit painter, and Thomas Bock who did portraits of the Aborigines.

Now came a new honour: Ronald was elected a Fellow of the Royal Society of London – the first Tasmanian resident to be so honoured – on William Hooker's recommendation.

'It makes all my life, my lonely years of work and discouragement, worthwhile,' he told Margaret, beaming with pride and pleasure. "Ronald Campbell Gunn, F.L.S., F.R.S.!" Who would have thought it?'

'I would,' said Margaret, and gave him a kiss. 'You must write and tell young Ronnie, he'll be so proud.' Young Dr Gunn, after practising in Melbourne, had left for the distant colony of Moreton Bay.

Since that youthful portrait was painted by Wainewright, twenty years earlier, Ronald's face and figure had filled out with middle age (though he still had 'a canny long head' according to Margaret), and a greying beard fringed his cheeks and chin. His hair, though dark, was receding, and though his mouth was still good-tempered, the large clear-gazing eyes of his youth were now narrower and more shrewd.

Yet he had become what he never could have imagined when he arrived as a penniless young man from the West Indies: a landed proprietor, a known and respected member of the community whose opinion was sought on all sorts of subjects, not only those connected with botany. He was in demand to open functions, make speeches, attend dinners, and was appointed Chairman at a dinner in the Cornwall Assembly Rooms to bid farewell to the Governor, Sir William Denison.

Margaret's eldest boy, John Jamieson Gunn, was now thirteen and at boarding school in Hobart. He had already decided that he wanted to follow his half-brother and make medicine his career.

'Not a botanist among them so far,' sighed Ronald Gunn. But Isabella showed a talent for drawing plants and painting them in watercolour.

Meanwhile Joseph Hooker, who had recently married, was deeply involved in the *Flora Tasmaniae*. He wrote to

an old chum yclept R. C. Gunn: that the same R.C.G. was more on his mind than almost any other person; and if he does not write it is not from forgetfulness of the glorious days we spent together in Tasmania . . .

Each plate of the *Flora* costs £10 plain and £15 coloured, a fearful price! to spend on perhaps 1200 species.

Joseph had seen Mrs Gell – the former Eleanor Franklin, now married to the Reverend J.P. Gell – '*awfully* fat, though thinner in the face', with a rose-cheeked baby; and Lady Franklin too, in bad health: 'No news of Sir John and she *must* have given up hopes . . . Jimmy Ross has just written, but as usual does not invite me down to his place . . .'

Later he wrote from Kew in delight over the Tasmanian Government's decision to vote a sum of £360 towards the *Flora*, as a result of Gunn's and William Archer's representations.

> . . . I have no regular employment but vegetate upon temporary pay as an assistant Surgeon . . . The collections are now fine and complete towards the V.D.L. Flora, to which I am about to devote all my energies. I shall send the proofs of plates regularly . . . I have £100 a year from my father, the most generous of men, and ditto from my wife.
>
> The grant from your Government is most timely as I am short of funds and want to do the Flora very carefully and critically indeed . . . It is so mainly a Flora of your collections, that I look upon it as part and parcel of your work and a most anxious to make it worthy of your labours.
>
> I see Lady Franklin now and then. Their family quarrels are miserable, I suppose both are at fault, but Gell latterly has committed himself most seriously.

At Eleanor's instigation, Gell had joined with her in demanding her share of her own mother's estate, declaring that Lady Franklin was using it to continue the search for Sir John in the Arctic. The quarrel had become bitter, for Eleanor also demanded her share of Lady Franklin's own property, which as a married woman had belonged to Sir John; while Jane steadfastly refused to believe that he and all his men were dead.

Jane Franklin, half-mad with worry and deferred hopes,

wrote asking for documents and deeds relating to 'our
property' in Tasmania. There were thousands of acres in
her and Sir John's name, at North Esk and St Patrick's
river, besides the Ancanthe estate at Lenah Valley and the
land let to tenant farmers at Franklin on the Huon river.
Lawyers agreed, she said, that the money invested by her
father for her benefit

remains mine; and the £5,000 sent out by him to Van
Diemen's Land . . .
Simpleton that I am, I did not put the money to a
separate account at Drummond's – from neglecting this
precaution I have become the victim of the Gells'
revengeful spirit. . . But the £5,000 I do claim exclusively
as my own. I brought to my husband about £16,000, in
spite of my poor dear old father's 'disinheritance'.

All these letters from London kept Ronald Gunn in
touch with what was going on – Philip Parker King, who
had accompanied him years ago on that expedition to
Recherche Bay, had been to Kew Gardens. Lieutenant
King wrote that Kew alone was worth going to England to
see – a splendid affair – the Palm House, 345 feet long, was
a most extensive mass of glass and iron frames, full of
tropical productions growing in the greatest, most inde-
scribable luxuriance – the laying-out of the grounds was
tasteful and the whole place well kept.
He added the news that young Dr Hooker had just been
appointed as Curator of the Library and Herbarium at £400
a year, while Sir William had obtained a grant of £3,000 to
commence building the Museum to house his collection of
Economic Botany.
Kew Gardens, with its extensive grounds and Herbarium
of over a million plants, was now the most famous botanical
garden in the world, 'and your pines are growing splen-
didly'.
Gunn did not write to the Hookers of the new worry
which filled his days. Isabella, who had shown such talent in

painting watercolour drawings of some of her father's specimens, had been losing weight and complaining of tiredness for some time past. She was not married and showed little interest in young men – not even her cousin Ronald, a handsome lad with black curling whiskers, though several years her junior, who had been showing her attention.

Then Isabella began to cough, and one morning she coughed blood. The doctor looked grave. It was that dread disease, tuberculosis of the lungs, or consumption, and prognosis was not good. By Christmas 1854 she was wasted away and too weak to do more than lie on a couch all day. She suffered from debilitating night-sweats which left her clammy and cold.

'This will be my last Christmas,' she said with a sad, patient smile that wrung her father's heart. He knew that it was true. He kissed her forehead where the damp curls of her dark hair were clustered.

'I have something to show you,' he said, and went away and brought her a perfect little greenhood orchid, planted in a pot. It curved its top downward, like a shy child hanging its head.

'*Pterostylis curta*.' He set it on the table beside her couch.

'I don't suppose you remember,' he said, 'but when you were a little tiny girl, about three years old, you found a rare *Pterostylis*, the *squamata* – described by Brown, but I'd never seen it. I was so pleased.'

'I believe I do remember. Thank you, Papa!'

She touched the frail green hood with her pale, almost transparent fingers. 'I think – I think I would like my drawing and painting things. Will you ask Claudia to get them for me? On the shelf in my room.'

He hurried away, feeling a new hope. She had been too listless to do anything but read, or be read to, and had not done any painting for months. It was a good sign. She must be getting better.

The watercolour was never completed. He kept the drawing, with its half-finished outlines, among his papers until his death. Isabella had tired before she got round to colouring it, and by mid-January she was dead. His old dread of death returned. First Robert, and now Isabella, of his first family, as well as baby William. Of Eliza's children, only Frances and Ronnie were left.

William Archer of Cheshunt wrote with his condolences. He was a masterly painter of orchids himself and had admired Isabella's work on a visit the year before. He had done sixty-five drawings of orchids for the *Flora Tasmaniae* but said he would be happy if a tenth of those appeared.

'How little,' he wrote, 'do we appreciate the sunshine of those we hold dear, until their death replaces it with a gloomy shadow!'

He was intending to leave Van Diemen's Land for England in the last week of April, and was looking forward to a holiday from politics:

Botany forever! With its wonderful and beautiful forms and its delightful associations. Politics are a necessary evil, however – but after the abuse and quarrelling of politics, Botany is a bed of roses.

28

MARY ANN, the eldest of the second family, had been much distressed by the death of her half-sister Isabella. She had accepted that old people and babies often died, until Robbie's accident. But he was eight years older and a boy, and they had not been close. Seeing Isabella's patient suffering, attending her and reading to her as she became weaker, she had felt rebelliously that life just wasn't *fair*. Why did God allow such things to happen; why should beautiful, gentle Isabella be taken when she was young?

To stop her moping, Margaret sent her for a holiday to stay with her cousins on the other side of town. She was 'outgrowing her strength' at the age of puberty, and was rather thin and tall for her age. She developed an intense friendship with her cousin Louisa, who was almost the same age, and whose second name was Isabella.

The younger children teased them as they walked with their arms twined round each other's waist, and insisted on wearing the same colour ribbons in their long hair, Mary Ann's as fair as Louisa's was dark.

'Here come the bosom friends!' young James and John, Louisa's brothers, would chant teasingly, while Elizabeth, the younger sister, felt left out. The two girls wandered in the extensive rose garden which lately Louisa's father had planted at Glen Dhu with his brother's help. They exchanged roses, which they pinned in their pinafore-frocks, with vows of eternal friendship. Sometimes they fell out, and would not speak to each other for a whole day. Their quarrels were fierce, but they always made them up, with many tears and apologies; 'I'm sorry, dear Louie; it was my fault.'

'No, no, it was mine. After all, it is your skipping-rope.'

'I was being selfish. Will you forgive me?'

'Of course, Mary Ann. We will never quarrel again over something so silly.'

But of course they did, and once more made it up with tears.

'Those girls are so soppy,' said their young brothers scornfully.

There were important visitors at Penquite when Mary Ann returned, and Papa was not to be disturbed in his small study. A deputation had come to ask him to stand as Chairman of the Launceston Patriotic Fund for the relief of widows and children of soldiers who had died in the Crimean War, which began in 1853 and was now drawing to a close.

He was also a board member of the Breadalbane Road Trust, and Vice-President of the Northern Agricultural Society. His days were far too full, though he now employed a travelling manager to deputise for him in the Lawrence Estate supervision. He was asked to present a petition advocating a Western Railway from Launceston to Deloraine, a dream that was not to come true for another ten years. He signed the petition himself, below the obligatory declaration that no female, child or servant was among the signatories.

As an acknowledged expert on the topography of northern Tasmania, Gunn was sent on a trip with the Government Surveyor, Mr Peter Lette, to report on the gold discoveries on the Calder, the Forth and the upper Arthur rivers; and to search out the best routes to the still undeveloped lands inland from the coast, between the rivers that flowed northward into Bass Strait. Though with wide estuaries, dangerous to cross, they were not navigable and could not provide a highway to the interior, which was still largely unexplored.

Setting off just before Christmas 1859 with one manservant to carry their provisions, they proceeded to the Calder river through a dense forest of sassafras and myrtle. Bad weather set in although it was midsummer, and they found little trace of the supposed gold in the Calder, so they returned to Launceston.

In January they set off again, with three men this time, for the Surrey Hills, proceeding across the Black Buff to the River Forth, through a series of thinly wooded, open forests and plains forming a sort of plateau at about 2,500 feet; and it was then that Gunn discovered the extensive plains to the east of the Leven river, open and treeless but with soil of good quality, to be named 'Gunn's Plains' in his honour.

The party noted that valuable timber in vast abundance occurred inland from the north coast: eucalyptus, myrtle, blackwood, sassafras, and celery-top pine. The most suitable access route to this rich country would be a track almost due south from Table Cape. And it was outside the Van Diemen's Land Company's huge grant.

Gunn found a few things for his friend Joseph Hooker, who had now taken over most of the correspondence from his father and was nearing the end of his work on the flora of Tasmania. Gunn had also collected some new specimens for his extensive herbarium of dried plants that he intended to present to the Royal Society of Hobart, formerly the Tasmanian Natural History Society.

He nearly lost all the specimens when crossing the Leven river near its mouth, not far from where the V.D.L. Company's surveyor had been drowned years before. They were caught by the turning tide as it raced up river in a tidal surge. Ronald felt his last hour had come. His feet were swept from under him, and he struck out for the bank hampered by the bag of specimens slung round his neck. He went under, swallowed some water, and surfaced again, floundering.

Peter Lette, who had already reached safety, turned back to help the older man out. At last they struggled to the bank, where he lay gasping and coughing.

Gunn was drenched, cold and shaken. They lit a fire and dried their clothes, but he could not get the chill out of his bones until the midday sun warmed him the next day.

'Why didn't you let the specimens go?' Peter Lette had asked him crossly. 'You could have drowned.'

'I know.' How to explain to someone who was not a botanist how important it was that they should not be lost?

But from this wetting he developed the arthritis in his hands and knees which increasingly troubled him in later years, until he could no longer hold a pen firm to write those long screeds, marshalling the words in neat serried lines that flowed across the page and in which he had so delighted.

Now a new interest absorbed him. He had started to build his long-projected mansion on the hundred or so acres he had acquired on the eastern side of Launceston, adjoining the North Esk river. He sold the forty acres of market garden and orchard in the small sheltered valley across town; he was going to concentrate on a botanic garden of exotic trees around his new home, with specimens that Hooker had promised him from Kew Gardens.

He could afford to purchase labour these days – even free labour, now that transportation to Van Diemen's Land had ended. The Penitentiary for the Northern Division in Launceston was gradually closed, and brother William retired with a pension to cultivate his roses at Glen Dhu.

Ronald planned a two-storeyed house with long windows framed by green-painted shutters, a wide front door with glazed panels, and on either side two large windows to let light into the hall, and a stone porch with steps. Gone were the days of struggling to raise a large family on a small income, when a debt of two or three hundred pounds was crippling.

When the building was completed, he named it Newstead House, after Newstead in Roxburghshire where he had roamed when a boy in Scotland. The house had a sweeping drive to the front door between the new trees he had planted, and he bought two Italian terracotta vases to stand on either side of the steps. Margaret filled them with white and purple petunias in summer, with pansies in winter. The centrepiece of the front garden was the Spanish Oak which he had grown from an acorn, and which was already a young tree.

For the first time he had a proper room for a study. The walls were lined with books, a large desk was set in a good light, where he could work at his writing. There was a glass case containing the herbarium of dried plants that he was still compiling.

Two cases of living plants arrived from Kew Gardens, including a magnolia, rhododendrons (which Joseph Hooker had brought back from the Himalayas), and a cineraria – all new to Tasmania. Besides establishing his own botanic garden on his land, he was President of the Launceston Horticultural Society and so responsible for the extensive public Botanic Gardens which had been established on the seventeen acres donated by Sir John Franklin for the purpose. Many exotic trees and shrubs were already acclimatised there. But he had less and less time for gardening with his appointment first as Registrar of Births, Deaths and Marriages, and then as Commissioner of Crown Lands. His days were endlessly busy. He had only one more ambition: to see the two volumes of the Tasmanian Flora in print, the crown of all his life's work.

Louisa Gunn, William's daughter, sat beside her cousin Mary Ann in the beautiful flower-filled, sheltered court-yard at the back of Newstead House. The two wings of the house enclosed a sunny space, scented with mignonette and lavender, thyme and sweet marjoram. Tall hollyhocks grew in the middle, and bright geraniums, shaded by a tall exotic palm-like tree, a pandanus-leaved richea which Ronald Gunn had brought from the southwest.

'I'm never going to get married and have children,' said Mary Ann, tearing a bright flower to pieces as she sat on the wooden garden seat. 'What's the use? It only makes you dreadfully unhappy when they die.' The red petals strewed the ground like drops of blood.

She had seen three of her family buried, and she was only nineteen. Louisa had been equally shocked by the loss of her cousin Isabella Margaret.

'Mary Ann, let's vow *never* to get married,' said Louisa intently, shaking back her dark curls.

'Never, Louie?'

'Never!'

They stared at each other solemnly, there in the sunlit courtyard where warmth and colour and light, the humming of bees among blossom, seemed to deny the hateful fact of death. Yellow butterflies drifted like leaves through the tranquil autumn air.

They went upstairs to Mary Ann's bedroom, and there with great secrecy drew up a document which read:

I, Louisa Caroline Gunn, of Glen Dhu, and I, Mary Ann Gunn of Newstead House, Launceston, do solemnly swear that we will never marry, but remain single all the days of our lives.

They rolled up the paper and hid it in a secret hollow in a tree in the garden. They did not tell Mary Ann's sister, who was only twelve. The next year they had a falling-out, as Louisa suddenly became interested in a young man, a friend of her brother Ronald's.

'Oh, Mary Ann, he has asked me to marry him!' she whispered to her cousin when they met in church on Sunday. 'Oh, it was so romantic! He went down on one knee, and kissed my hand.'

'He must have looked stupid!' whispered Mary Ann crossly. 'And what did you say! I hope you told him – '

'I told him I would have to think about it.'

'*Think* about it! In her indignation Mary Ann spoke aloud and someone in the pew in front turned to glare at her.

After church, and a walk in the cemetery to visit Mary

Ann's sisters' graves, Louisa still refused to promise that she would give the young man his congé. Mary Ann went home in a huff, and cried herself to sleep.

However, on the young man's next visit to Glen Dhu, Louisa decided that he did look rather stupid. Romantic friendship prevailed over romantic love, and she renewed her vow to remain single.

Five years later it was Louisa's turn to get upset, for Mary Ann was being wooed by Alfred Douglas, while Henry, his younger brother, was making eyes at Jane, who was pretty and dark and nearly eighteen.

Mary Ann at twenty-five felt it would be nice to be asked for her hand even though she might decide not to give it, so she did not discourage him. Louisa Gunn would not speak to her after the engagement was announced.

But Alfred who had looked so robust, developed Bright's disease, and died in a coma before the wedding date was even settled. Jane married her Henry after a suitable period of mourning, and within a year produced a first grandson for Ronald Gunn, naming him Ronald Campbell Gunn Douglas. Her father was delighted.

After a while Louisa and Mary Ann were reconciled, and renewed their vows of celibacy.

In May 1860 the long-awaited *Flora Tasmaniae* was published, in two volumes. It was nearly Christmas before a ship arrived from England with the precious cargo, the result of many different men's devoted work on opposite sides of the world.

It had been worth waiting for. As he lifted the first of the two volumes reverently from its packing. Ronald Gunn's eyes were moist. It was the best Christmas present he had ever received.

In the same ship which had brought the *Flora Tasmaniae* came news from London that Lady Franklin's long search for her explorer husband was at an end. A last vessel sent out by her under Captain McLintock had resulted in the discovery at Point Victory of a small, rusted canister containing a message; the ships had been hopelessly caught in the pack-ice; Sir John had died on board in 1847. The next year the ships had been deserted by the men, who then walked south to their deaths. It was little enough, but for one who had waited fifteen years for news it must have been an enormous relief.

So that was the end of *Erebus* and *Terror*, the naval ships which had survived two dangerous voyages to the Antarctic, and which had brought his friend Joseph Hooker to these shores for the first time! With the publication of the *Flora Tasmaniae* the *Botany of the Antarctic Voyages* was complete: one volume of the flora of the Antarctic islands, one on the flora of New Zealand, and two for Tasmania. It was a work which fulfilled Sir William Hooker's criteria for a volume of Natural History: 'It should be so carefully produced, and so accurate, that it will stand as a reference work forever.'

Gunn had not felt well lately, had premonitions of death, and had feared he would not live to see his life's work embodied in print. He could scarcely see to read the opening dedication in Joseph Hooker's Introductory Essay:

To Ronald Campbell Gunn, F.R.S., F.L.S., and William Archer, F.L.S., this Flora of Tasmania, which owes so much to their indefatigable exertions, is dedicated by their very sincere friend, J.D. Hooker, Royal Gardens, Kew, January 1860.

There was his name, Ronald Campbell Gunn, immortalised as long as Hooker's magnificent book existed; and that was surely 'as long as men can breathe, and eyes can see'. Then Hooker's preface in which he had said:

There are few Tasmanian plants that Mr Gunn has not seen alive and collected with tact and judgment, and transported to England in perfect preservation. His

251

notes display remarkable powers of observation such as few experienced Botanists possess, and he has collected indefatigably.

More than two thousand species were described, with 412 illustrations including 200 beautifully drawn and coloured lithographic plates. Of these, thirty had been done by William Archer, to depict species of Tasmanian orchids; and two dozen embodied the name of Gunn in Latinised form.

But by far the most interesting thing about the *Flora Tasmaniae*, he realised, was the introductory essay. Alfred Russell Wallace and Charles Darwin had read a joint paper to the Linnaean Society in 1858 on Natural Selection, Darwin expounding his theory of the 'survival of the fittest'.

Now Hooker affirmed that he had been aware of Darwin's theories for the past fourteen years; they had discussed the theory of natural selection in the fernhouse at Kew Gardens back in 1845, and had kept in touch all their scientific lives.

Darwin's epoch-making work, *The Origin of Species*, had appeared in November 1859, causing a furore in the scientific and religious world in England. But Hooker, defending his friend against some of the attacks by churchmen and creationists, explained that he had arrived at the same theory quite independently, through studying the distribution of plants, just as Alfred Russell Wallace had done with animal life.

His essay was written before the *Origin of Species* appeared. It was a reasoned statement by a philosophical botanist and great constructive thinker, based on the relations and the mutability of species, especially on islands, and the geographical distribution of plants. The flora of Australia and its islands was particularly suited to testing this theory, he said.

Ronald Gunn, reading it, was fascinated to find how some of his own discoveries had led Hooker to his assumption that species were derivative and not immutable.

His essay showed how difficult it was to explain the facts of plant geography except by the theory of natural selection working on inherited variations. And really, when you thought about it, any student of natural history must doubt the legend of individual creation for every genus, every species, which existed on the face of the earth. The infinite variety of mosses alone, the variations in butterflies and birds, the sheer number and beauty of tiny plants which grew in dank gullies or on windswept peaks – for whose eyes had they been made?

29

WRITING, WHICH used to be such a joy, was now becoming a painful chore. It made his shoulders ache, and it had become increasingly difficult to hold a pen. He wrapped a strip of cloth around his favourite steel-nibbed Gillott pen and managed a limited correspondence.

He wrote apologetically to John Gould in London (who had asked him for a map of his latest discoveries, including Gunn's Plains).

> I write now with such pain and stiffness in my hands and fingers that your letter has remained unanswered . . . If you were here for a day I could answer all your queries easily – but I cannot *write* them, my dear Gould.

He had written, of course, to Joseph Hooker after receiving the two magnificent volumes of the *Flora Tasmaniae* with their flattering dedication.

Before increasing stiffness in his knees forced him to give up all but the briefest walks around his large garden, Gunn made a last expedition to Ringarooma in the north-east. It was the same country he had explored, alone, the first white man to see it, back in 1848. Now, accompanied by the Government Surveyor and the Colonial Secretary, he went by way of the coast from George Town.

Crossing the Piper's River to Bridport they went south to the Ringarooma valley, already settled with timber-getting towns.

To his distress – though of course it was inevitable – the

great gloomy forest hung with mosses which once filled the valley was being cleared. Someone had rediscovered the Ringarooma in 1855, had taken up five thousand acres of virgin land, and was steadily clearing it for its valuable timber. After ten years it was becoming a cradle for the dairying industry, and cows grazed on the green pastures flourishing in the rich soil which had supported those enormous trees.

The year was 1865: thirty-five years since he had arrived in the island, then covered in virgin forests and dangerous with implacably hostile natives. Much had changed. Tasmania had become an independent State, with a burgeoning apple industry, and export cider was brewed at the Cascades here the women convicts used to be incarcerated. Of the original Tasmanians only five survived, most of them old women.

It was the year which marked the end of his botanical excursions, the year that his old friend and correspondent Sir William Hooker died in London after a few days' illness. A letter from Joseph arrived at the end of the year, with a moving eulogy of his father.

I shall never see his equal for liberality and genuine kindness, utter absence of self-esteem, and single-minded devotion to Science. He had not a single enemy, but friends all over the world.

Joseph said in his letter that Sir William had been buried in the open air in the churchyard at Kew Green, as he had asked. The hymn sung at his funeral was 'What though I know each herb and flower . . .'

Ronald Gunn sat for a long time with the letter in his hand. Even though Joseph Hooker, now to succeed his father as Director of Kew Gardens, had for years taken over as his principal botanical correspondent, Ronald felt that with Sir William's death part of his own life had ended.

He would never go exploring Tasmanian lakes and mountains again, and he would never see Kew Gardens. The great work on the Tasmanian flora which he and the

Hookers had worked on was complete and safely published. And his old mentor was dead, at the ripe age of eighty years.

For himself, he did not wish to live so long. His elder sons were grown up, two of them practising medicine, though to his regret neither had become a botanist. Young John had elected to stay on in England after getting his degree, having fallen in love with his cousin Isabella Gunn, Robert's youngest daughter. William Edmund, the youngest, was still a schoolboy. His last son, Robert George – it was an unlucky name! – had died in infancy, and of the little girls, Louisa and the second Isabella, neither had survived childhood.

He thought about death, and how some died as soon as they were born, as if God had changed his mind; and some were cut off in their prime, like Robert Lawrence; and others lived like Hooker an active life into their eighties.

There was a time to live and a time to die, and he hoped that when his own time came he would be ready. Lawrence at least had never known the pains and disabilities of old age. Mere long life without the joy of living to the full did not have much to recommend it.

On his sixty-eighth birthday Ronald Gunn retired from all public office. He had held several important positions – Registrar of births, deaths and marriages, Lands Commissioner, and member of the Board of the Western Railway, which commissioned him to collect the unpopular tax on the landholders of the district served by the new railway. He came down on the side of the landowners, and refused to collect the tax.

Painfully, he wrote a last letter to Joseph Hooker. He dipped his pen once more and scrawled some lines from Ben Johnson he had learned as a boy, long ago in Scotland:

> It is not growing like a tree
> In bulk, doth make man better be;
> Or standing long an oak, three hundred year,
> To fall a log at last, dry, bald, and sere.

The lily of a day
Is fairer far in May,
Although it fall and die that night,
It was the plant and flower of light.

He closed the inkwell and put down his pen on the inlaid desk. Framed on the wall above his head were two beautiful colour plates, one of the crimson bell, blandfordia, and the other of the yellow mountain buttercup, the *Ranunculus* named after himself by Sir William Hooker.

Ronald Gunn was to live another five years, through increasing pain and disability.

Nursed by sturdy Margaret, still hale and rosy-cheeked, he hobbled about the garden as long as he could, and when he could no longer walk, was wheeled in his chaise-longue out to the back porch, opening on the courtyard where he could look at his beloved plants. His daughter Frances, Fanny Eliza of his first marriage, had died years ago after giving birth to twin girls, having produced nothing but daughters. Her surviving girls were now grown up – their father had married again – but Jane Franklin's boys, little Douglases, came to visit. They clambered over their grandfather's chair, bumping his sore knees under the rug, and bringing him flowers and frogs and beetles to look at, clutched in their sticky little hands. Jane already had five sons.

Her seventh child, a daughter, was to be born only a few days before Ronald Gunn died.

By the time Margaret came to die in 1895, only one of her nine children survived. The last to go was Jane (named after Lady Franklin), who had been left a widow and was in poor health. She came to stay at Newstead while Mary Ann, a devoted aunt, looked after the four youngest children at the old home of Penquite.

257

Margaret was fighting a losing battle against cancer.

At first she had refused to give in, to take to her bed, but now she lay in her upstairs room, too weak to get up; her once bonnie rosy complexion yellowed and wan, her face bony, with sunken, shadowed eyes. Then as a final blow her daughter Jane, who had been up with her mother during the night, died of a heart attack at two in the morning.

Margaret's niece Louisa Jamieson, who had been helping to nurse her aunt, and the housekeeper did not dare tell her. They sent for Mary Ann to break the news.

'Dear Lord!' cried Margaret passionately. 'Is there no end to it? First my dear husband, and all my sons; and now poor Jane! Why was I not taken, before I saw my bairns die one by one? You're my only chick now, Annie, the only one left. . . Ah, but I'm weary, weary with it all.'

The sudden flash of spirit with which she had cried out against circumstance was the last spurt of a dying flame. At eleven that morning, while Mary Ann sat beside her reading the 23rd Psalm, Margaret slipped quietly away.

The last words to reach her consciousness were, 'He leadeth me beside the still waters. . .'

She was dreaming that she was young and active, striding along a sandy beach by the Tamar with her skirts tucked up and her feet bare, finding seaweeds for Ronald's collection.

Jane Franklin and her mother were buried in the same ceremony at the Presbyterian cemetery where Ronald had preceded them fourteen years before. Mary Ann brought the three youngest Douglas children – the 'baby' of the family was only ten – back to Newstead, and the house was lively with young voices. Besides 'Aunt Annie' there was 'Aunt Louie', Ronald Gunn's sister-in-law, and Louisa Gunn, Mary Ann's cousin, who often came to stay – three unmarried ladies to look after them, as well as the motherly housekeeper, Miss Beecraft. Then Ronald Thomas Gunn, Louisa's brother, moved in and there was once more a man in the house.

The children grew up and married; the last great family gathering of the Gunn descendants was for the wedding of

258

Margaret Douglas, with a marquee in the grounds and her eldest brother, Ronald Campbell Douglas, giving her away. Soon there were great-grandchildren, descendants of Ronald Campbell Gunn's two marriages, scattered all over Australia and abroad. But not one bore the surname of Gunn, out of all the seed he had planted in his lifetime.

Epilogue

MARY ANN, the last of her father's two families left alive, sat with her cousin Louisa Gunn on the rustic garden seat in the courtyard at Newstead House. It was the summer of 1911, fifty-five years since they had made their vow of eternal friendship at Glen Dhu.

In the great empty house behind them, Ronald Gunn's extensive library of scientific books remained largely unread. He had presented his Herbarium to the Royal Society of Tasmania in 1876, when most of the orchids he had collected forty years before were still in surprisingly good condition; many of them looked as if they had been collected only a week before.

Today, on the thirtieth anniversary of his death, Mary Ann had brought out her scrapbook which contained things like old invitations for her father to attend vice-regal dinners or farewells, the record of Sir Joseph Dalton Hooker's knighthood, some old letters from Governor La Trobe of Victoria and Governor George Grey of New Zealand, and thanks for donations received by the British Museum over the years.

She turned the pages to a collection of newspaper cuttings pasted together, and read out:

March 17, '81: The Funeral of the late Ronald Campbell Gunn left Newstead House at 3 p.m. on 16th for the Presbyterian Burial Ground, where the remains were placed in the family vault. In accordance with his wishes, the funeral was very plain. It was attended by the principal heads of public departments, and many business establishments in Launceston had their shutters up as a mark of respect.

Mr. Gunn had been crippled by arthritis for some time before his death, and retired from public life in 1876.

'That was the year Queen Truganini died, the last of the Tasmanians,' said Mary Ann.

The next cutting she had taken from her father's notebook, and it was ringed with faded black ink:

The death is recorded in Derby, England, on 6th November, 1878, of Dr. John Jamieson Gunn, M.D., only surviving son of Ronald C. Gunn of Launceston.

'Poor father!' sighed Mary Ann. 'If only he had died a few years earlier! To lose all his sons was very hard.'

'What happened to the eldest – your half-brother?'

'Ronnie? He died only the year before in Queensland. But we had not been in close touch with him. He died of the plague, thought to have been brought by rats off a ship. And poor William died the same year; he was only twenty-four.'

'So your father lost three of his sons in two years? Ah well – the name Ronald Gunn was carried on by my brother.'

'And at least we have kept up the garden. Father's memorial is in all these beautiful trees and shrubs and flowers – though my mother was the great one for growing flowers – and the dozens of plants and species named Gunnii.'

She nodded at the strap-like leaves of the orchid, genus *Gunnia*, growing in the fork of a Gunn's acacia. In spring the tree would be covered in golden puffballs of wattle blossom, and the sweet-scented raceme of Gunn's tree orchid would spill down the trunk. 'But what will happen when we die, Louie? Now that your brother is gone? There'll be no Gunns left to keep the place up.'

261

'I don't know. Perhaps Louisa – she's only fifty.' Louisa Jamieson was away in the south, staying with the family at New Norfolk.

They stared despondently at the brilliant geraniums and pelargoniums, the richea palm now reaching to the level of the second-storey windows.

'Don't you go and die first!' said Mary Ann. 'I'm older than you, don't forget.'

'Yes, about eighteen months.'

'But I'll be seventy next year, my three-score years and ten.'

'You'll live to be about eighty, like your mother. Good Scots stamina.'

'Then *you* must be prepared to live to eighty-two.'

'All right. Let's make a pact, shall we? Like the one we made ages ago not to get married, remember?'

'Yes. And do you remember the Christmas at Penquite, it must have been about 1847, I was only five I think – and you and I both had the most beautiful wax dolls in our pillow-cases.'

'Yes, I remember. It was very hot.'

The two grey-haired cousins sat in the sun, playing their favourite game of 'do you remember?' The red and the white valerian which Margaret planted thirty years before still bloomed in the courtyard. And in front of the house the Spanish oak, grown from an acorn sent to Ronald Gunn from Kew Gardens, had become an enormous shady tree, spreading its branches as high as the roof; while on the other side of the drive rose the blue-grey form of *Eucalyptus gunnii*, the shapely cider gum.